Taking In Water

Pamela Johnson

Published by Blue Door Press

Cover design: Sam Sullivan

Copyright © 2016 Pamela Johnson

All rights reserved.

ISBN: 10:1534627243

ISBN-13: 978-1534627246

Praise for *Taking In Water*

"I loved the setting, with the prowling sea, the studio, the house where Lydia has made her retreat. Lydia is a woman who has been burned by the intensity of the spotlight and knows that it isn't safe for her to stay in it. But she is still fully alive as an artist. Most striking is her energy, the way she lives from an inviolable creative core, her survivor's instincts. *Taking In Water* is thoughtful, sensuous, so illuminating about what makes an artist and what can destroy her. I was completely caught up in it."

Helen Dunmore

CONTENTS

March 2002	**3**
September 2002	**261**
Acknowledgments	276
About the Author	277

This house has been far out at sea all night
from 'Wind' by Ted Hughes.

March 2002

1

'It's the gate,' Lydia said out loud, relieved to have identified the source of the noise.

How come it was open? She could have sworn she'd locked it. She removed her eye mask and, as the lighthouse beam passed over the window, checked her clock – 2 am. The banging gate meant a storm on its way. She'd have to shut it, couldn't afford a sleepless night if she was to get on with her search before high tide tomorrow.

Wide awake now, she was alert to every sound. The gale coming in off the sea plucked at the roof timbers, a creaking above her that snatched the years away, each gust pitching her back to Grandma H's house – peeping through the letterbox, watching the sea swallow the road, spray leaping above the garden gate, how could a gate keep out the waves?

Pulling the duvet over her head to deaden the sound, she shut her eyes, called up the wreck; it was the only way to stop images of that night filling her head.

No bodies, no funerals.

She'd made herself imagine the wreck because she couldn't bear to think of her family forever drifting, pulled apart by the currents. There's no wind, no rain, no weather at all on the bottom of the sea. She liked to think of them, serene on the sea floor gazing through swishing curtains of fish. Her wreck is rusted, encrusted with barnacles, but it's solid, bedded in the soft sand of Dogger Bank, out there where the sea is shallow.

Luc was the only person she'd ever told about her ghostly wreck. Telling him her fantasy led to the art they'd made and a different kind of storm. She'd never managed to tell anyone else about the other images that lived in her head, images of that night that she didn't make up; that had taken years to surface; that she didn't want to invade her right now – her father climbing on the table, prodding the ceiling with a poker, her looking down on Grandma H's sitting-room as the sea rushes in to grab an armchair, the table's floating like a boat, everything's floating: Grandma's spectacle case, father's trilby, the doll's arm – images that flickered like stills from a film out of order until she had to hum that tune, that silly hymn. Otherwise, the images might splice together, speed up towards the last frame. She didn't dare run the whole film. Not yet. If she could make this new work, maybe then she could admit what happened.

A drumming on the skylight cut in, told her the downpour had arrived. She'd have to tog up if she was going to fix the gate. Here, she was hundreds of feet above the shore, no chance of any waves forcing themselves through her gate, however big the storm. And, a storm meant stuff was being washed up at Slayton. There'd be plenty to find after a night like this.

Downstairs, she pulled on her fleece and a waterproof and stuffed her feet into cold wellies.

'Torch, torch?' she muttered to herself then remembered, 'Bugger – it's in the studio.' Well, the lighthouse beam would have to do. If she didn't get out there soon the gate would be off its hinges.

2

Next morning, ignoring the sea fret, the thin mist rolling in with the tide, Lydia pulled off her gloves and crouched down. She wasn't leaving until she'd dug this out.

A familiar curved metal handle protruded from the packed sand, close by the ruins of the wartime pillboxes at the foot of the mud cliff. A teapot, she was sure. She scooped away, revealing the lid skewed to one side, the hinge just holding. With this she could now begin the new piece. Her skin tingled.

She checked her watch: fifteen minutes before high water.

The big storms of last week had done their work, giving the sea more strength than its regular slap and suck. The mud cliffs here at Slayton had been shoved around and things long buried had worked loose. Every day this week she'd found fragments as the cliff released its hoard. Now, the storm last night had given her this, a teapot that seemed intact. She must preserve it. Like an archaeologist she scraped away, mud and sand clogging her fingernails.

'Take your time,' she muttered, pawing at the edges of the stuck spout, easing it from side to side, and there it was: flattened, scoured, but whole. It was too smeared in mud for her to read the words she knew were engraved on its side: *The Marine Hotel*. She cradled it in both hands, as if it were a newborn thing, and she was seven again.

Come on Lydia – how many more holes can you dig? Time to go. Help me polish the silver, and then we'll make scones for tea.

If she looked up now would she see her mother, in her

wellies and old trench coat, the belt tied in a knot because the buckle was broken. Her eyes burned. She wouldn't cry, not here. She sat down on the broken concrete slab where she'd left the old mailbag, used to gather her beach-combings, and laid the teapot carefully on top of her other finds.

If she was to take the short cut to the cliff-top she must make a move. She glanced up to check how close the water was.

'Oh – ' she held her breath.

The figure was quite still, standing a few feet away, watching her. Not her mother. A man in a long leather coat. He looked like some spy lurking in the mist with a dog at his side.

How long had he been there? Her pulse thudded in her neck. She stood to face him. As she caught his eye his expression changed in an instant.

She froze at the surprise in his eyes.

He opened his mouth to speak, but before he could say a word she grabbed the mailbag and ran.

3

He'd recognised her.

Up on the cliff top path she hurried along, her breath mingled with the mist.

How could he when she'd not been in the papers for years?

She stubbed her toe on a half sunk rock and stumbled, her heart knocking under her collarbone.

'Slow down! Don't run,' she said out loud.

Anyway, there was nowhere to run. Her house was the only building between here and the lighthouse. On a clear day she'd be able to see it. All she could see now was the path immediately ahead of her, grass worn down by hikers and sodden by months of rain. Her boots squelched on the springy, uneven ground.

There was rarely anyone on the beach this early. On the cliff, yes, she'd sometimes nod a 'good morning' to walkers tackling the coastal path, or bird-watchers. He was no bird-watcher, in his leather coat. Black, well cut, fitted at the waist, long, not beach gear. She pulled her scarf across her mouth. Too late to hide her face but it slowed her breath, warmed her nose.

She listened, expecting to hear him call out, as so many had before, her other name: *Layla*.

Nothing but the thump of waves hundreds of feet below and the screech of sea birds.

She'd not mistaken his look: sudden recognition on the face of a stranger. As a child she'd seen it:

Both of them – mother and father?
Yes, and the grandmother.
Poor mite.

And again at seventeen, when she was with Luc, the surprise in the eyes of people who'd seen her on television, in newspapers or magazines, and acted as if they knew her – *Hi Layla* – when they didn't even know her real name. They knew her face that was all. The flash of recognition – Luc loved it, she hated it – made her feel as if she were a fish plucked from the water by a hungry gull. That's how she'd felt when the man on the beach stared at her just now, walking towards her out of the sea fret. *Don't fret, love.* Her father's voice, soft so she won't hear the fear. *Don't fret, Lydia. Hang on. It'll be like hide-and-seek.*

Except, in hide-and-seek, the seeker must come back.

She kept up a steady pace. The strap of her full bag cut into her shoulder. She shifted the weight of it to ease the strain in the small of her back. A sign of age she'd rather ignore. Fifty-seven this year. In her head she was no age and every age at once: seven, seventeen, fifty-seven. She would not let go of what she'd found on the beach. *Hang on, Lydia. Hang on.*

Ahead, through the thinning mist, she made out a solid patch of red: the side of her beach-hut studio, the slope of its roof, the veranda rail. With home in sight she stopped a moment; sweat trickled down her spine. She eased her scarf, damp with breath, from around her mouth. The fret meant mild air had clashed with the cold sea, a sign that warmer weather was on its way. Once it cleared there would be a fine morning. Perfect for a session in the studio. March. There couldn't be a better time to begin a new piece. How she hated the first two months of the year. Fifty years, next year, since the storm that January. It had been well into February before she'd been conscious of the world again. Half a century of years that, for her, started in March.

Now she can walk every day, out at first light. Rising early comes easy, a habit from childhood, woken then by dawn deliveries to the hotel, the throb of the bread van's engine or the clatter of crockery on the morning tea trays.

Sometimes she took the cliff path to the lighthouse. Other days she dropped down to the shore, to the small bays cut in the steep chalk cliffs. Or, like today, she'd walk beyond Flampton, beyond the chalk to Slayton where ancient clay hugged a wide sandy bay. That's where she'd been when he appeared.

She slipped her hand beneath the flap of the bag, ran her fingertips over the crushed metal.

Who was he?

She checked again to make sure the gate was firmly shut, and her shoulders eased. This was the safest place she'd ever known, even though her house stood not much more than fifty metres from the cliff edge. Closer still to the edge was the beach chalet she'd rescued and turned into her studio. This place was nothing like her grandmother's bungalow nor any of the hundreds of homes destroyed that night in '53, homes that had got too close to the water, families snatched from their beds as they slept. Here, high up, she looked down on the sea, she knew its ways, didn't trust it an inch.

When she'd first moved in there'd been no gate and no fence. She'd installed it to solve the ambiguity of the coastal path, a public right of way, which divided in two around her property. Was it meant to veer inland around her house, an inconvenient loop for the walkers, or carry straight on? Both appeared on local maps. Straight on meant strangers cutting across the rough ground where her garden ended and the wild growth at the cliff edge began. When in the studio she liked to keep the doors open. She'd be deep in work, or gazing out to sea, and she'd hear the squeak of waterproof trousers. Twitchers. They'd stop to chat, ask questions, assuming she was photographing the puffins like everyone else that brought a camera here. Eventually, she'd put up a low wooden fence to encourage the walkers to make the loop round her house, which didn't seem like too much to ask. Painted white, it formed a semi-circle enclosing house, hut, garden: her place.

Of all the places she'd lived, only this one had she been free to choose for herself; this white house with its blue entrance porch that faced inland, a porch designed to greet people in all weathers. However, Jean and Howard, her only regular visitors, knew to use the red door on the cliff side, so the porch had become her woodshed, stacked with driftwood, mainly for the fire, though some was interesting enough to use in her work.

Damn. She'd left the driftwood. Just before the teapot she'd found a hollowed out log inside the pillbox, something that might have been more than firewood. Never mind, she had the important stuff.

She headed down the side of the house towards the studio with its back to the land. In one stride she was up the few wooden steps at the end of the verandah.

There was a satisfying clunk of metal as she put the bag down on the bench, all of it silverware from The Marine. She pulled off her woolly hat and ruffled her fingers through her cropped hair.

She unlocked the hut, took the teapot from the bag and went inside. The sink had only cold water; under its icy flow she rinsed mud and sand trapped in the grooves of crushed metal. Even with the mud washed away the metal had a brownish tinge, something more than tarnish from the years it had spent buried in the cliff. The word *Marine* was still legible, etched in loopy copperplate script, but *Hotel* was partly erased, scoured out by stones and mud.

Somehow it seemed all the more significant for having been found down by the pillbox ruins, the concrete slabs she'd photographed when she'd first come back to live here, pictures that had started her *Failed Objects* series; pictures of stuff the sea had damaged or washed up. This teapot was not for *Failed Objects*.

She patted it dry with paper towels, laid out a sheet of fresh white paper and set the thing on her worktable. Later. She needed to come back to this slowly. She needed to work with no fear of intruders.

Out on the verandah she inspected the rest of her finds, laying each piece carefully on the bare boards: some odd fragments that seemed to come from toast racks, four forks with bent tines, a couple of large serving spoons, two odd handles that might have been sheared off tea trays, everything pitted and scored by the weight of earth but still recognisable.

'Take your time, take your time,' she whispered and leaned on the verandah rail, scanning the water below.

It had been such a fleeting memory of her mother down on the beach. A vivid fragment – there were so few. She ran her hand along the rail. Flaky paint peeled off, easy as dead skin, exposing the wood. The hut had taken a battering this winter. Her hands were shaking. She was lightheaded, hungry and had slept badly all week; couldn't quite trust herself when short of sleep.

Had she imagined the man?

She sat down on the bench and closed her eyes. Lean, tall, though not much taller than her, dark hair, short at the back, longer at the front so it flopped onto his face, which was shaded with stubble. The dog stood apart from him – was it his dog? A wheezy old thing, she remembered paw prints in the sand. The man was real all right, but too young to know about Layla. Late thirties, maybe; early forties at most. By the time he could read a newspaper she'd stopped being Layla.

Yet he knew her face. It chilled her all over again to see the sudden fix of his eyes. She hadn't imagined that. And if she'd stayed, let him speak, what would he have said?

'Coffee, that's what you need,' she said aloud, reassured by her real voice.

She looked up towards the garden that lay between the hut and her house. Fifty metres of ground she'd cleared back to the beds laid by the first owner. The snowdrops were hanging on. A path, edged with smooth white pebbles, curved from the hut to the red door of the house. 'Coffee and a good breakfast.' She'd prepare herself for a day in the studio.

Glancing to the other end of the verandah – she couldn't help herself – she checked out the path.

Nobody.

4

Steven sat beside the pilot, a map of the coast spread over his knee. Only occasionally did he glance at it, though, because he was keeping his eye on the line of the cliff edge, determined to be the first to spot the chalk stacks. They were almost there.

'Look what's coming,' said the pilot.

No sooner had he spoken than they were in it: mist surrounded them. They could be anywhere. With no cliff to watch, Steven felt trapped in a bubble of noise.

'Let's chop it up,' shouted the pilot above the high-pitched whine, and he increased the speed.

Steven had been warned about this guy – 'He's a dickhead, a real show-off.' And he knew Steven was a trainee. The spotless work boots gave him away, hard new leather, stiff as lumps of concrete on his feet.

On this initial site visit Steven wanted to show his boss he was up to the job, his first since graduating. He'd gone through months of applications before he landed this one. He knew how lucky he was to have been selected. And, with Northern Geophysics being an independent consultancy, he also knew they'd cut him no slack. *Perform or you're out.* Today was part of his induction into CoDMaS: the Coastal Defence Management Strategy. He'd done the intensive report-writing course; this week it was site visits alongside his boss, then he'd be on the project for real. He'd show that he knew how to be a team player.

He glanced at the radar, tried to remember what he'd been taught. Judging by the clutter on the screen he guessed they were probably just above the cliff edge. He peered out from the cockpit bubble for confirmation. Now, when he needed to look closest, he could hardly see anything at all. He struggled to piece together glimpses of cliff, visible where the mist was patchy, trying to maintain the lie of the land in his mind's eye. It seemed they were above a house; no point looking for chalk stacks.

They were here today to get an overview, to note the winter damage to the stacks and arches below Flampton. Later, there would be onshore site visits to monitor erosion hot spots, to note the level of saturation in the cliff edge after the winter's unprecedented rainfall.

At Uni he'd excelled in geology and soil mechanics, fascinated by processes that shape the land. His enthusiasm had come through at the interview, his boss had told him. This was his chance to show off his knowledge for real. But right now the only person showing off was the pilot. Steven was hardly aware that the idiot had moved the controls, but each cell in his body registered the shock of the sudden manoeuvre. Instinctively, he clutched the panel in front of him. Blood clamoured to his head. His gut rose, he was turning inside out. The pilot laughed, mouth wide open showing stained teeth.

'Bit rough?'

Steven tried not to react, but knew his discomfort must show on his face. His head was pounding. The pilot had dropped a couple of hundred feet in seconds.

They were hovering above the house below.

'Is that where she lives then, that artist woman?' asked the pilot as they hovered.

Steven stared down on a small white house and a well-tended garden with a pebble-lined path leading to a beach hut, perched near the cliff edge. A woman hurried from house to hut.

'What's that you told me?' The pilot shouted over his shoulder to the boss, 'Used to paint her tits? Loopy.'

The boss cleared his throat but said nothing. Last week, he'd briefed all the CoDMaS team about 'sensitivity' when dealing with Habitation Assessment and Community Liaison. It sounded as if the boss'd been less than discreet with the pilot.

Dealing with people affected by their project was part of the job for which Steven had little experience, except he was good at sussing people out. He knew the pilot was a dick and that his boss could be pushy. But putting himself forward, speaking up, he'd have to get used to that. He'd like to ask why they were flying so low over this woman's house, but said nothing.

'Who'd put a beach hut on a cliff?' said the pilot. 'Let's have a closer look.' This time Steven was prepared, and the drop was not so steep, but still the blood flooded to his skull. It helped to look down.

The woman was on the verandah of the beach hut, bending, picking things up. As she headed back to the house, she stopped, glanced up and then stared at them.

'Barking,' said the pilot.

Steven was familiar with mad people. His mother worked at the day centre. He'd worked there himself as a cleaner, the first summer home from Uni. Mad people tend to shuffle, looking at things that aren't there. This woman moved with purpose.

The pilot kept the helicopter low, circling. Round and round, until the discomfort Steven felt was more on her behalf than his. He'd be happy to return his unstained boots to his locker and spend the day back at his desk entering figures on spreadsheets. The pilot must be breaching regulations flying so low, with no good reason, over a private house.

Steven said nothing.

5

Warm air hugged her as she peeled off the layers – scarf, hat, waterproof and fleece. Calmer now she was home, she hung her gear carefully on the coat stand.

In the kitchen the phone rang.

Him? How would he get her number? She let it go to the machine and listened.

'Hi, Lydia, it's Patrick. Are you there?'

She laughed with relief and ran to pick up the call.

'I'm just back in from my walk.'

'Glad I caught you. Look, I know you don't like to deliver to order but how many of your *Horizon* series you could let me have?'

'Ooh, Patrick –'

'Think about it this once. I have a client very interested; he's collaborating with an architect on a new college library, needs contemplative pieces for a presentation, wants to show examples of the work, not just PowerPoint. He liked what we have in the gallery, particularly the *Horizon* images, but I've only a couple here and he'd like six to make an impact.'

'*Six?*' She generally let them go in ones or twos. 'Let me have a think and call you back.' She hadn't time for this, really, she had to get into the studio.

As she hung up she noticed there was another message.

Hi, Lyd. Listen, I'm not going to make it this weekend. Got a gig in Paris. There was a pause before Howard carried on. Something odd in his tone. *Anyway, talk soon. What about if you come to London – week after next?* Impossible.

In the bathroom she stripped to her underwear and filled the basin. She scrubbed mud and sand from beneath her fingernails, splashed under her arms and scooped water over her face, catching sight of herself in the mirror. *Good bones. With your looks people will come to you.* Her cousin Bea's words, all those years ago, had turned out to be prophetic.

Her face. That's all he'd have seen – the spy – framed between her woolly hat and her waterproof. Good bones, yes, but look at the lines around her eyes. Ruddy from the walk, she smoothed moisturiser into her weathered cheeks.

In the bedroom she grabbed jeans, a clean t-shirt, another fleece. It would be chilly in the studio and she needed to concentrate. No distractions, just plunge in, follow where the hotel objects took her.

She hurried down to make breakfast, ignoring the dirt and the sand gathering in the cracks between the stone flags of the passage. Her usual March blitz following the anniversaries could wait; she'd waited long enough to make this work, nearly fifty years of keeping a secret; seventeen years the silverware had been buried in the cliff, almost as long as she'd lived in this house.

Up from London in 1985 to discuss the future of The Marine after the collapse of the ridiculous dining-room extension, Jennifer had pushed Lydia to release her share of the business. *I don't want you getting your hands on any compensation*, not in so many words; her body language said it all. Jennifer had never wanted Lydia as a sleeping partner and certainly not since, *your episode. You have to be on top in this game.* One mild afternoon, tired of her aunt, and without much thought except knowing deep inside she had to do it, she'd gone down to the beach huts below the hotel, stripped to her underwear and swum out, as her father used to, towards the headland. Afterwards, she'd never felt more alive. Since her 'episode' she'd had bad patches but never enough to put her in hospital again. She'd got by, living in Bea's house in London, taking in lodgers. She'd existed.

That afternoon swimming in Slayton Bay she was suddenly alive again, facing out the real thing and not cowering from a sea that, in London, filled her head. If she could do this every day she might get well, might even make new work. And in that instant she'd decided, yes, she'd sell her half of the hotel and buy the Clegg house at Flampton. After years of holiday lets, the solitary place on the solid chalk cliffs was up for sale. It was far enough away from Jennifer but would keep her connection to this coast. She could keep her eye on the sea in a house that was well out of its reach, set far above even the highest waves. It was a reliable looking home, built in the 1920s by Alfred Clegg as a refuge for his shell-shocked son, Eddie. Poor Eddie who couldn't settle to the family carpet weaving business in Bradford, cringing at the clatter of looms, yet could lose himself in the sound of seabirds. It was from Eddie Clegg that her father had learned to distinguish their calls. *Listen Lyddie, you can spot birds with your eyes closed.* And it was from Eddie that her father learned how a guillemot chick and its parents call to each other even before the chick is fully hatched; they learn to recognise each other's voices. After her father had disappeared in '53 she hadn't seen much of Eddie, until, ten years later, about to leave for Art College, she'd come across him up on the cliff path.

'Is that young Lydia? Whatever's the matter?'

She'd been shouting into the wind, calling into the sea, *Bring them back.*

'Nothing,' had been her tight-lipped teenaged reply, when really she'd wanted to ask: How do you do it? How do you survive? As they stood listening to the clacking of gannets, she'd willed him to read her silence. Eventually he'd said:

'I didn't think this is how my life would go. You carry on.

You'll find a way.' Finding a way, for Lydia, was still a work-in-progress.

In the passage by the kitchen she straightened the line of photographs ranged along the white walls and considered which of them she might let Patrick have. *Horizon* was an open-ended project. In London she'd lived high enough to see the city skyline, the dome of St Paul's on a clear day. In New York, working out on the roof, she'd got to know Manhattan's jagged skyline. Here there was no skyline, only horizon, an uninterrupted line, where sea appeared to end and meet the sky, unreachable, untouchable but reliable. Her spirit level. In these photographs there were no objects, only sea and sky. Thousands, she'd taken, all from the same spot on the verandah. Same sky, same sea, but always different and never quite enough. Setting the tripod in the same place, she captured what she could.

It was like a diary, days recorded by how the light was, the height and density of clouds or the texture of the sea's surface. Not every day, but regular enough. She loved to catch operatic moments: the dark towering mass of cumulonimbus before a storm, or high wispy cirrus on a bright day. Cloud forms so particular they could be named even though they didn't last. Each shot was taken facing the horizon. This was the limitation, the challenge she set herself: how many permutations of sea and sky could she capture within that space?

This pair she might let Patrick have. One that was mostly clear sky with fluffy cumulus breaking up and only the narrowest band of sea, dotted with whitecaps. The next one showed muscular, oily mounds of water and barely a strip of sky. The stormy ones sold particularly well; dangerous weather to hang safely indoors.

Looking was what mattered. Paying attention, keeping an eye on the tussle between air and water, pattern and chaos, reminding herself it was physics, not portent or punishment but moisture clinging to particles of dust, building into clouds. When the load got too heavy the water got dumped. Round and round it went – rain, river, sea, rain – the same water. But it was also her connection to the family. She often wondered: had the sea that swallowed them, dissolved them all, been back as rain, tapping on her window? Was that all that was left of them? She was no scientist, no meteorologist, she wasn't religious but her work was devotional, a lifetime's work, a labour of love. And now the hotel stuff was asking her to step away from what she did everyday.

The new piece had to be in three dimensions. And it had to be something more than the assemblages she often made from her beach-combings. That kind of work she did because Patrick could easily sell it. Also, there was satisfaction in the making itself, giving new life to stuff abandoned by the sea. But that work could never say what needed to be – had to be – said.

She poured a second cup from the cafetiere and sat back from the kitchen table, resting her arms on the arms of the pale-oak carver. Her father's chair from the morning-room at The Marine. She'd often wondered if he'd visited here when it was Eddie Clegg's home. Perhaps her father had once sat here, watching, though as far as she remembered they usually met him out walking the cliff. *Lives like a hermit, does Eddie.*

Nothing wrong with being a hermit. *My hermit*, Howard would tease her. She'd rather say nothing to anyone about the new piece, but she'd have to let Howard know why she couldn't possibly come down to London next week.

She slotted a slice of bread into the toaster, growing aware of a noise outside, coming her way.

A helicopter.

Someone in trouble? The caves in these chalk cliffs were as

big as cathedrals, easy to get cut off if you didn't know the tides.

The noise came closer. She shivered. That sound could signal the end for someone. It wasn't only the drowned she was thinking of. When a rescue failed the living were changed too. Right now someone might be having breakfast, unaware of a line being drawn across their life.

She jumped as the toast popped up.

Hurrying along the path to the studio, she couldn't see the helicopter but it was close, getting louder. Quickly picking up the stuff from the verandah she took it all inside her studio, laid the battered bits on the worktable with the teapot. She came out, locked the door and looked up. It swooped like some monstrous dragonfly, the slender tail kept it steady as its blades spun so fast they seemed to form a solid disc and sent out a force that thumped in her chest.

'Who are you?' Futile, her voice was swallowed by the noise.

The light was against her, but someone must be looking at her behind the blank, bug-eyed stare.

No chance of working now. She carried a cup of coffee to her bedroom. She needed to be high up. She'd had the ceiling knocked out of the room because she couldn't rest with the dark space of the loft sealed in above her as she slept. In her bedroom she was as high as she could go. Her lifeboat, she called it. The boat-builder who'd helped with the renovation had made the most of the space: a cabin bed with cupboards beneath, and all around the bed a shelf, now cluttered with books, CDs, radio, a bottle of brandy – whatever it took. She put the mug on the shelf then climbed the small ladder to the bed and lay back, propped on pillows.

The helicopter moved off. She kept her eye on the skylight. The mist was clearing, there was the first patch of blue.

The room's white walls were hung with photographs from her *Surface* series. This work, close-cropped, captured nothing but the state of the sea's surface: curling, dimpled, ridged, smooth. She searched out a flat-calm to focus on.

It was back, circling. The whole house vibrated.

'Make up your mind: either land or go away,' she shouted at the skylight and pulled the duvet around her. Think how the morning had been before all of this, before the fret: the steely light over the sea, crisp air on her face. She'd found a pebble and had paused to study it: pinky brown, veined, egg-shaped. She used to collect pebbles when she'd first moved back, arriving home with pockets stuffed, but they'd dried to something that was no longer the thing that had attracted her. Now, she left them, content to have noticed. Pebbly moments, tucked away in her photographic memory. Images to meditate on when troubling images pressed in.

It wasn't working.

She couldn't shake off the image of the man on the beach. How long had he been watching her?

Luc and Layla, long since forgotten, she'd thought. But there were images out there, images from their story, that always did have a life of its own. A *story,* that's what it was. She was a player in it, but it wasn't her true story.

The helicopter circled again; pressure building in her head.

The threat is never where you think it is, Luc had kept saying in the weeks before he jumped. Maybe it's something to do with the man in the leather coat? Thirty-five years this summer since Luc killed himself, she calculated. Why would anyone still be interested? And yet, thinking about it, the leather coat said *media*. Press. A journalist, had to be.

6

Martin slid the key into the lock, entered the house and listened: snoring from the half-open door at the top of the stairs; she was still asleep. Too early to make phone calls so he'd make coffee, think how to put this to his editor.

'Good girl, Barley,' he whispered, patting the head of the old Labrador. The house smelled of dog, overlaid with lily-of-the-valley air freshener. He hung his leather coat on the hallstand and, just in time, remembered to take off his shoes. *Mind my new carpet, Martin.* Meanwhile, Barley ambled ahead to her basket in the kitchen, padding sandy paws over the pale-green pile.

He dug out a dustpan and brush and made a cursory sweep, his thoughts filled with the woman on the beach. He wouldn't allow himself to call her Layla yet, not until he'd double-checked names and dates. If that was Lydia Warburton he'd just seen then, according to Judi Noone in her 1968 *Flex* interview, she was also Layla. What name did she go by now? It would be good to get to the bottom of those single names. Luc and Layla – a product of their time or something more?

In the kitchen he filled the kettle, his unshaven face reflected in its spotless chrome. Behind him the table was laid for breakfast, cups upside-down in their saucers. Even though weak from flu, his mother, Eileen, persisted in her rituals. Each day followed an indelible pattern: dusting, Hoovering, sweeping the front path, walking the dog, and before bed, laying the kitchen table for breakfast. On Fridays she bought a lottery ticket and chose a new detective novel from the library, and, on the last Thursday of the month, had a night out with her friend Monica.

The noise of the kettle rumbling to a boil seemed loud enough to wake Eileen. The sound of her muffled coughing stirred Barley from the basket by the boiler.

'Stay, girl,' he patted the dog's head, filled a bowl with fresh water. 'Let her sleep.' Otherwise she'd be on at him about the new washing-line contraption. *I need it fixed, Martin. I'm days behind with the sheets.*

He spooned instant coffee into a mug.

The woman on the beach was a creature of habit. He'd seen that now for himself. Last night her daily beachcombing had been a topic of gossip in the pub.

'Dead spit of your dad, y'are. More like Bill every time I see you.' Jack Powell, his Dad's old fishing partner, had been leaning on the bar of The Northern Lights.

'Same again?' Martin had nodded to Jack's empty glass.

Since his father had died, coming back was never easy but a drink with Jack had been preferable to an evening in front of the TV with Eileen and her probing about the situation with Francine. *It doesn't add up. You're either living together or not.* It soon will add up. If Francine could raise the money he'd let her buy his share of the house; no need to discuss it with Eileen until the deal was done. Besides, going to the pub meant an opportunity to ask around about the Warburton family and The Marine Hotel.

'Don't mind if I do,' Jack said, lighting a cigarette from the one he was finishing, smoke swirling around him. How could he do that having watched Bill die the way he did?

'How's your mam?'

'On the mend.'

'Nasty, that flu. Good of you to come, Martin.'

He shrugged. Yes, he was here because Eileen had been ill and it was her birthday at the weekend, but, for once, it suited him. He had the Warburton connection to follow up and he was out of Francine's way.

Even after all this time it still felt odd to be in the Lights without his Dad's cheerful teasing. *How come a son of mine is seasick on anything but a flat-calm?* At least his dad had quietly respected his academic life. Unlike Eileen, who was either parading his cleverness, showing it off to her friends like a new appliance or getting at him for his chosen subject. Modern art was something else that *didn't add up.* And why had it taken him so long to get a 'proper job'? *You could have done anything with all those A-Levels.* For years his working life, though far removed from his father's, had been as financially precarious – bits of part-time teaching, the Artists' Voices project, curating, reviewing, all freelance, all short-term – a 'portfolio' that finally landed him a lecturing job. Now he was a Reader with time for research; when he'd finished this book he'd be on his way to becoming a Professor. His publisher was expecting a manuscript by Christmas. He was halfway through his sabbatical but nowhere near halfway through his book.

'I was coming at the weekend anyway for her birthday.' Then, eager to get off the subject of Eileen, he asked: 'Jack, you know everything that goes on around here – what do you know about the Warburtons who ran The Marine?'

'Not much, only what everyone knows.' And Jack reeled off information that Martin, as a schoolboy, had been vaguely aware of, stories of The Marine often being in the *Evening News*: how the Waburtons had taken the place upmarket, built a reputation and could fill rooms when many were closing. 'She were forever expanding, had that extension added.'

'That would be Jennifer Warburton?' The name gleaned

from the news cuttings he'd gathered.

'Went too far if you ask me, building that thing – it were like some giant conservatory.'

'You think it was the building that caused the mudslide?' Martin asked.

'Who knows? Anyway, she put up a fight, blamed the Council. Compensation in six figures, so they say. Mind you, what good did it do her? Dead within a couple of years, she was.'

'And Lydia Warburton, she was Jennifer's daughter?'

'Sort of thing our Kath would know about, or Eileen. Ask your mam.' Jack raised his pint to his lips, as if to say: enough women's talk.

Asking Eileen was not an option. She thought artists were a dangerous bunch and the exhibitions Martin had worked on, well, pornographic some of them, if you asked her. *With your brains you could have been a lawyer, a doctor. They say you can retrain.* Martin kept an invisible electric fence around his work, with a tacit agreement, each to stay on their side. Asking Eileen about Lydia Warburton would set sparks flying.

'Pint, is it?' Jack offered, lighting another fag.

'No thanks. I'll be off.' Fond of his dad's old friend as he was, he needed air. 'Take care, Jack.'

'Odd woman. Bit of a recluse.'

'Who?'

'The Warburton woman. Daughter, was it? Had something to do with The Marine. She still lives out Flampton way. Has a house on the chalk cliffs. I've seen her when I'm coming in with the boat – a couple of times this week. Early mornings, here at Slayton. Beachcomber. Saw her yesterday rummaging around the old pillboxes.'

Up in his room, Martin spread his papers on the bed, flicked through the file of photocopied articles he'd brought from

London. *Rolling Stone*, September 1967. Under the heading 'Barefoot Muse' the photo-caption piece was all speculation: Why had Luc's 'blue muse' fled, barefoot and bleeding, across Washington Square only hours before Luc had killed himself? Where had she gone? The photograph showed Layla dressed in jeans, a sleeveless t-shirt and barefoot, blood streaked down her arm. Something had made her turn her head. She glared at the camera, eyes full of fear.

The same eyes he'd seen this morning.

When Barley had pestered him to go out first thing, he'd walked the dog along the beach, headed off towards the pillboxes at the end of the bay, thinking about what Jack had told him and what he'd most like to ask her if this Warburton woman turned out to be Layla: how had *Taking In Water* come into being? What had it been like to work with Luc? And – something that had always intrigued him – what did it mean, that scooping gesture? With each staging of *Taking In Water* Layla had improvised how she'd arranged herself on the mound of salt but, no matter what position she adopted, as the soundtrack got louder, she'd turned on her side and, with eyes closed, scooped a hollow in the salt. When he saw the woman this morning he'd been afraid to disturb her, absorbed in her task, delving, scooping at the sand with her hands. When she'd finally looked up, he couldn't quite believe his eyes.

He laid out colour stills of the last performance of *Taking In Water*, good-quality photocopies from the limited edition book that Luc's dealer had produced. There were black-and-white movies of each performance in Garth Sarton's private collection, which Martin was still hoping to persuade Sarton to have transferred to DVD, make them more available. Last September that had seemed too much to ask after Sarton had been so generous, welcoming Martin into his home once it had become impossible to return to Manhattan. In between keeping up with the news and the grounded planes, Martin had played each reel, over and over, making notes, trying to build a visual memory of the performances. Luc's images and the soundtrack of the sea had started to merge in his mind with the billowing dust of the falling building. A building that, only hours before, he'd been in. Thinking of it now, of the what-might-have-been, of the luck of his close shave, he still found himself anxious for the Japanese family who'd been ahead of him in the queue, the twin girls giggling, excited. The thought of them brought on the familiar twist in his gut, a discomfort that contained both nausea and relief. It spread through his body, filled his skin.

He shook his head to free himself of the memory and returned to the images. He studied carefully the one that had been shot just after the performance, a close-up of the mound of sea-salt, carrying the impress of a human form. Layla's. And, beside it, the small hollow she'd scooped out – he'd love to know more about that gesture. He picked up another one showing the whole thing: around the walls hung sheets of canvas with the blue imprint of Layla's body. These alternated with images of huge waves and of Yuri Gagarin, first man in space, his fresh face encased in his helmet, clear-eyed. Luc had repeatedly silk-screened this newspaper photograph and, with each new image, had cropped closer in on the eyes until that was all you saw, Gagarin's eyes. Of course, with the movie came Layla's movements and the soundtrack. It started off a soft lapping of water and built until the sound of crashing waves filled the performance space.

Here, somewhere in all of this material, he knew there was a book to be written. With the ice caps melting and sea levels rising, *Taking In Water* was ready for re-examination. The question it posed was more urgent now than forty years ago – how do we live in a world that is mostly water? A subject that gave him scope to develop his ideas around the sublime, the vastness of nature and the limits of what the mind could take in. For Luc the sublime had encompassed space travel and technology as well as nature. Since last September, the sublime, that sense of awe and wonder and horror, had acquired further meaning with the need to understand the new cult of death. What notion of the sublime made someone fly a plane into a building?

The threat is never where you think it is – Luc peppered his interviews with get-outs, always avoiding questions. On 10 September, when Sarton had refused to talk on the phone, Martin had felt certain that his project was about to be sabotaged. Hadn't all the e-mails he'd exchanged with the curator, Alex Markovski, about access to Sarton, and the collection and archive up in Connectucut, been enough? Waiting for Sarton to make up his mind had led him close to disaster. He felt sick to think of it: him standing in the lobby, calculating how long it would take to get to the head of the queue.

Now, Martin was struggling to keep to his plan to return from his sabbatical with a manuscript delivered and lectures arranged here and in the States: professorship guaranteed. But, was he about to sabotage himself; so desperate he was imagining Layla in the face of a stranger? And yet, despite the waterproof, the woolly hat, the woman on the beach had commanded attention. A striking face, those wide-apart eyes. Older, yes, but unmistakable.

His pulse quickened as he flicked through his files to find a still from the video he always showed during his *Introduction to Post-War Culture* module. Layla's face framed by curtains of straight hair, sitting behind John Lennon – the first global satellite link-up in the history of television. *All you need is love*, beamed round the world live, June 1967, in the Summer of Love. Martin would have been eight.

It was the same face.

He should know it. He'd watched this film often enough. His students tittering at the clipped vowels of presenter Cliff Michelmore; Martin making the point that mass media speeded up linguistic change and how distinctions between high and low were fast breaking down: the symphony orchestra backing the pop group; people from humble backgrounds shot to world fame – Warhol, The Beatles – the rise of a new celebrity class. Luc and Layla. 'Consider the context,' he'd explain and underline the word, *technology*. They'd had mobile phones since primary school but could they imagine how it had been when television, Telstar, jet travel were brand new? Mass media needed spectacle. Luc and Layla became the spectacle after *Taking In Water*; the work got left behind.

Tracing connections was Martin's work. *Taking in Water*, a serious piece, ahead of its time, had been overshadowed by spectacle and gossip, and neglected ever since. He wanted to trace all the connections that led to the work, get behind the gossip, show the art in a new light. There was, too, the connection to his father's death, but that was for him to know.

Coming up the stairs, the sound of Barley's rasping breath. He went out to the landing.

'Shsh. Go back.' He could tell by the dog's determined, arthritic progress that Barley was having none of it.

'Martin, what time is it?' His mother's sleep-filled voice.

'Too early for you to get up,' he said, keeping his tone cheery, encouraging.

He put his head round the door to her room, blocking the dog's way.

'Barley needs a walk,' she mumbled from under the duvet.

'It's all right, I've already taken her out. Why not have another hour?'

'Really? Well, I don't mind if I do.'

'Good, I'll look in on you in an hour or so, OK?'

'Has she had water?'

'Yes, I filled her bowl. You rest,' he crossed his fingers behind his back, closed her door and eased the dog towards the stairs. 'Go girl, back to your basket.'

If that woman was Layla he *had* to speak to her. Others around Luc had been dead by the mid-Seventies: drink, drugs, suicide. She was the only credible witness left. It would be a coup, remarkable to have her testimony. Needing time to interview Layla called for an extension to the deadline. This was primary research. And, since there were no recordings of Layla's voice, no interviews of any kind, the Sound Archive would be interested. Eight-thirty, Nick wouldn't be at his office yet. He reached for his mobile, selected Nick's home number.

'Hello?' It was Nick's wife.

'Hi Angie, it's Martin. Is Nick around?'

'You're up early.' He could hear their three children in the background squabbling.

'Sorry to bother you, wanted to catch him before – '

'Oi, stop it you lot!' Angie shouted. 'He's not here. Conference in Cambridge. Back tomorrow. Try his mobile. Sorry, got to go.'

He selected Nick's mobile but it went to voicemail. No. Before he made a move he needed to go over the new information, the press cuttings he found in Slayton Library, make sure he'd joined the dots in the right way.

Finally following up on Judi Noone's *Flex* interview he'd begun by checking the name Warburton on the microfiche in Slayton Library yesterday.

'Family tree?' The librarian had asked. When he'd explained what he was looking for she'd brightened, seemed keen to help.

'Oh the Warburtons of The Marine Hotel. We've quite a file on the hotel and the family – victims of the '53 flood, you see.'

'Flood?'

'It doesn't get talked about much any more. A terrible business. Hundreds died.' She'd produced a folder full of cuttings going back over sixty years including a piece from the *Norfolk News*. He took out the copy and read it carefully once more.

Norfolk News, **6 February 1953**

HOLIDAY GIRL SAVED BY SONG

Our reporter on yet another remarkable survivor

of last week's tragedy

Seven-year-old Lydia Hutton was in Norfolk on a family visit when the storm surge struck last Saturday night. She was discovered, late the next day, alone in the loft of her grandmother's shorefront bungalow near Cromer, clinging to the joists, singing *All Things Bright And Beautiful*.

"I thought I was hearing things," said volunteer rescuer, Mr Robert Slater. It is unclear how she managed to climb into the roof. Her parents, Mr & Mrs Edward Hutton and grandmother, Mrs Eustace Hutton, are all missing, presumed drowned.

The child collapsed in Mr Slater's arms and was rushed to hospital. She remained unconscious for several days. Now physically well, the voice that saved her has fallen silent. She has not yet spoken since regaining consciousness.

"It's the shock," said the girl's aunt, Mrs Jennifer Warburton. She has travelled from Yorkshire to Norfolk to comfort her niece and awaits news of her own sister, Mrs Alice Hutton, the child's mother. "She was pregnant," confirmed Mrs Warburton. "I'm praying for news of her, of all of them."

Mr & Mrs Hutton, proprietors of The Marine Hotel at Slayton Bay, on the Yorkshire coast, had travelled to Norfolk on a hastily arranged visit to Mrs Eustace Hutton. Edward Hutton's mother had been due to visit the couple in Yorkshire but ill health kept her at home. Instead, the couple decided to make the journey to Norfolk.

Mrs Warburton plans to take Lydia back to Yorkshire and to stay with her at The Marine. The popular cliff-top hotel is currently closed for the winter but Mrs Warburton believes that being in familiar surroundings may encourage the child to speak. She has yet to be informed of the fate of her family.

Lydia is not alone in facing devastating news. It's believed that nearly five hundred perished in Britain, with three times that number in Holland. The final death toll could reach two thousand.

The statistics caught his eye ... *five hundred perished in Britain, with three times that number in Holland. The final death toll could be over two thousand.* Over two thousand, almost as many as perished last September in Manhattan. It was the first he'd heard of this disaster. If the surge tide had run all the way down the east coast, had it affected Slayton? He wished his father were here to ask; he would surely have remembered such a night. Then, thirty years on, the sea hit the family again.

Yorkshire Post, 1985

MARINE HOTEL LANDSLIDE – LATEST

Hotelier and Council at loggerheads

Hotelier Mrs Jennifer Warburton is seeking compensation from Slayton Council for the damage to her property caused by the recent cliff landside at Slayton Bay.

Mrs Warburton claims that poor maintenance of drainage to Council land, adjacent to the hotel, was the cause of the landslide. She refused to comment further for legal reasons. "But, I would like to say how thankful we are that no lives were lost. Thirty years ago I lost my sister to the sea."

Her daughter, Lydia Warburton, co-owner of the hotel, lives in London and was not available for comment.

The original hotel building is intact. Demolition of what remained of the dining-room is now complete, its contents lost beneath the mud.

In the *Slayton Evening News* he'd found pictures and diagrams that told the story across four pages: a photograph of the cliff slumping beneath the Pitch & Putt in Marine Park, 'The ground was saturated due to unusually high rainfall,' said a spokesman; cracks appearing in The Marine Hotel's dining-room extension, photographed by a guest; hours later a picture taken from a boat showed the front of the dining-room sheared off. 'Tables set for breakfast stood untouched, white linen fluttering in the breeze,' said an eyewitness. Architect's plans showed Jennifer Warburton's ambitious extension: a conservatory-style corridor running from the main building to a rectangular construction close to the cliff edge.

'Our diners enjoyed the sea view,' said Mrs Warburton.

'An inadvisable development,' said a planning official.

There were diagrams of drainage pipes in the cliff – had they been adequate? 'Instability in cliffs composed mainly of glacial mud is to be expected,' said a spokesman.

The final photograph showed The Marine Hotel open for business as usual.

'We'll carry on,' said Jennifer Warburton.

Other articles followed the row that rumbled for a couple of years. In the end Jennifer Warburton was awarded substantial compensation.

Martin needed to get the facts clear in his head before he took this further.

So, in 1953 a Lydia Hutton, an orphan, goes back to Slayton to live with her aunt in The Marine Hotel. In 1985 a Lydia Warburton is co-owner of the same hotel. It had to be that Lydia Hutton and Lydia Warburton were the same person. 'Daughter' a piece of sloppy journalism, a fact not checked? Or perhaps she'd been adopted by Jennifer? It fits with what Jack had said in the pub. The dates work: Lydia's age fits with what's known of Layla. But Lydia Warburton had lived in London in 1985. If the woman on the beach was Lydia/Layla why had she moved back to Flampton? Given what had happened to her family, why would she want to live by the sea?

He could hear Eileen mumbling endearments to Barley, baby talk, as she made her way to the bathroom, then the flush of the lavatory. He gathered up his papers.

'Martin?' Eileen called softly then shuffled into the room, ample in her turquoise housecoat and sheepskin slippers.

'It's late, Martin, gone nine. You shouldn't have let me sleep on,' she said.

'You need to rest.'

'Busy with your papers already?' She peered over his shoulder.

'It's research.'

'How much more of this *research* have you to do? I hope you're not going abroad again. You're not, are you?'

'Come on, I'll make you a cup of tea.' He slipped the cuttings back into the folder and guided Eileen out of his room and downstairs.

'Barley's paws are full of sand. Wherever did you take her?'

'How are you feeling?'

'You've never had her down the beach?'

'Why not? I'm a Londoner, I needed the sea air,' he grinned at her. 'Barley loved it.'

The dog seemed to be panting, her breathing caught in an odd rhythm.

'She needs one of her pills.'

'*Your* medicine must be doing the trick. You're looking much better. Shall I book a table at the new Italian place for your birthday?' *I know it'll be hard for you coming back, but you'll look after your mother,* his father had said as he was dying. Martin had been a year into his PhD. He'd never missed her birthday since.

'We'll see.'

In the kitchen Eileen climbed on a chair to reach Barley's pills, kept on the highest shelf. As if the dog were likely to take an overdose.

'Let me,' he offered.

'I'm used to doing things on my own.'

Eileen, landing heavily, as she stepped off the chair, held her hand to her chest.

'Are you all right?'

'My pulse, it's racing.'

'I'm not surprised. Sit down.'

'In a minute. Here, girl,' she slipped a pill into Barley's mouth. 'It keeps happening, this fluttering.' She sat a moment, stroking her throat. 'It's passed. One egg or two?'

'I'll do breakfast,' he offered.

'It's all right. I'll do it. I know where everything is,' she insisted.

He watched her resigned movements from fridge to bread-bin to toaster, a well-worn pattern. She'd never been the same since his dad died. There'd been no raw aching grief, not that he'd seen, only a continual, rumbling depression, a lowness relieved by small pleasures: detective novels, needlepoint, chatting to Monica. She was sliding into the role of an old woman. Sixty-nine wasn't *that* old. He thought of the woman on the beach, made a calculation. If she was Layla, she'd be heading for sixty.

'You've a lot of papers up there,' Eileen cracked eggs into hot fat. 'Wouldn't you be better working here on the table?'

'I'm fine upstairs, thanks.'

'I got used to your dad going out to sea but these nutters, Martin, they're everywhere. Tell me you're not going back to New York.'

'Not in the immediate future.' She'd known he'd been in New York that day but she didn't know he'd been in the lobby of the South Tower less than an hour before the attacks.

'I mean you're not safe in London, are you?'

'Who said life was safe? There are no guarantees. I'll be off to the library soon, need anything from town?'

'Again?' She put plates under the grill to warm.

'I've a book to finish.'

'I was hoping you'd put up that new rotary drier. The forecast is giving warm this afternoon. I could get the sheets out.'

'You're not well.'

'The machine does the washing. But don't worry, I can see how caught up you are with your – *research*. It doesn't add up, Martin. I mean, that folder under your bed, those pictures. Disgusting. They look like what's kept on the top shelf at the newsagent.'

7

Lydia added the morning's haul to her collection, arranging the fragments on the shelf that ran along the back wall of her studio. They were beginning to form a kind of still life.

In her sketchbook she listed the new things: *half of a toast rack, 7 forks with bent tines, 4 serving spoons, 2 handles, off a tea tray?* She recorded the place, time, date, then jotted down images, thoughts: *teapot trapped in the sand, dug out with my hands, lid still holding to body. Sea fret. Sinister man in leather coat.* The spy was now attached to the experience. *Mother in her trenchcoat – calling to me.* So few memories of her mother and now this fragment, called up by the teapot.

Midday. Almost three hours since the helicopter left and the mist had cleared. Maybe she'd overreacted, crawling under the duvet like that.

She lifted down the teapot but left the window shutters closed, couldn't bear more interruptions, not now. Setting the thing on a sheet of black card on her worktable, she spot-lit it with the table lamp. The digital camera would be fine; this was not about perfect pictures. It was about getting close up yet remaining objective, starting to know the thing as it is now.

She zoomed in on the sheared spout, the flattened belly, the hinge of the lid; studied it forensically from all angles. She turned it over, propped it up against an old paint pot.

She could do this. She'd had a sense of her mother down on

the beach and *not* felt the terror. If she kept working there might be more memories.

In a large sketchpad she made quick marks: draw what you see, not what you think you know, focus on each dent, crease, scratch. Maybe the memories would come if she stayed with the details. Drawing was more intimate than working with the camera; drawing created a space where time slowed. After a while, she started to draw with her eyes closed, feeling with her left hand, drawing with her right; translating the sensations of rough metal that had once been smooth.

Luc had taught her to do this, said she was wasting her time with life classes. *Close your eyes. Feel.* She'd cupped his balls, felt the smoothness of his hardening prick. *Draw what you feel.* Afterwards, they'd admired her sketch, its energy quite different from her studies of the college model. *Find other ways to know a body*, Luc had said. She hadn't known then how her body would feature in his work. Right now it wasn't helpful to think of *Taking In Water,* though Luc had been right about drawing blind: *know your object and you'll find your subject.* Her fingertips searched the untidy pleats of crumpled browned silver, the jagged edge of the spout and she was back at The Marine.

Back from school. Afternoon tea. *Remember to smile at the guests, Lydia.* Aunt Jennifer's on at me to clear tables. *And be sure to thank Miss Battersby.* Tea served in the Garden Lounge, with its high-backed chintz chairs and fine sea view; French windows open onto the lawn that runs down to the cliff edge. Tea on the lawn today – white Lloyd Loom tables and chairs. I'll do it because when it's done there's the washing-up and arranging the tea services in the pantry, and that's when I can be alone.

It's warm. End of May or early June. Miss Battersby from Bolton is here. These are her two weeks, same each year and has been since Jennifer and Bernard's first summer. The walkers and birdwatchers aren't yet back, it's the less active guests, wanting a fresh pot or another scone. That scarecrow Miss Battersby always wants something. Miss B's all bony shins and hair pulled back in a French pleat, so tight she has a look of permanent surprise.

Thank you for my gift, Miss Battersby. Can't bring myself to say: the white gloves, the hair grips. She's big on 'grooming'. She'd left the packet at reception. Gives me something every year. So far, I've managed to avoid her.

My pleasure Lydia, you are growing up so fast. I'm almost sixteen. 1961. White gloves?

Miss B is reading a magazine. It's spread open on the table at a page that shows pictures of Yuri Gagarin. FIRST MAN TO ORBIT THE EARTH – WHAT DID HE SEE? His face is framed by the helmet of his cosmonaut's suit and he's smiling, bright-eyed. Everyone's talking about him. Those same pictures are pinned up on our Current Affairs board at school. Gagarin saw that the Earth at a glance is mostly blue, mostly water, *a tremendous blue.*

Odd to think now that, as she'd peered over Miss B's shoulder, she'd no idea that she'd soon see those images of Gagarin again, in Luc's studio. Gagarin's eyes, his words, Luc obsessed on them. *An unprecedented encounter with nature.* Words they both obsessed on.

Not Luc. Not now.

Back to her mother, back to tea on the lawn. Is there more?

More tea, Miss Battersby?

She looks up from the article.

That would be lovely. Thank goodness some things don't change, she says, gazing out at the calm expanse of water. Miss B, like everyone, avoids direct mention of 'it,' my past, my lost family. I once heard her telling another guest: *the sea is God's anger. There was no sea in The Garden of Eden, it came with the Flood.* I wanted to kick her bony shins and shout: What have my parents or my grandma done? Why would God be angry with them? Believing in superstition is tempting, easier than living with all the random stuff.

The sea doesn't have feelings, I want to tell her – tell myself too – the sea just *is*. *Another scone Miss Battersby?* I say, but inside, I'm thinking: Looks pretty now but come back in winter when the wind's been up for days. The thump of a wave over Marine Drive would snatch a stick like you.

I clear the table, carry the tray to the kitchen.

Jennifer doesn't talk about my family either. But I think of them every day, try to hold on to anything I remember. Things around the hotel remind me. So I don't mind clearing up the tea services, laying them out in the pantry.

Jennifer wants to update the hotel, wants to update me too. I might be Lydia Warburton on the school register, but I'm still Lydia Hutton, crouched inside myself, hiding, waiting.

In the pantry I sort the teapots from the milk jugs and sugar bowls, and form neat rows. On the shelf below there are silver cruet sets, blue glass mustard pots set in filigree; below that, drawers lined with green baize: knives, forks and spoons lie snug in separate compartments.

I stroke silver polish onto a teapot, so I can stay here longer; I do it like Mum taught me; I do it to forget Miss B; I do it till I feel my mother standing next to me, smell the cologne she wore, *4711*, a fresh smell that mingles with the sharp tang of silver polish. It's as if I'm six again, I pretend that we're getting ready for the spring opening, the teapots are brown inside, *tannin*, she calls it, and tells me it's all right, but we must buff away the winter tarnish on the outside. I can't see her face, only her hands, neat fingernails, and the yellow duster. I'm asking Mum to explain why tannin inside is all right but tarnish outside isn't.

That was it. Gone.

If she'd known they only had a few months left she'd've have studied her, learned her mother by heart: the colour of her eyes, every freckle, the fall of her hair.

Lydia opened the door and shutters, then, spreading her sketches out on the floor, she selected those that interested her and pinned them to the wall. The rest were too tentative, self-conscious, but these four surprised her, talked back to her.

She put the teapot on the shelf and rearranged her still life. If she could work through more memories of *before* the storm, could she then go back into the storm and tell it all? It began quietly enough: domestic, yes. A sitting-room. Drinking cups of tea around an open fire. Wind roaring down the chimney. Go on. How? At least with the teapot she'd made a start; this thing that was here with her right now, and had been there before the storm, polished by her mother. Damaged though it was, it was real, solid. Tomorrow she'd try drawing from memory; draw the teapot as it had once been.

She needed more objects but she couldn't simply select a bowl of fruit here, a jug there, she'd have to wait for what the cliff released.

Two-thirty. It was warm, a balminess had nudged away the misty morning. The sun was strong in a clean blue sky. Outside she set up the tripod with her old Pentax. No need for the meter, this kind of light she knew by heart. She looked through the viewfinder, made adjustments: equal sea, equal sky. A fine balance. Click.

She scrambled down to the small bay, dwarfed by the chalk cliffs. Above her, puffins fluttered, gannets swooped and cried.

The tide was right. Swimming safely was all about timing, knowing where to leave your clothes, where the water would be by the time you'd finished. She waded up to her knees, her feet and shins hardly registering the cold. The next breaker would reach her waist. She inched forward, waiting for the shock against the soft inside of her thighs. Her knees folded, plunging her shoulders under. Divine iciness, it burned. Numbness below as if her legs didn't exist, though they must be doing something, she was travelling away from the shore. First swim of the year. Stiff-muscled at first, out of practice, but reaching, stretching, her body soon remembered.

Out in the bay she didn't look back. All that mattered was hugging the water, staying intimate with its inhuman bulk.

8

Martin was thirsty. The mist of this morning had given way a bright, warm day and the walk to the lighthouse, a gradual climb from Slayton, was taking longer than he'd imagined. The ground was sodden from months of rain and his suede shoes were caked in mud. If he found her place he'd hardly pass for a hiker.

Lives on the chalk cliff, Flampton way, Jack Powell had said. Between the Flampton turn-off and the lighthouse. There couldn't be more than a handful of houses.

Off to the left, a track struck out across a field to picnic tables beside a wooden building. A café? Beyond that was the track to the main road. What did he think he was going to do – knock on her door and ask for an interview? Ridiculous. He'd get a drink and walk back to Slayton along the road.

'Sorry,' said the woman. Her bright voice matched her bright eyes. She looked directly at him, not hostile but firm. 'We're closed until next week – start of the season.'

Of course, The Bird Centre. Opened long after he'd left.

Unruly grey hair flopped onto the woman's weathered face as she pushed and pulled at the jammed door. On the ground sat a stack of cardboard boxes.

'Swollen wood. It's the damp,' she said. 'Would you mind having a go?'

'Okay.' Shoulder to the door he shoved hard and, on the third attempt, it swung open onto a counter stacked with postcards of sea birds and the chalk cliffs. Farther in, the walls were lined with information panels: the puffin, the gannet, the guillemot. Behind the counter hung a row of binoculars and a sign: *for hire*. With binoculars he could do a reasonable impersonation of a birdwatcher.

'Thank you. Could I ask another favour? Then I'll see if I can find you a drink?' The woman gestured to her car, its hatchback open, packed with more boxes. It looked as if today he was destined to perform good deeds. He'd thought fixing Eileen's washing line had been heroic especially after her remarks about 'dirty pictures.' He realised the futility of explaining that the portfolio of images – including Layla naked on the mound of salt at the centre of *Taking in Water* – represented the triumph of his research in New York; he ought to tell Eileen that, thanks to the rescheduling of Alex Markovski's morning, getting those images had saved his life.

'Almost in Connecticut before the first plane,' he'd assured Eileen, which was almost true. 'No way I would have been in the area, Mum,' he'd said on 12 September, when they'd finally made phone contact. Wouldn't she love the drama of his close shave, something to chew over with Monica? So he'd put up the washing gadget and made his escape.

'Rummaging around Slayton Library again, is it?' Eileen had said as she'd pegged the first sheet. Of course, she hoped the library was a cover story, that he was really shopping for her birthday present, even though she protested: 'Don't waste your money on me.' She'd be mortified if he took her at her word. The present was already sorted. A silk scarf bought in London at Liberty – Francine's suggestion. It was one of a repertoire of gifts: scarves, bath salts, soap, notepaper, dog books. Things that said: *I didn't forget your birthday*. She bought him gadgets from one of her catalogues. The electric sandwich-toaster from Christmas was still in its box. He'd leave it for Francine when he moved.

No library or shops. He'd set off along the coastal path, passing where The Marine Hotel had once stood. Where the cliff had slumped beneath Jennifer Warburton's dining-room extension, the ground had been smoothed and grassed over. The old hotel building remained, now a conference and wedding venue. Hard to imagine Layla there.

Locating the beachcombing woman's house would, at least, give him a sense of her – and an address. When Nick was back from his conference, he'd phone him, make an official approach to the Archive.

He'd set off, striding out as if he were one of those serious hikers who came here drawn by the bleak vistas, the cool, grey light. This stretch of coast had a stoic beauty, austere, industrial-strength. Farther north the beaches were strewn with coal. Beyond the clay cliffs of Slayton Bay rose the more attractive, towering, chalk cliffs. As a child he'd spent many chilly Sundays on Slayton beach where the dull mud cliffs were always on the move, slipping and slumping. *Not too far back.* Eileen, ever alert, would pitch their windbreak well clear.

The cliff path rose steadily, a tougher walk than he'd anticipated. Here, at The Bird Centre, the chalk stood 400 ft. He was halfway to the lighthouse but still no sign of what might be her house.

'Thanks,' said the woman, as he brought in the last of the boxes. 'Jean, by the way, I'm Jean Thornton.' She offered her hand. He shook it.

'Martin Dawson. Have I earned my drink?' He nodded, gesturing towards the door beyond the information desk to a café area where blue plastic chairs were stacked on tables. 'A glass of water would do.'

'Take a seat,' she said, pointing to the picnic tables outside.

'Here.' She came back holding up a carton of long-life orange juice.

'Thanks,' he said, trying to rub the mud off his shoes.

'Not the best footwear given all the rain we've had.'

'So I heard.' Every phone call to Eileen began with a gloomy weather report. *Stair rods, Martin.*

'You don't live here then? Only, you sound as if you might.'

'Originally. Just visiting.' Though he'd tried, he hadn't entirely rounded out his vowels. As a student he'd read aloud, anything – the newspaper, cereal packets, lecture notes – to cultivate a neutral voice. Even though by then it was cool to have a regional accent he hadn't wanted his. Didn't want to hear his flat vowels pitching him back to where other boys went shagging girls on the beach while he studied for A-Levels. *Marty smarty pants.*

'Beginner?' she asked.

'Oh, I'm no twitcher,' he laughed. 'Just out for a walk, spur of the moment thing, hence – ' He pointed at his shoes. 'Thought I might make it to the lighthouse.'

'You might see puffins today, they're coming in fast. Why not visit our viewing points?' She opened one of the boxes and fished out a leaflet, 'hot off the press,' and explained what he might see along the track to Flampton lighthouse.

'Noisy,' he said.

'Contact calls, finding each other. They come in hordes, check out nesting places then fly off until it's time to lay. *Then* it's noisy.' He should be sure to notice the gannet colony on one of the chalk stacks. 'Looks like nothing but heaps of bleached seaweed, but each pile is a home with an owner about to return. Amazing, isn't it, how they know?' she enthused.

He struggled to imagine what it felt like to have a homing instinct.

'How much?' he said, pointing back inside at the binoculars.

'But we're not open – oh, well since you were so helpful. Got a credit card? I won't charge you but I need a deposit. Not that I don't think you're honest, but it's amazing how people get carried away, forget.' She jotted down his details. 'You can return them any time up to five. With this lot to unpack, I'll be here until then.'

'Thank you,' he said and finished the warm orange juice.

'Is there still a cafe on the cliff, past the Flampton turn off?'

'It shut a while back,' she laughed.

'So what is there between here and the lighthouse?'

'A couple of derelict cottages, and Marine House.'

'A hotel?'

'A private house. You're thinking of The Marine at Slayton, it's a conference centre now. You've been away a while, then.'

Martin rejoined the path and stopped where a sturdy wooden platform afforded a fine view along the coast. Birds screeched, patrolling the cliff, sounds that bounced off the rock and amplified to a cacophony of anxious chatter that filled his head. *Dirty pictures. Adult material.* How adult was it for him to still think Eileen needed indulging with protective lies? He steadied himself against the rail and leaned over. A skyscraper of a cliff, sheer, etched with thousands of fractures and ledges, the drop to the sea below, hundreds of feet. His head spun as he recalled those who'd jumped from the towers at such a height. He leaned over as far as he dared, unnerved by the danger and yet there was a moment of exhilaration, of almost wanting to leap, thinking he might fly and dive like a gannet. He stepped back and trained his binoculars towards the sky.

Last September. A clear morning and awake at 4am with jetlag, anxious because Sarton was still checking him out, wanted more information about his research, his proposed book. As he'd showered, he'd gone over the conversation he'd had with Alex Markovski.

'Don't worry. I'll get back to you,' she'd assured him, the previous day.

She took his research seriously but only now, since Martin had actually arrived from England, could she finally organise access to the Collection & Archive *and* Sarton himself. 'Mr Sarton only deals with what's in front of him – too many time-wasting grad students.' She'd paused a moment then added. 'I have a telephone conference with him booked for first thing, then I plan to take work up to Connecticut. The car will be leaving around midday. No promises but I'll just say, have a bag ready. If all goes well, we'll collect you.'

He'd packed a holdall: laptop, notes and a change of underwear. Alex had implied he could be staying over for a couple of nights. Sitting around felt too much like waiting for a call from a lukewarm lover. He'd walk off the jetlag, get some breakfast. No point in wasting a morning. It had always been part of his plan to explore Luc's territory. He could do that and be back by noon.

Not long after 5am he walked across Washington Square, stopped at the fountain to consider the spot where Layla had stood; then headed down Thompson but hadn't been able to work out which building Luc had jumped from, the sort of information he'd find among papers in Sarton's archive; he'd taken photographs up and down the street, shots he hoped would give him focus when he came to write.

He carried on walking south, the clear morning clearing his head, until a half-formed idea of maybe going up the World Trade Centre became a plan. He'd go up to the top, get a bird's-eye view of the Village, an overview of Luc's neighbourhood.

Almost there, he passed a diner, stopped for coffee and eggs over-easy.

'You're from England aren't you!' the waitress exclaimed with pride at locating his accent. 'Headed for the Towers?'

'I am.'

As soon as his coffee was emptied she'd offered a refill.

'Thanks.' He'd looked up, smiled, noticed her name badge.

'If I were you, I'd get in line early,' Dosha advised. 'It's awesome to be first up and it's such a beautiful morning.'

His neck ached as he gazed skyward, taking in the glass and steel structure towering above him, the geometry of it, the scale. Dosha was right, inside the lobby a queue for the Observation Deck was already forming. He joined the line behind a Japanese family – mother, father, twin girls – and watched as workers poured in, already talking on their phones, take-out coffees in hand. He was impatient to join them, to get high up. Now that he was here, he wanted to look down on it all, even if he wasn't going to be the first. He checked his watch. Eight. How much longer before they started handing out tickets?

Then: the vibration in the pocket of his jeans. He couldn't hear the ringtone, what with the hubbub of voices around him, the Japanese twins chasing each other round and round their patient parents, giggling and shrieking with delight as the one caught the other. Who would phone at this hour? Eileen, something wrong? The relief when he heard Alex's voice.

'Good news,' she'd said, 'a change of plan.' A rescheduling that saw him sitting with Alex Markovski in the rear of Garth Sarton's chauffeured limo, headed towards the Interstate, when the first plane hit.

'What's that all about?' Alex commented as low-flying helicopters and police cars, sirens screeching, passed them, headed towards Manhattan. Martin took a cursory glance, shrugged and settled back into the soft leather seat.

'And you're sure Mr Sarton's okay about me viewing the Mantella films?' If he saw nothing else while he was there, he had to see those films.

'Relax. It's all fixed,' Alex reassured. 'The guest suite is ready for you and I've had Mr Sarton's PA set up the projector in there so you can view at your leisure.' At Sarton's place in Greenwich,

Connecticut, the housekeeper ran out to greet them.

'Thank the Lord,' she cried and hugged Alex, then hurried them into what seemed like an office; TV blaring in the corner, another woman, who turned out to be the PA, glued to the set.

Martin stared at the screen not quite believing his eyes. And in that moment the South Tower collapsed. This must be some disaster movie. This isn't real, his mind said.

'Oh, Martin. To think – ' Alex exclaimed.

His stomach lurched. He closed his eyes. *Breathe, breathe, breathe*, ran the voice in his head to stop his breakfast returning.

'Sit down.' Alex was saying, offering him a chair. He slumped to the seat, head between his knees. Alex's voice, explaining the sequence of their morning, sounded far off. There was talk of Sarton busy making calls, checking on his daughter, his staff, all in Manhattan.

It was a relief to be alone in the guest suite. He poured a whisky, tried calling Eileen and Francine but the lines were jammed.

Eventually, to blot it all out, he began to watch the *Taking in Water* films. It helped for a while to focus on the images playing before him, Gagarin's face, close-ups of the sea, waves cresting to the soundtrack of the sea. But, he couldn't help it, every so often he had to turn on the TV.

He lost count of the times he'd watched the building fall and fall again, his body flooded with a mixture of nausea and elation, a twist in his gut. He looked in vain among the wailing, dust-covered crowds for the Japanese family, as if somehow he needed to witness they'd been saved, could hardly bear to think of those little girls or the workers he'd seen showing their passes, going up in the lifts, most of them would have been at their desks. He allowed himself to believe Dosha would survive; after all, she was a block away.

It was compelling and indecent, his need to keep staring at

what looked like grey snow; and people with jackets or shirts over their faces, coughing, running, dwarfed by the surge of dust. Dust everywhere. What with the jetlag, the whisky, the shock, the more he watched the more he went back in his mind to where he'd stood just hours ago until it seemed as if he could smell the burning, feel the dust catch in his throat. As the building fell for the umpteenth time, the billowing dust became a sea surge, his mind lifted above his body and he saw his father, the way he used to imagine him when he was a child, as if looking down from space, seeing his father a speck in a boat, out fishing on a globe of water, his tiny boat riding the huge waves.

He'd woken in the small hours shouting, *no, no, no*. Then, relief to realise it had been a dream: him running to stay ahead of the surging sea only to be swallowed up by a cloud of dust.

Leaving the viewing platform he found the path again. He was in no hurry to go back inside Eileen's bubble of anxiety. He needed to walk off the memory of that day, compose himself. He didn't want the nightmares to return. His shoes were wrecked, anyway. He might as well carry on having come this far.

Ahead, the land sloped gently down as the highest part of the chalk eased into an uneven stretch of gullies and bays. He could see a white house. He glanced over the cliff to the inlet below where a boulder-strewn beach turned sandy at the shoreline.

There was something in the water. Jean Thornton said there were seals along here. He looked through his binoculars. Not a seal, a person. He scanned the shoreline; no one else was down there. Thoughts of rescue flicked through his head. Who would he call: ambulance, coastguard?

He focused the binoculars. The person was treading water with no sense of panic, rather the opposite, the swimmer had command of the water. Warm though he was from his hike, he couldn't imagine stripping off, plunging in.

The swimmer pitched forward into an easy crawl, heading for the shore and, just short of the beach, stood up. A woman, naked. Tall and graceful as she strode through the shallows onto the sand.

He re-focused as she moved, heat rising in his neck.

It was her.

She flung a towel around her shoulders, arched her spine as she rubbed her back, a movement that emphasised the roundness of her breasts, the curve of her hips. A little fuller now, but that was a body he knew. Unbelievable!

He dodged back from the edge as she made her way towards the path that led to the wooden steps up the gully to the cliff top. He crouched in the undergrowth. A few feet back, along the way he'd come, was an information board. He scrambled towards it for cover.

He read one word at a time, as if this would make him invisible. *Do not pick the wild flowers.*

9

Steven sat at his computer, a new blank document open on the screen.

'It's only a draft,' his boss had emphasised. Still, Steven wanted to get his assessment of the chalk stacks below Flampton right. 'In your opinion, Steven, what are the implications for our onshore investigations? Onshore work means dealing with the public,' his boss'd leaned in, eyeballed him, 'Listen, managing the erosion is the easy part; it's managing the human beings that eats the time and my budget.'

Earlier that morning Steven had sent out letters to property owners in the project area flagging up the possibility of a ground survey on their premises next week. Luckily, there weren't many homes in their unit but one of the letters must have been for the woman whose house they'd flown over.

Steven was preparing himself for the fact that he now had a job that involved *real people* as well as the geological processes he'd studied with such interest. At Uni, he'd been fascinated to learn the ways in which six billion people were eroding the Earth. Human activity was now classed as a geological process, second only to water as an agent of erosion, a fact that thrilled him, in theory. In practice, with this project, he'd be dealing with individuals who might be adversely affected by their work.

For the moment Steven was in a people-free zone. He glanced round the empty, open-plan office. Everyone was down the pub for a pint and a pie. He wanted his draft finished by the time they came back. *In your opinion.*

'Opinions will differ, Steven, so back yours up with sound observations.'

He was beginning to understand the project as a whole: the national strategy for coastal defence and, within that, how the work of Northern Geophysics in this region fitted in. Here, the coast had been divided into units and the one he'd been assigned to was the stretch from the end of Slayton Bay to Flampton lighthouse, which formed a discrete whole because of its geological structure: chalk. Formed by a slow build-up of microscopic particles, the skeletons of ancient sea creatures, billions of micro lives, shed to form those massive cliffs.

He opened the spiral-bound pad with his notes from the trip. This report was a small task in a complex project involving weeks of work in phases outlined on the flow-chart above his desk: DATA ACQUISITION: MARINE AND TERRESTRIAL ZONES > ANALYSIS OF PROCESSES > STRATEGIC OPTIONS > IMPLEMENTATION. His draft report would be a minute section of marine zone data.

'What are we dealing with, Steven: damage due to wave attack or atypical precipitation?' That's all he had to focus on, he'd better get on.

He'd followed the arguments on both sides: the increase in severe weather events was part of a natural cycle – there'd been floods in Mediaeval times; floods yes, but no cars, no industry, no holes in the ozone. His view was that the climate was changing and most likely it was a manmade problem: if we could lash it up, we could put it right. Or at least have a go.

No need to worry about his bad spelling, the computer could sort that, though he'd had to instruct it to learn: coccoliths, silica, Upper Jurassic, Corallian.

Who needed to be good with words when the layers of the Earth could be read like a book? Next to the flow chart was a geological map of the region, chalk shown as a swathe of grey.

The cliffs at Flampton were evidence of strata that ran miles inland, beneath rolling fields grazed by sheep. The band of purple, to the north of it, indicated glacial clay in which dinosaur prints had been found.

Chalk and clay behaved differently when attacked by the sea, which was why the clay formed a separate unit, to be dealt with by others on the team. He was glad he wasn't on that unit, clay being much more unstable. A while back, there'd been a controversy on that patch concerning poor drainage with the local authority held liable for the damage to some hotel.

Nothing so dramatic on his chalk unit: a different formation, from a different era. So, how had it been affected by weather and the sea? Human activity was not significant at Flampton because so few people lived there, which simplified things. His boss was pleased to have at least one sparsely populated unit in his brief.

'Makes our job easy if there are no property issues.' Which meant they could proceed smoothly to 'strategic options' and 'implementation.' The boss was in line for promotion: *on time and within budget.*

In Steven's opinion, comparing photographs they'd taken from the helicopter with pictures taken five years ago, the instability of the chalk stack below Flampton could be due to excess water retention following unprecedented precipitation. *Precipitation.* He liked the way this word covered all forms of falling moisture.

The cliffs just beyond Flampton and up to the headland, where the lighthouse stood, were slumped chalk, between 100-200 ft. They were substantially lower than the cliffs in the direction of Slayton. Between Flampton and Slayton, the higher chalk reached a vertical 400 ft. In his opinion, this section was not a problem. On balance, he believed their ground investigations should focus on the slumped area, perhaps extending somewhat towards the higher chalk as a precaution. This, he calculated, would leave the woman's house off their patch. Just.

10

At the kitchen sink, Lydia held her mouth under the running water, cold tap full on. The sea had left her throat dry; all that water and yet she was parched.

She wouldn't boast, not even to herself, but she was quietly pleased. First swim of the year, a good session in the studio, and she hadn't let this morning's panic take hold. It was tempting to go back to the work for an hour but she knew she'd had the best from herself and, besides, she had calls to make. Howard had left another message while she was out. And Patrick – she'd quite forgotten. She shivered, her hands tingling pink; first, a hot shower.

The telephone rang, she could see it was Patrick, must have read her thoughts. She dried her hands, lifted the handset off its cradle and walked as she talked.

'Patrick, hi. I hadn't forgotten you,' she fibbed, trying to keep her tone light.

'You know I try not to pressure you for work but – '

'Framed or unframed?' Unframed, she might manage to put together six.

'Framed would be better – '

'I can tell you now I've only a couple of framed *Horizon* I could think of letting you have – '

'Whatever you can spare. *Surface* images would be his next choice. He was less keen on *Failed Objects*.'

'Not pretty enough?' she laughed.

'If that's what you have, then send them. As much as you can spare from each series – I can always sell them.'

'Well, I can't get over to York.' Too much outside world if she was to burrow down into the new work, but she couldn't mention that, didn't want Patrick getting curious. Not yet.

'I know it's short notice but Ross will be over your way tomorrow morning.' She could tell by the enthusiasm in his voice that this meant a lot to him and he wasn't giving up. 'He'll collect. Okay?'

'Okay.' She couldn't let Patrick down. 'I'll get something together when I've had my shower. I'm desperate for a shower, I've just been swimming.'

'Don't tell me you've been in the sea, already?' He mock shuddered down the line. She pictured him in the warm, white space of his gallery.

Already? She hadn't swum since October, a warm spell before the bad weather. Warm and wet, or crisp and dry, it was all decided in the tussle of air masses high above the Atlantic. The warm October that let her swim late brought a stormy, wet winter. There was always more interest in her photographs after storms especially with the publicity weather gets these days, as if it were some celebrity bad boy.

She wasn't desperate to sell work, hadn't ever sought a gallery, that wasn't why she took pictures. Patrick had found her through Jean's daughter, Sally. At first she'd let him have her assemblages, her 'doodles', fashioned from what the sea threw up – rope, shoes, cans, driftwood, worn shells – pleased to find a home for work that only satisfied her need to collect and to make. She'd refused to let him have photographs until they'd stacked up, begun to swamp her. Patrick was generous with support too. Once she'd given up doing her own developing and printing he'd advised on the best lab, made suggestions on paper quality. He'd also persuaded her to buy the computer and digital camera. If the digital shots for this new piece turned out to be more than studies Patrick would know where she could get technical advice. She would make an effort to find something for Ross to collect.

In the bathroom she took a fresh towel from the airing cupboard and spread it on the wooden seat beneath the window. The sun caught the window's tinted border, casting a blue shadow on the white wall. Her skin was tight, itchy with dried salt. She slid open the shower door, let the water run hot and stepped into the flow, stretching as it drenched her hair, streamed over her face and dissolved the patches of salt all over her body.

Out in the bay she'd soon fallen back into the rhythm of swimming, letting the sea lead while she followed, familiar partners again. It was easily done, thinking the sea was a creature, muscles the size of a mountain range, didn't know its own strength. So dumb it thundered across the road, didn't stop to knock on Grandma's brass shell knocker, the door no sturdier than a piece of paper under its heft. That was how she used to think of it, a living monster. Now, the sea seemed more like a vast cloth. Sometimes flat as bed sheets but more often a bolt of silk forever unfurling and slumping; she'd learned to embrace its folds.

She turned up the temperature dial and squeezed the last blob of shampoo, pearly white stuff with a whiff of coconut. This morning she'd finished off the bread in the freezer; it was time to stock up on supplies so she could settle down to work. She slid the shower door open, flung the empty bottle on the seat so she wouldn't forget. Swimming each day would keep her steady as she sunk into the new work.

She rinsed her hair then smoothed foaming oil into her skin, easing her muscles, paying attention to the stiffness in the small of her back. If Howard were here he'd find the spot, play her spine as he played his clarinet, a delicate, accurate touch, he always knew where to put the pressure. Had she read too much into his voicemail?

What about if you come to London?

There'd been something odd about that last message, a shift in tone that she couldn't put her finger on. Come to think of it, last time he was here, he'd asked, 'theoretically' would she ever consider coming back to London to live? She'd laughed it off. What a thing to ask. But now this. What was he hinting – that they become a conventional couple? What they had was just fine. 'Safe sex,' they'd joke – safe from attachment. Not a couple, they'd both agreed. They moved in and out of each other's lives. If he weren't her tenant and 'caretaker' of Bea's house – never her house, even though Bea had been dead for twenty years – they wouldn't even have had this. He came here to see her when he could, between gigs, said he enjoyed getting right away from London. When the orchestra toured abroad they might not speak to each other for weeks, though with e-mails back and forth, it could seem as if they had. 'Your virtual lover,' Jean called him.

Out of the shower she pulled the towel around her, warmth spreading through her, blood pumping oxygen to every cell of her body, filling her head with clarity and an eagerness to be back in the studio tomorrow. It was time to go further, take risks. Howard would understand her need for solitude, as she'd so often left him alone to his work.

A tap at her door below made her jump. A twitcher wanting water, no doubt. It often happened when the weather changed. She wound the towel around, pulling it tight across her breasts, tucking in the ends. Opening the window she looked down on the head of a young man, binoculars slung over one shoulder.

'Hello?' she leaned out and he looked up.

No leather coat, no dog, but it was him. The spy.

'You? Who the fuck are you?' she blurted out before she could stop herself.

'Sorry, sorry,' he said throwing back his head, a nervous flick of his hair. The binocular strap slipped from his shoulder, he caught it, looped it round his neck. Had he watched her swimming and followed her? Bloody stalker.

'Look, I'm sorry to intrude,' he said, polite, softly spoken.

'You're not a birdwatcher,' she pointed, an accusing stab, at the binoculars. 'So – which newspaper?'

'Newspaper?'

'TV then. What do you want?'

'What, sorry?'

'Not a journalist. Then what are you, a stalker?'

'No, of course not – '

'– and that helicopter stunt this morning – what was all that about?' 'Helicopter? I'm sorry – *helicopter?* Look, I'd better go.' He turned to leave.

'Wait!' Not so fast. She needed to know who he was, a name. 'Wait!' The word fixed him. He stood, awkward, on the path. 'I'm coming down.'

She unwound the towel and pulled on her bathrobe, tying the sash tight. Her feet thumped on the wooden stairs. Pulling the door closed behind her so he couldn't snoop, she was outside before she realised she was barefoot.

'So?'

'Sorry, I can see this isn't convenient,' he gestured to her bathrobe. 'I've gone about this entirely the wrong way. I ought to have written formally.'

'What do you want?'

He opened his mouth to speak. Nothing came out, as if it wasn't physically possible for him to finish the sentence. He studied her; the kind of look she'd seen many times before, but not for years. Looking at her as if she weren't real, as if he was checking her against a mental image, against images seen elsewhere.

'You were at Slayton this morning with that old dog. You followed me here. Why?'

'Sorry.' His hands went up as if protecting himself from her onslaught.

'Who are you?'

'Martin Dawson,' he said, offering his hand to shake. She didn't take it. He reached into his pocket, pulled out a wafer-thin metal case, snapped it open and handed her his card. Dr Martin Dawson, letters after his name. Reader at London University, the address of his college, Department of Art & Cultural History, phone, fax, mobile, e-mail. He produced another card. Dr Martin Dawson, consultant, Artists' Voices Project, National Archive of Sound.

He began to explain about some project: would she consider contributing to Artists' Voices?

'What makes you think I'm an artist?'

He gestured towards the hut.

Had he been here earlier?

'You've watched me working as well?' Then she remembered, even if he had been here, she'd had the shutters closed all morning.

'No, no. Of course not.'

She stood her ground, arms folded, looking him in the eye, waiting for an explanation.

'I didn't expect to find you,' he said.

'*Find* me?'

'It was a hunch – I mean – Luc,' he paused. 'The artist – '

'Oh, Yes?' she said.

He looked at his feet, then looked up at her.

'You're Layla.'

So, she'd been right, not paranoid. She took a deep breath.

'*Was.*'

She followed the ripples in his throat as he swallowed. His serious eyes regarded her, not blinking, as if looking through her, back down the years for someone who wasn't quite there anymore. Checking her against the press cuttings, the footage, no doubt he'd seen Warhol's screen test and, of course, the work itself. Enough images to make him think he knew her story; enough images to make one up. Did he think if he stared hard enough she'd become Layla?

'My name is Lydia. Lydia Hutton. You'd better come over here a moment.' She led him to the bench on the verandah of the hut. They sat down. She must stop this, now, set the record straight. 'Layla was a long time ago,' she looked him in the eye.

'I'm a historian.'

'And you're interested in Luc?'

'Yes.'

'In the gossip, or in the work?'

His hand pushed nervously through his hair again, his dark eyebrows raised furrowing his forehead, as if to show he was serious.

'My area of interest is the post-war years, the art world, cultural change. I'm interested in – ' He talked fluently, knowledgeably, about how Luc had been part of a pivotal moment in cultural history, when art and mass media collided for the first time. She'd been there, an eyewitness. It sounded like a lecture and also a pitch. What could he possibly want?

'Eyewitness? You make it sound like a – a crime scene.' She turned away from him, stared out to sea. She was witness to enough already; to events more significant than Luc.

'Your story's important,' he said, there was enthusiasm in his voice but did he mean it or was he simply trying to coax back her attention? She carried on staring at the horizon and said:

'To who?'

Taking In Water

'Lots of people – and academics, like me.'

'Is that what academics do now, stalk the ex-lovers of dead and forgotten artists?' she turned back to face him. 'Just how did you find me?'

He shifted uncomfortably, took a deep breath, and launched into another spiel, '*Taking In Water* is key to my current research interests. Last year I was in the States.' On he went about some archive, some university, Memphis State, its collection of underground magazines from the Sixties, some interview with Judi Noone.

'That bitch Noone?' An ex of Luc's, always did have it in for Lydia. 'What did she have to say?'

'That you – er Layla was actually Lydia Warburton, from a British seaside town called Layton or Clayton – Noone didn't get that right, but –' he carried on. Lydia was only half listening: to think Luc's ex would come back to haunt after all these years. 'Being from round here – the name Warburton and well, it seemed a coincidence.' How he'd wondered if Noone had meant Slayton and that he knew he would have to check it out.

'But why? Why go to all that trouble? And, by the way,' she'd better make this absolutely clear, 'I'm neither Layla nor Warburton. Right?'

He nodded.

'You were part of a key moment.'

'The moment has long since passed. I've moved on,' she stood up.

'You were part of his major work,' he stood beside her, 'a work that received international acclaim. Luc's was an interesting career at an important turning point. *Taking In Water* is a key piece that's been overlooked. A great piece, in my view, that's just as relevant today – '

'You think so?'

'Of course, what could be more relevant – the collision

between natural and manmade forces?' He was off again, sounding like a lecture. She could hear Luc's words in his: *exploring the sublime without romanticism, and the manmade without cynicism.*

'It was an ephemeral work,' she said, knowing it was well documented in a lavish book and there were the movies Mantella had shot of each performance.

'There is documentation – ' he said.

'So you don't need me.' She indicated he should walk ahead of her but he paused on the verandah steps, turning to try again: 'I'm interested in your view – of Luc, of how you worked together, the period, the first staging – you were there. Not everything is in the sources that remain.' He was blocking her way, not aggressive, more like pleading. 'You'd be creating a valuable archive.'

'Archiving voices – doesn't the work say it all, as I think you've just proved?'

'Eyewitness testimony is invaluable.'

'I don't want to be a witness to Luc's life.' She had enough archiving and witnessing of her own to deal with. 'Luc was a fraction of my life, barely four years and a *long* time ago.'

'The Sound Archive would want your story, not just Luc's. You can check their website.'

'Like I said, it's in the past. I've moved on.'

'I'm sorry,' said Martin.

'Stop saying sorry.' She waved her hand, made it clear he must move, go.

'Forgive my intrusion.' He fingered the strap of the binoculars and she noticed the sticker proclaiming them to be the property of The Bird Centre. What was Jean doing supplying binoculars to a stalker? Wasn't the Centre closed? The breeze caught her bare leg and she shivered.

'Do you mind,' she hurried him now. 'I'm going in. Luc's

been written about. It's all been said.'

'Not your version.'

'If you're the expert, you must know Layla never spoke.'

11

What made him think he could barge in like that? Back in the bathroom, Lydia thrust one leg then the other into her jeans. She hung her bathrobe on the hook behind the door, and fished in the pocket for his cards: *Dr Martin Dawson*. Academic or not, it was still prying.

He'd followed her, watched her swimming.

She'd given herself up to the water to forget about him spooking her this morning and he'd been spying on her, again! So what if he'd seen her naked, he must be familiar enough with her body. Her younger body. No, it was the invasion of her solitude; it was him dragging up Luc and all because of some snide remark by Judi Noone back in 1968. He'd followed a trail from some yellowing underground magazine until he knocked on her door today. How could that be? Was it possible?

Luc, that episode of her past, was the last place she needed to go. *Eyewitness*. She had that other past tugging at her: sole witness to events that night, all evidence gone without a trace.

Across the landing in her work room the computer sat on a desk by the window that faced inland, up the track. She pressed the start-up button and, while the computer got its brain in gear, busied herself browsing through stacks of framed photographs propped against the far wall. Patrick wanted *Horizon* and most of these were *Surface* and *Failed Objects*.

She opened the *Horizon* drawer in the plan chest that stood in the alcove. It was filled with neatly stacked pictures, printed on matte A3 fine art paper, a layer of tissue between each. All one-offs, she'd destroyed the negatives. Which of these did she not want back? Each was a moment in time she'd thought worth contemplating. She made a selection, trying not to think about what lay in the bottom drawer: a folder, fat with old newspaper cuttings, the pristine copy of *Taking in Water Documented*, the book Mantella had produced and which Dr Dawson had obviously studied. He claimed to be an academic but that didn't guarantee he wasn't some oddball.

She picked up the phone and punched in Jean's mobile number.

'Jean?'

'Lydia?'

'Where are you?' It came out sharp, a demand.

'At the Centre – '

'But you're not open yet.'

'I've been setting up. What's the matter? You sound annoyed.'

'Did you hire out any binoculars today?'

'Well, yes, there was a young man – '

Lydia took a deep breath to steady her voice, 'I think he might be – well – some kind of a stalker.'

'What? He seemed harmless, pleasant enough. Helpful, actually.'

'He was watching me down on Slayton beach this morning, and this afternoon he knocked on my door. He wants to interview me about – ' more hesitation. They avoided the Luc part of her past; Luc who'd driven a wedge between them all those years ago. They avoided most of the past since both, for different reasons, had returned here to start again.

'A journalist – oh, I don't think so.'

That note of hand-patting reassurance in Jean's voice said:

are you imagining this? Not long after Jean had moved back, one evening, the wine making her bold, Lydia had talked about her time in hospital, her 'episode,' thought Jean ought to know. But she'd not been bold enough to tell Jean what her hallucinations had revealed. That would have been too much to dump on her old friend who, back then, was still bruised from her divorce. Besides, she was still testing their friendship, had to discover if she could trust Jean so soon after becoming re-acquainted.

'Not a journalist, an academic. He claims. Did he return your binoculars?'

A pause. She heard concern in Jean's silence.

'Yes, he did. I'm sorry, Lydia. I'd no idea. Oh – ' Jean said, her tone shifting, as if suddenly remembering something. 'Now I think of it he did ask – '

'What?'

'Nothing that would have alerted me that he was after you. He wanted to know was there still a café at Flampton, and about any houses along the cliff.'

'See, he was snooping!'

'I'm finished here. Let me lock up and I'll come round.'

'It's all right.'

'No, I feel awful now.'

'No need. Come anyway for a drink, then you can do me a favour – could you stop by the mini mart? I need a few things.'

At the computer she checked her inbox, found messages from Patrick and Howard.

Hope you're glowing from the shower. That's great you can sort out work – as much as you like – it always sells. The weather is on people's minds, if not consciously then not far below the surface, there's always a demand for work that taps into that. Also, see attached – thought it might interest you. I've been asked to put forward the names of artists who explore water and the weather – any interest? I know you don't usually go for this sort of thing but this looks kind of different. *Ciao,* Patrick.

She clicked on the attachment. *Every Last Drop* – a multi-media event – exhibition, performances, conference – bringing together those whose work explored water. There was a call for contributions from artists, writers, dancers, musicians and academics. It wasn't happening until next spring. She could hardly think about tomorrow let alone next year.

Thanks for info about *Every Last Drop* - sounds interesting. A bit too far ahead for me to think about but keep me posted. Thanks, too, for putting me forward for the library commission – I've made a selection of work. I'll be out first thing so late morning would be good – say, 11.30? If Ross wants to come earlier I'll leave them in the studio – key under the verandah. Let me know what suits. Thanks, L

Lydia, hi

You're off the radar – what's up? Can you make it to London? Ray's agreed to keep an eye on the house while I'm on tour – maybe it would be good to sort out a few house things with you here? How about you turn on your mobile??? Talk soon... x Howard

'Howard, it's me, sorry. It's been the weirdest day. I was swimming when you phoned before.' In London swimming meant an overcrowded chlorinated pool at Swiss Cottage.

Howard didn't ask what had been weird, but chatted on about his rehearsals, more dates added to the Italian tour and wasn't it a good job Ray could keep things going at the house?

'So what about coming to London, sort stuff before Italy – '

'Things?' That sounded like more than the house. Why did he want to involve her suddenly when he'd always taken care of sub-lets; it was the deal they'd had for years. His voice had that edge again, distant, no warmth, no affection.

'The house and – ' he hesitated, whatever was coming after 'and' she wasn't sure she wanted to hear.

'Howard, I'm sorry,' she cut in, 'but London is the last place I can be right now. Something's come up – a piece of work I've just started and I really –' the word crave was in her mind but that sounded hysterical, 'I really *need* to be here, to be on my own...'

'More than usual?'

Silence.

'What was it you wanted to say?' she asked.

'It can wait. I'll call you once Max has decided about the final briefing – might get away in time to come up late on Saturday.'

In the sitting-room the fire was going well. Salt dried in the driftwood crackled, giving off sparks. Jean would be here soon. She went to the kitchen to find a bottle of wine. What was it that bothered her most – that Howard wanted her to move back to London or that she really did prefer her solitude to time with him? She had to make this new work, alone; make something, hands on, that would hold what she needed to put down.

No moping, Lydia. Her father would say on wet days. *What's the cure for moping?* And she'd say: *Making.* Out would come the flour, butter, sugar, jam and he'd let her mix and roll and cut out the jam tarts for tea.

She needed to *make* this new piece.

Reaching up to the shelf above the fridge, she lifted down a blue cup, coated in dust. All these years and still she kept it. She blew the dust away. Rough, handmade, such a sad thing. She'd rolled clay with the heel of her hand, to and fro, exerting an even pressure to form a rope that she'd coiled into a cylinder and then smoothed the joins. She'd meant to make it bigger. At least she'd made it. This *made* thing had let her return to the world. The day it came whole from the kiln in the Occupational Therapy workshop, she'd discharged herself. Now there were cracks in the glaze. The handle was too small, the rim turned in on itself, a tight-lipped cup. A teacup to hold the storm.

12

'This is cosy.' Jean settled into the armchair by the fire.

'Cup of tea, or red wine?'

'Well, it's gone six, why not a small one.'

Lydia poured them both a glass.

'I'm sorry about the binoculars. Martin, that was his name.'

An uneasy silence gathered around the name – *Martin* – and all that his appearance implied. She didn't want to go into that, the reason this Martin had turned up.

'You weren't to know,' Lydia smiled, sat back on the sofa. 'Oh, let's forget about him,' she raised her glass. 'I went in today. To my first swim of the year and to a successful season at the Centre. Cheers!"

'Cheers. Rather you than me.'

'Oh come on, it's fine once your shoulders are under,' Lydia smiled thinking she sounded like Jean when they were ten. 'That's what you used to tell me.' She stretched her legs along the sofa. At ten, she'd been afraid to go into the sea but the summer before Grammar School, Jean had coaxed her into the water. Like sisters they'd been. Until Luc came along.

Back then she'd practically lived at Jean's house – after school, in the holidays and sleeping over on a Saturday night. The Thorntons' semi was on a new estate away from the front. Compared to the hotel it seemed a dolls' house, with its tiny kitchen and a toaster that took only two slices.

Jean's mum and dad treated her as part of the family. Mrs

Thornton, a fine dressmaker, took commissions: wedding gowns, communion frocks, smart suits. Her mouth was always full of pins, a tape measure draped round her neck, the dining table spread with fabric, a row of bridesmaids' dresses, peach satin, hanging from the picture rail waiting to be hemmed. Mr Thornton, an amateur photographer, would sometimes take the wedding pictures. If the red light was on above the bathroom door they had to use the outside loo. It was Jean's father who'd taught Lydia how to develop and print.

Left to their own devices, she and Jean would put giant rollers in each other's hair, trying out new styles, or practise jiving to Elvis. They'd fetch battered cod and thick chips from the chippy to eat straight from the newspaper, watching TV. Aunt Jennifer would've been appalled. Lydia also liked to watch the fish in the Thorntons' tropical aquarium. Tiny, colourful fish nuzzling around a miniature wreck. What if her family had found a wreck, all of them, stayed together? The thought comforted her. By the time she'd headed for London and Luc, she and Jean had grown apart, but thoughts of the wreck lingered and flourished.

After Luc died, she and Jean had met up in London, a few weeks before Jean got married. It hurt then and could still rankle, to remember how distant Jean had been that day, as if 'Layla' had been more real to her than her old school friend. Then the distance became physical as the newlyweds left for Australia and Jean continued to follow Mike's career, having three children, each born on a different continent. Her reward: ten years ago, Mike found himself a young post-graduate student. Jean had come back to Slayton to recover, start again and, like Lydia, make the best of things. They mostly stuck to the present, to who they were now.

'It's not getting shoulders under that bothers me, it's the coming out,' said Jean. 'You won't get me in the sea until June.

Anyway, I'll be too busy at the Centre. Can I put you down for a few hours?'

'Why not – then I can vet who gets the binoculars.'

'I'm sorry. He seemed harmless. Are you sure he – ' That tone, again.

'He knocked on my door. Look.' She offered Jean his cards. 'Wants to interview me for some Archive.'

'Oh, the *Sound Archive*.' Her stress on the word seemed to say: *There, I told you. It's all right*. 'Huge collection of bird calls. Highly respectable.'

'He was no ornithologist. This was for some artists' project.'

'Lydia, it's part of the *National* Collection of Oral History,' Jean went on to explain how some new hot-shot Director was collecting stories from all walks of life: scientists, sex-workers, butchers, bankers, writers. And wasn't that a marvelous idea? 'So now they're collecting artists lives too? It's become rather grand with all this digital recording. You should be flattered. What did you say?'

'Told him to go away.'

'Oh, well, that's it then,' said Jean.

'How's Sally and the baby?' asked Lydia, and Jean was off about the board books she'd bought for little Annie.

'Six months, but she can turn the pages.'

'And your mother, how is she?'

'Much the same but they've put her on antibiotics, another chest infection.' Suddenly, Jean looked weary.

'Look, I haven't much to offer but now you've brought me some eggs I could make a Spanish omelette. You look done in?'

'Thanks but I promised to look in on Mum.' Jean finished her wine and stood up.

'Give her my love –' Lydia stopped herself in time from saying – remember me to her. Edna Thornton remembered very little these days.

'I will, thanks. You know, I think she must remember something because yesterday the whole time I was there her hands were never still, running along the edge of the bedsheets, fingering the cloth as if she was turning a hem.'

'She's well looked after. You can't do much more.' What must it be like? To be an adult and still have a mother. 'I hope she's comfortable.' She gave Jean a hug.

'Are you sure you're all right?' Jean turned back as she reached the door.

'I'm fine. Thanks for coming.' But she'd really like to say: *Be a sister, please stay.*

Alone in the kitchen, she sat at the table and picked at her omelette, looking out on the dark. Her reflection in the window stared back at her. She pulled down the blind, something she never did, but tonight she couldn't shake the feeling she was being watched. If he were out there what would he see? A woman alone. A sad spinster, like Miss Battersby who stayed at the hotel? Miss B never touched a drop. She poured another glass of wine.

I've moved on, she'd said to Dawson. From Luc, maybe. Harder to leave behind was the dark space in her head, dark as the caves below the cliff. Night, blackness, the howl of a gale, thundering water as the sea crossed the road. *Eyewitness.* She had to make a piece of work to give a shape to what she'd witnessed; to what she'd never been able to tell anyone.

She was scared, scared as hell but she was going to do it.

Martin Dawson's cards lay on the table. She hadn't heard the last of him. Pushing him away had probably made him more determined. *I'll write formally.* She had a sixth sense about this man. He would be back. She didn't want him snooping round her new work. She'd better check out this 'highly respectable' archive. Maybe get in first, make a deal: give him something on Luc on condition he left her alone. Give him something to get rid of him so she could get on with her work. She couldn't be forever wondering if he was watching her. She couldn't always work with the shutters closed.

13

Martin turned his back on the chintzy lounge, pleased, at least, to have a window seat. The only thing grand about The Grand was the view. Along Marine Drive, a string of pearly lights flickered into life; towards the harbour, a fluorescent rainbow of electric blue, lime green and acid red flashed against the dusk, some hellish funfair contraption. He couldn't stomach it, not after the meal he'd just eaten. He wanted to do his duty by Eileen's birthday, really, he did, but at the same time he'd rather be anywhere but here.

He stared into the growing darkness.

Lydia was a few miles down the coast, away from the hustle of the resort, alone out on the cliff.

He hadn't expected her to be so forthright, opinionated. *Doesn't the work say it all?* What had he expected – the mute young woman at Luc's side, an airhead? Not a term he'd use but that's how the tabloids had portrayed her, and some of the serious critics. It was her body, not her mind, in Luc's work, they said. He'd like to know what had gone through her mind as she'd lain on the pile of salt, always rolling on to her side to scoop out a small hollow, a space she then cradled with her other arm. Luc would never be drawn as to why. *It's a space for you to fill.* He couldn't go back to ask her, and what if she wasn't alone? The way she'd leaned out of the window, maybe she'd been expecting someone. A lover? Her cropped hair, wet, hugging her head had outlined the stark beauty of her face, those wide-apart, dark-blue eyes. She was unmistakably Layla, despite the greying hair, the weathered face.

'They've everything in there,' said Eileen, her face flushed from the overheating, her mouth a gash of hastily applied lipstick. She lowered herself into the armchair opposite. '*Eau de toilette.*' She extended her wrist for him to sample the fragrance, a sweetness at odds with the lingering smell of cooked breakfasts and deep-fried fish. She was enjoying this, he reminded himself; it was what she wanted.

'The Grand'll do fine,' she'd insisted when he'd offered the new Italian place. 'I know what I'm getting.' Even though this was his treat, Eileen wanted the Early Bird Special: a three-course meal with coffee plus mints, half-price for two if you booked before 6.30 pm. *You know I can't eat late, Martin.* Eileen and Monica had a Special at The Grand on the last Thursday of each month. 'Girls' night out.' And, for Eileen, The Grand held memories. Forty-odd years ago his father had proposed in this room. She didn't mind the fallen grandeur, the 'wicker' furniture made of plastic or the vinyl parquet floor – *well, they're easier to clean* – it was still the place where Bill had said: *What about it, Eileen, you and me?*

'Coffee and mints for two.' The waiter set down the tray.

'I'd like a brandy please,' said Martin.

'That'll be extra, sir,' cautioned the waiter who, according to his plastic badge, was Jason.

'Of course.'

'One brandy. Marvellous, thank you. Anything for Madam?'

Eileen fidgeted with her new scarf, a fine silk covered in frowsy pink and white peonies. The gift had been a success.

'Brandy for you too, Mum?'

'I don't drink spirits, as you know, Martin.'

'A port? It's your birthday.'

'Go on, then,' she chuckled. He didn't say port was wine fortified by brandy.

'One brandy, one port,' said the waiter.

'Make the brandy a double,' said Martin.

'Wonderful, thank you.' Jason pivoted away.

Martin set each cup in its saucer and noticed a brown ring in one of them.

'To tell you the truth, I'd love a cup of tea. Coffee's no good to me. I'll be up all night.' He didn't say there was just as much caffeine in tea.

'You should have said.'

'But it's included. The coffee, I mean.' All part of the deal: tomato soup, followed by a choice of scampi or plaice, desserts from the trolley. A familiar, school dinner of a meal.

'It's your birthday. If you want tea I'll get you a cup of tea.'

'Don't make a fuss. It's a set menu.' *Rules are Rules, Martin.*

'It's not carved in stone.'

Jason returned with the port and the brandy.

'Jason,' he couldn't help it, 'my mother would like a cup of tea, please. And can you change this?' He lifted up the dirty cup.

'Sorry about that, sir. Tea for one. Milk or lemon?'

'Milk, please,' said Eileen.

'Wonderful, marvellous, thank you.' It must have been part of the training.

Martin took a slug of brandy, glad of its numbing warmth.

He'd knocked on Lydia's door unprepared, unprofessional, and now she had him down as a stalker. He recalled the figure swimming in the bay, at ease in the water, gracefully wading the shallows to the beach. Comfortable in her nakedness, her body fuller, rounder, but it was the same figure he'd studied. Layla, posing in the studio before Luc daubed her with paint, her long hair falling around her shoulders or reclining on a pile of salt, mining a small hollow. She'd been digging with her hands when he'd come upon her on the beach. What he'd give to sit and sip a brandy with Lydia and ask why she'd scooped out the salt in *Taking In Water*? What was she working on now? What had she been so eager to dig up that morning on the beach?

He settled back in the armchair. Eileen raised her glass of port. 'Cheers.'

'Compliments of the house,' Jason returned with Eileen's tea. 'Sorry about the dirty cup.'

The lounge was filling up. An elderly couple sipped coffee and stared past each other. A group of women, all around Eileen's age, came through from the dining-room, laughing. He should have invited Monica. With Monica here Eileen would have had a laugh.

'You'll be off back to London now I expect,' said Eileen.

'Actually, I was thinking of staying a bit longer, if that's all right with you?'

'I keep forgetting you're on holiday.'

'Sabbatical.'

'It's time off.'

'For research.'

'They pay you?'

'I'm working, you know, on my book.' He could hear the electric fence crackling between them. He was going to have to touch it soon, tell her to keep out of his room, leave his papers alone. He'd glossed over the 'adult material' comment the other day because she'd been ill.

'Only, you're usually so eager to get back. It's Francine isn't it? If you don't mind me saying Martin, those pictures you call 'work' – well, no self-respecting woman would want those lying around the place.'

'Mum. Those images are of a work of art. Okay, not to your taste – ' Leave it. Today was her birthday. 'And I've told you.

Francine and me, it's over.' These things happen.' Six years they'd been together, ever since Francine had joined the English Department at his college. Of course, Eileen had expected a wedding and grandchildren. Now that Francine was seeing someone else and her father was buying Martin's share of the house, it wasn't going to happen. 'Anyway, if it's all right, I'll be here for a few more days.'

He'd hang around, see whether Lydia responded to the formal request from the Archive. In the two days since his blunder, he'd done what he could to find another way in. Yesterday he'd spoken to his friend Nick, Director of the Archive of Sound.

'I've found an excellent subject for Artists' Voices.'

'I thought you were doing nothing till the book was finished.'

'It's a rare opportunity.' He'd explained about his meeting with Layla, though he played down his binoculars routine.

'You just knocked on her door without an appointment?'

'I know, I know –'

'You're sure it's her?'

'Absolutely.'

'Who's paying?' Nick never lost sight of the Archive's "funding challenges."

'I'll do it for nothing, donate it. I know it's central to my own research, but it would be a coup for the Archive.'

'Well we wouldn't simply want her time with Luc, we'd want the whole life.'

'Of course – and what a life.' Martin had explained what he'd gleaned from the press cuttings, losing her family, raised by an aunt. 'It makes me even more curious about her role in the work – so many connections, can't you see – '

'I can see how your book would lift off. For us it would have to be *Taking In Water* through the prism of her life. But if she's

Taking In Water

not willing –'

'An official request from you might make a difference. She's wary of the press – was convinced I was some hack doorstepping her.'

'I'm not surprised. What possessed you?'

'Oh, come on, wouldn't you have tried it?'

'And, what about production costs?'

'I've said I don't want a fee, surely it's important enough for you to meet the cost of feeding it into the system?'

'It should go to committee first.'

'Why? She's an A-list subject, I'm donating my time - '

'E-mail me her details, I'll send out a formal request, but it might take me a day or so, I'm up to my eyes. I'll let you know when it's been sent.'

Eileen leaned forward: 'If you don't mind me saying so, Martin, you seem, well, preoccupied.'

'Do I?'

'It's beyond me, still living in the same house when you're not a couple.' Eileen wound the end of her scarf round her finger.

'I've other things besides Francine on my mind. You like the scarf then?'

'Liberty. Very nice. You shouldn't have.'

His mobile rang. The elderly couple glared at him and Eileen jumped.

'For goodness sake, Martin.'

'Sorry. It might be work.' He walked out of the lounge, putting the phone to his ear.

'Dr Dawson?' An unnecessary emphasis on *doctor*. 'It's Lydia Hutton.'

14

'Whoever was that?'

Eileen was drinking the last of her port as he rejoined her in the lounge.

'Work,' he said, keeping the lid on his excitement.

'I thought you were on holiday.'

He let that pass, thought better of saying it was the woman in his 'adult pictures.'

'Would you like another?' He nodded at her glass hoping she'd say no.

'No thanks. I'm thinking this one was a mistake. I feel peculiar.'

'Oh?'

'This fluttering, again. I'm wondering, Martin, do you think it's my heart?' She laid her hand on her throat.

'Is it a pain?'

'No. It's fluttering, like butterflies in my neck.'

'You've no pain, you are sure?'

'No, fluttering, a sensation. I can't say it's a pain, though I'd rather it wasn't there.'

'Indigestion, most likely.' All that batter.

'I hope so. If you don't mind, Martin, I'd like to go home. I want to phone Monica. Then I think I'll turn in. That was a lovely evening, thank you.'

Grateful now for the Early Bird dinner, he headed out of Slayton along the coast road, trying to remember every word Lydia had said just now on the phone:

'I've checked out the website, of this Artists' Voices thing. I'd like to know more – what it would mean, if I agreed.'

'Shall we meet?' He'd suggested the wine bar down by Slayton Harbour.

'I'd prefer it if you came here.'

'Tomorrow?'

'What's wrong with now?'

He wasn't entirely happy about leaving Eileen with her 'fluttering' but then he'd remembered the kidney failure scare last year that turned out to be a touch of anaemia. She hadn't mentioned the fluttering on the journey home, and he'd left her chatting happily to Monica.

Now he'd passed through the clutch of houses that formed the hamlet of Flampton, he turned down the unmade track to her house. The pitch dark was punctuated by beams from the lighthouse, strokes of light across a black sky, round and round, like spokes in a wheel. It lit up the hedgerow, bushes with branches, sculpted horizontal by the prevailing wind. How could she live here?

She led him through to her sitting-room, the embers of a fire glowing in the grate. There was no one else in the house, it was so obviously her place: distinctive, private.

'Sit down.' She pointed to a deep sofa scattered with cushions, all different sizes and different shades of blue. On the white walls hung photographs: a single glove on a rock, a shoe washed up on shingle, cloud formations. 'Would you like a drink?'

'No thanks, I have to drive. That track,' he laughed suddenly self-conscious. The woman he'd studied for so long was here, talking to him, had invited him.

On the coffee table she'd spread out browned newspaper cuttings – more spilled from a dog-eared buff envelope – and a pristine copy of *Taking In Water Documented*.

'You've seen all of this?'

'Yes,' he said trying to stay neutral, holding back the excitement at seeing the real thing again, having worked these past six months with photocopies.

'I've had nearly forty years of living since I was Layla, and I'm not Layla now.' Wearing old jeans and a zippered black fleece she'd made no attempt at glamour yet she had presence, was so obviously the woman he knew as Layla.

'Yes, I understand but – '

'So what more do you want to know, I mean that you can't get from all of this?' She lifted up the book.

'You were present at events that others want to know about. The Archive wants your version of those events, it would make a difference –'

'To what?'

'The body of knowledge, around *Taking In Water*, and the period. A unique perspective.'

'And what's in it for me?' She got up to throw another piece of driftwood into the embers.

'A good question.' One he'd been asked before, so he confidently told her that most people got something from it, remembered things they'd forgotten, sorted things out, reviewed their life.

'Why don't you bring me a machine, leave it with me?' She laughed, then added, 'And I'll talk to it, like Andy used to.'

The hairs rose on his neck. Always Andy, never Warhol, to those who'd been there.

'I think you'll find that might be a lot harder than doing an interview.'

'What if I don't like your questions?'

'Okay, interview isn't quite the right word – I won't be asking questions.'

'Really?'

'It's not like a journalistic interview.'

'But still an interview, right?'

Sensing interest in her, he chose his words carefully.

'I'll suggest areas to talk about, prompts rather than questions. It's up to you how far you go.' Thinking fast how to keep her engaged he suggested three broad areas they might explore: her life before she met Luc, her work with Luc, her work since Luc.

'Sounds a lot – how long will it take?'

'Well, an average Archive interview is eight hours, over a number of sessions – to suit you, of course.'

'That's more than I'd had in mind.' He heard the reluctance creeping back into her voice.

'Why don't we do a couple?' he said, knowing that one session wouldn't get very far. 'See how it goes.'

'How about I do one session first – do I get to listen to it afterwards?'

'I could send you a transcript, if you want to check it out,' he offered rather too quickly, not thinking through the work it would involve.

'One session, you send me a transcript and then I'll consider doing the second one. All right?'

'All right. Would Monday suit you?'

'Sooner the better. Monday's fine.'

'Good.'

'But once it's done, that's it. No more interviews. I'm agreeing to this so I won't get pestered again. I have work I need to concentrate on. Understood?'

'Understood.'

He was ready to agree to anything. It was getting late and he still had the drive along the dark track to navigate. Also, at the back of his mind, pushing its way forward, was a concern about Eileen's heart.

15

'Absolutely confidential,' Martin reassured, 'until you sign the release form.'

On the table between them sat the machine. He was tempted to press *record*, but knew he must let her set the pace. Sitting in an old oak carver, her hands resting on the chair's arms, Lydia stared out of the window at a low, grey sky, silent for a while. Then she turned, looked straight at him with her dark-blue eyes.

'How can it be *absolutely* confidential? I mean, you'll have heard everything,' she smiled.

Heat rose in his neck, embarrassment that surprised him. What was it – the aura of Layla? He was here to get behind the myth, not be drawn in by it.

'Material from this recording cannot be used by anyone unless you sign the release. Your choice,' he repeated, looking down to fiddle with the volume control while his face cooled, not wanting to contemplate the implications of her refusing to sign, which would keep the material out of reach, embargoed until after her death. The Archive got him in here but might just as easily shut him out. 'For now, think of this as a private conversation.' What mattered was getting a good life story, putting her at ease, gaining trust. 'You're in control.'

'We'll see.' She looked away.

He wasn't sure he was quite in control, barely holding back questions he was longing to ask: How had she felt making a screen test for Warhol? Was Luc's French identity a pose? Why the compulsive scooping? Journalistic questions guaranteed to scare her off. What was close up to him through research was a lifetime ago for her. *Forty years since I was Layla.*

She gave him a cautious glance. Pensive eyes. Not quite the haunted look in the picture of Layla, pursued by a photographer across Washington Square. *Barefoot Muse.*

Lydia wouldn't be pursued. The woman opposite was determinedly Lydia, not Layla, the figure in the art. But for him, she was both Layla and Lydia. Layla, naked, draped on a mound of sea-salt, an immortalised figure like Botticelli's Venus or the Mona Lisa. Yet time had etched fine lines around the living Lydia's thoughtful eyes. Lydia, a woman in her fifties, was dressed for comfort in a purple sweater, grey tracksuit pants, had her hair cut short and silver hoops in her ears. Forty years ago, her hair falling around her shoulders, naked and daubed with blue paint, she'd made love with Luc on sheets of white canvas on his studio floor. The marks of their lovemaking became *Traces*, owned now by Garth Sarton, who had most of Luc's work. Last year, when Martin had viewed *Traces*, he'd had to wear gloves to handle the piece, studying it under the watchful eye of Alex Markovski. Untouchable Layla. He'd noted how the paint lay on the cloth, caught in its loose weave, an indelible record, chaotic marks: her buttocks, his knees. Now, only Lydia's face and weathered hands were bare.

She shuffled in her chair, as if she'd read his thoughts, crossed one leg over the other, both hands clutching her ankle. A careful move, like a yoga pose, holding on to her guarded, private centre. The feet that walked bare across Washington Square – why no shoes? – were concealed in thick black socks.

Four days ago he'd nearly sent her running. His job now was to listen and the story worth listening to would be the one she wanted to tell.

'I'm not sure –' she closed her eyes.

'It's understandable, visual artists often aren't easy with words.' Words couldn't always translate the world. Everywhere in her house hung her photographs. There were no people in her pictures but he sensed a narrative. What was the story? He had to get her started, knew that the power of her own memories would engage her. The most reticent often gave the best stories in the end. 'Dates, things in order, don't worry about any of that, just try to *be* there, inhabit the memory. Do you see what I mean?' He didn't want her simply listing exhibitions, performances, death. He needed Lydia to collapse time, be present at events. The chronology was easy, he had all that on file: Luc's college dates, early photos of the studio floor after making *Traces*, performing *Taking In Water* in Mantella's loft space off Canal Street, but he must start further back. Nick's words played in his head. *How did she get to be the person Luc collaborated with?*

'As you go back into a memory, say what you see. Start with an image if it helps. I mean, things you might think trivial could be important – the clothes people wore, food, furniture. The sort of things that puts you back there. May I?' He offered her the microphone.

She clipped it to her sweater.

'Let's start with life before you met Luc.' He pressed record and began with formalities, stating the time, date and place. He asked her to say her name and, if she wouldn't mind, her date of birth. Fifty-seven. In every way she seemed younger; the way she moved, talked, the way she lived.

Normally he'd open with a question about grandparents or parents but having read the cuttings he needed a subtler way in.

'Can you talk about the hotel where you grew up?' If he could get her talking about the material world, he was sure, bricks and mortar would soon dissolve into people.

16

'Martin, can I come in?' Eileen nosed round his bedroom door. 'I thought I heard a woman's voice – ' She spoke to his back, hunched over a folding picnic table he'd found in the shed, a makeshift desk.

'I'm transcribing an interview – ' He pressed *pause* on the recorder.

'Only, I was wondering, are you sure about the Hoovering?'

'Absolutely. We talked about that yesterday.' *And I'm not going to engage with the subject again.* Before he went back to London he'd clean his room so she'd never know he'd been there, but meanwhile, could she please leave his papers where they were, especially those laid out on the floor which he needed for visual reference?

'Right, well, if you're sure – '

She'd told him last night she'd a busy morning: an appointment with the chiropodist and her library books to change.

'Bye, then.' As his hands moved back to the keyboard he glimpsed the hurt in Eileen's eyes. She wasn't happy with him being here yet not here, buried all day in his work.

'You're stopping in, are you?

'For a while – ' And he wasn't going to account for his movements either.

'You'll let Barley out if she needs to?'

'Of course.'

'Shall I make you a sandwich?'

'No thanks, I'm fine.' Why couldn't he be more accommodating; why couldn't she simply leave him alone?

'Bye,' she said 'I'll drop round to Monica's on the way back.'

And he could imagine the conversation they'd have.

He waited for the thunk of the front door, grateful for her ingrowing toenail. The 'fluttering' hadn't been mentioned since the birthday dinner.

He needed to e-mail the transcript to Lydia, give her time to consider whether the second session, pencilled in for tomorrow, was still on. He knew from experience how off-putting verbatim scripts could be, the meandering, the indecision, so he'd tidied it up, edited the worst of the *ums* and *errs*. Now, one more read-through to make sure he'd been true to what she'd said.

The Marine – well, it was two different places to me. The hotel my parents ran was different to what it became with Jennifer and Bernard in charge – my aunt and uncle. It was smaller in my parents' time, fifteen rooms, I think. Open March to October. We lived in the basement. Life revolved around the kitchen and our sitting-room next to the kitchen, cosy with an open fire. We called it the 'morning-room,' though we used it all day. And there were storage cellars stacked with giant catering cans – grapefruit segments, peach slices, maraschino cherries – oh, yes, and stone jars of marmalade. There was a walk-in pantry where – you know … we kept the … I remember the pantry … shelves lined with silverware, I've been thinking …

I remember waking each day to the smell of bacon frying but I wasn't allowed in the kitchen, not while he cooked the breakfasts – my father, that is. I knew what he was doing from the sounds: eggs sizzling, the rumble of the potato peeling machine, the clatter of the washing up. And him whistling, always whistling. I'd peep round the kitchen door and he'd hand me a couple of rashers and a piece of toast. He'd have the window open, the sea air cool over the kitchen heat, and the sound of the birds. Hear that, Lyddie, *kitt-i-waake*. He knew all the calls. After the breakfasts were done, he'd come into the morning-room for a cigarette before making a start on lunch. Out would come the little roller and his tin of tobacco. He showed me how to do it, let me tuck in the tiny strands. He'd sit back in his chair, light up. Always the same chair, this chair I'm sitting in now.

She'd stopped at this point, gripped the arms of the pale-oak carver and looked out of the window as if Martin hadn't been there. He'd seen this happen before with a new subject, the past becoming painful. It was a fine judgment – check she was all right, or leave her to find her own way forward? Even though she hadn't spoken for some time, he'd said nothing. Eventually she'd carried on.

My dad would sit in this same chair, read the paper, drink his mug of tea. Always the same mug: blue and white stripes ... the hotel had been in my mother's family, it was run down but they took it on. I don't know – home, work, it was all the same ... that's the sense I have of it ... homely ... My parents were easy-going with guests – mainly walkers and birdwatchers. Dad liked to talk birds. We had keen bathers too. Dad swam for most of the year. There were wooden steps from our garden that joined the cliff path down to the beach. We had beach huts. That's one of them out there, my studio – Jennifer changed the place, built a huge conservatory, a dining-room to give guests a better sea view... Did you know about that, the landslide a few years back? It was after that, that's when I had the hut moved here ...

I'd sit in the beach hut, watch my dad swim... out of season we'd have afternoons down there, take a flask of tea and the ginger biscuits we'd made together. We'd collect shells, dig in the sand then sit in the hut drinking tea. Or we'd walk the cliff to watch the birds ... gannets clacking their bills. 'Old married couples,' he'd say... told me how they mate for life and always come back in spring to find each other... Puffins – at the end of summer we'd watch for when the puffins had left. They leave in the night, you know ... you never see them go, one day they're just not there ...

... another thing, I can see it now, the brass dinner gong that stood in the hall beneath a huge gilt-framed mirror. There was a knack to it; my father let me try when we were closed for winter. You begin with light, quick taps, then pick up speed, building to a crescendo.

I'd hit it too hard, it fell over. *Practice makes perfect*, he said. *When you're older you'll sound the dinner gong.* That must have been just ... you know...

She'd stopped again, looked out of the window. *You know –* Her voice flat, expressionless. In this pause he'd sensed distress, had been tempted to lean across, touch her arm, bring her back to the present. He needed to check whether she wanted to carry on, so he'd paused the machine.

'Do you mind if I get some, some water?'

'I'll get it,' he'd offered, feeling the load that the word carried for her.

'No, it's all right.' She'd taken a glass from the cupboard, filled it from the tap, sat down again.

'I'm sorry,' she said. 'Do you want one?'

'No, thanks. Do you want to stop now?'

'No, it's all right. You can switch it on.'

The Marine was just a business to Jennifer and Bernard. She was determined to expand. They turned the morning-room into an office. No more toasting crumpets on the fire. Bernard had a pipe. I wasn't to touch his pipe paraphernalia. He smelled of stale smoke and aftershave. Jennifer bought a desk and a filing cabinet, wanted to throw out my father's chair. I sat in it and cried, wouldn't move, so she let me have it in my room. I've kept it ever since...

When the hotel was closed for winter, the heating was off except in the basement. Bernard would say, *Lydia, fetch the paper.* I'd climb the stairs, dreading the shock of cold air. It was dark in the hall. I'd imagine people staying upstairs, ghost guests. I'd pull the newspaper from the letterbox and wave it ahead of me. *What kept you, Lydia?* Jennifer had a sharp tone. You were guilty until proved otherwise. I once heard her talking to Bernard, sizing up my room. *We could get a double bed in there.* Over the years they added bits, had the gardens redone. Bernard had a brochure printed. I must have been about ten or eleven. My friend's father was an amateur photographer, he took the pictures. Bernard arranged us

in the garden as if we were having the holiday of our lives. Aunt Jennifer sitting in a Lloyd Loom chair. They made me lie on the lawn, stretched out reading an Enid Blyton, *Famous Five*.
Much later, probably around 1980, she added a kind of glass corridor from the main building to join the conservatory that overlooked the sea ... it was so ugly... I didn't mind when it fell down ... except that, things got buried in the mud ... the other morning on the beach, when I saw you, I found ... I'd like to stop now.

She'd seemed to be in full flow but then this abrupt ending. He'd read in the reports about the contents of the dining-room being buried in the cliff. Her distress was about more than lost silverware. He had a feeling, a sense of her fear. She was afraid. But of what?

17

Lydia ambled up the narrow inlet off Dunwick Bay, eyes scanning the sand. She couldn't help it even though stuff from The Marine would have sunk long before it reached here, but the cliff at Slayton hadn't disgorged anything since the teapot.

Early this morning she'd been back to the pillboxes half-hoping to find the gong, a piece of it at least. *Say what you see.* She'd carried on seeing the gong after Martin had left: the gong, the gilt mirror and her wearing the cardigan Grandma H had knitted, multi-coloured stripes, made from the odd balls of wool Grandma had saved. This morning, reading the transcript again, she'd remembered opening the fat parcel on that Christmas morning.

He'd kept his promise, sent the script. Her words tidied into sentences and paragraphs. She'd read it several times. It was like a book she'd been waiting to read but couldn't have written for herself. He hadn't intruded, hadn't pressed her, not even when she'd stopped at the mention of the teapot and seeing him on the morning she'd dug it out. Why had she stopped there? It was more than not wanting to talk about the new work; mentioning their meeting on the beach had reminded her of his presence. It had been easier to talk when she'd forgotten he was there.

She'd broken her first rule of survival – *Say nothing* – but there was something compelling about talking this way to a machine. One more session, see where that took her. He was supposed to have come in the morning but phoned to ask whether she could shift it to the afternoon, something about his mother, a doctor's appointment. Having found nothing at Slayton, late morning, she'd walked here with her camera in search of *Failed Objects* and *Surface* shots.

Dunwick Bay was wide, gouged between two fault lines in the ragged stretch of slumped chalk that started just beyond her house. At Dunwick, the cliffs had lost their height; one headland was undermined by caves and the other by a crumbling arch.

Patrick had phoned to say the client loved what she'd sent, wanted more from each of her series. She wasn't going to attempt a serious session in the studio until she'd finished with Martin, so she might as well take shots for this commission.

With the tide out, she lingered in the deep inlet. It had been a cave until its roof collapsed. Its sides leaned inwards. She searched among the boulders. Some, pure white, were knee high, many more were the size of footballs, then came smaller pebbles. They ranged from white to a dark grey. Here was a coil of orange rope, manmade fibres, that had failed to secure a boat; part of the sleeve of a waterproof, royal blue – somewhere a person was wet, or worse; three crumpled oil cans with green-and-yellow labels. There'd been a time when she would have run towards such a heap, her mind configuring a body.

She crouched. Close-in, slightly out of focus for abstract colour, or sharp, magnifying the surface detail? Fingertips lightly on the rim of the lens, she adjusted the focus, sharp on the frayed end of the plastic rope, its tough orange fibres unwinding, splayed against scoured white chalk. Click.

Over the weekend, she'd done more drawings of the teapot, how it was now and, from memory, how it had been. She'd photographed the memory drawings with the digital camera. With these images uploaded to the computer, there must be a way to layer the material, animate it. When Patrick called she'd sounded him out.

'I'm wondering how to merge images or maybe create

layers.' She had drawings, photographs, found objects, and possibly text and sound. 'Could I maybe scan in actual objects?'

'Is this new work?'

'Early days, Patrick. I'm exploring possibilities – '

Patrick talked willingly about the scope of working digitally, of software she could use. 'Image, text, voice, music – once digitised it all exists in the same element, so to speak.'

'Like water, fluid?'

'Sort of. You can play round, merge, layer. Sounds like a departure for you?'

It would be, if she dared to do it. If she could animate the fragments it might be a way to project images, to represent the film in her head. It started with the soundtrack: the roar of water, splintering wood, her father's voice, *hang on, don't fret*. And, the crying. A ghostly sound. Frail, bewildered. A chair, a cup and saucer, a spectacle case, Grandma H's knitting. Familiar things in the wrong place. They're floating, the soundtrack is out of sync, the crying carries on.

She turned her camera towards the oil cans, concentrated on framing the image to stop the film in her head.

'Is she having a crap?' voices behind her.

She turned, toppled on her side, just managing to hold the camera clear of the sand.

'Watch it. She's coming.' Two fat schoolboys with clipboards stood at the entrance to the inlet, their voices amplified in the confined space. An army of red and blue waterproofs was massing on the beach, a chorus of chafing nylon leggings. Dunwick Bay attracted hordes of school kids.

'Right everyone,' shouted an enthusiastic teacher. 'See over there? What's that?' All heads turned to gaze across the bay. Reluctant, kagool-clad arms rose.

'An arch, sir,' said a tall girl with a stud in her nose.

'Good. This is a high-energy coast. A few more storms off

Norway, twenty-footers, what'll happen?'

'Fall down, sir,' said a flat, bored voice.

'And what's left behind?'

'A stack, sir,' the tall girl again.

'Exactly. A finger of chalk poking up from the sea. A piece of lost land.'

Lydia put the cap on her lens, eased her way through the group.

'Did you see her?' whispered one a fat boy. 'Taking pictures of rubbish.'

'Nutter,' they laughed and she smelled chewing gum on their breath as she squeezed past.

She headed off to the far side of the bay, picking her way through rock pools, watery hideouts exposed as the sea rolled back, filled with stranded creatures longing for dark and the weight of water. A world in each pool: barnacles, crabs, seaspiders, hiding among coralweed and bladderwrack; then an alien flash of blue. She peered through the clear saltwater at a child's flip-flop, thong broken, the blue rubber sole smoothed away, its toe trapped under a stone. She shifted round, found the angle that would avoid the glare on the pool's surface and took a couple of shots.

The school party had broken into groups, all busy with worksheets. *Nutter*. She scrambled up the headland rocks towards the arch. The tide was not quite low enough for her to round the headland so she waited, eyeing up the water for *Surface* shots, but it was thick with litter: a carrier bag, a Coke can, swollen bread rolls. Disposed of, then brought back on the wind. Disposed of. Disposal of the dead. She hadn't been able to dispose of her dead in any other way than stowing them on the wreck. 'An image remembered in detail,' Martin had said more than once. She had many, some real, some imagined. She'd made up the wreck, starting with the toy boat in the Thornton's fish tank, the fantasy had developed, become real to her. She 'visited' the wreck often; saw it clearly in all its detail. It wasn't an image she could inhabit for Martin. He'd have her down as mad.

Nutter.

Now, the water was low enough. She stepped down the chalk ledge, made her way round the headland to where she could be alone with the open sea, to where waves had cut ledges in the chalk that rose like steps and where rain had made pyramids of the topsoil. Strange, magnificent forms. That first time here she'd felt as if she'd stumbled on a lost civilisation. Aztec City, she'd named it. From here she could see the full stretch of chalk, the high cliffs beyond Flampton standing tall, where her house stood, holding out against the sea.

There was nothing to find here, nothing stuck except limpets. She hesitated, not wanting to step on them, eyed them through her lens, zooming in on the crusted rocks.

Why don't limpets let go? My seven-year old fingers are determined to pluck one free. My seventh birthday – end of summer. Mum's pregnant – did I know that then? She's in the deckchair. I can see that her stomach is round. Dad and me are searching the rock pools, we don't know this is our last summer.

Let's go for a paddle, he says.

We go back to Mum and leave my bucket and fishing net.

She's fallen asleep.

Shh, Dad whispers.

It's hot. My bathing costume, knitted by Grandma H, is itchy. I run into the sea to cool down and it sags.

But why won't they let go. I can't believe that all of them are stuck. *It's how they survive so the sea can't wash them away. It's a tough life where they live.* He explains how one minute the limpet's home is on dry land; next, it's submerged by sea. *They've adapted.* They make a little dent in the rock, worn down by their single rubbery foot, a suction pad. *They won't budge Lyd, no matter how hard you try. If the sea can't move them, you can't.*

We walk the shoreline, me running in and out of the water.

Wait there. He fetches the camera to take a photograph for Grandma H of me in my costume.

Look this way.

I turn towards him, a tremendous thump on my back, the wave flings me onto hard sand, face down. Salt stings my eyes.

Dad laughs. A kind, coaxing laugh.

It's all right. He scoops me into his arms. I cling to his neck, howling. *Don't fret. Sh, sh.*

Mum wakes, lumbers up from the deck chair, holds a towel open but I won't let go of Dad's neck. I hang on, wanting to be high up, away from the water. *Come on now, little Miss Limpet. Lydia Limpet,* he laughs, *Let go!*

The name sticks. The last thing he said to me: *Hang on, Lydia Limpet, don't let go.*

Whitecaps feathered the sea. She scanned the water through her lens. The wind was getting up now, agitating the surface. A wave thumped the ledge, its spray wetting her trainers. Time to go. She packed up her camera. Looking towards the cliff top she noticed a group of men in hard-hats and reflective waistcoats, a livid citrus yellow, walking the path in the direction of her house.

As she made her way back, the whole class had gathered round the teacher blocking her way. She waited, let him finish.

'Who can name the forces at work here?'

The tall girl with the stud in her nose put up her hand: 'Wave attack, attrition, rain, sir.'

'And one more?' he asked 'This one's less obvious because we can't see it.'

Not even the tall girl knew the answer.

'Compression,' he said. A few keen pencils scribbled on

worksheets. 'When the sea rushes into a cave it compresses the air inside. A tremendous pressure, greater than we can imagine.' He paused, allowing them to imagine. 'Then, the sea rushes out and the air expands again, so fast it has the force of an explosion, ripping at the rock inside, making the cave bigger. Everybody get that?'

'Yes sir.'

'Just because we can't see it doesn't mean it isn't there, doing its damage,' he said.

Lydia pushed past him.

18

Steven had been sent on ahead.

'A brief introduction, that's all, gauge the mood,' his boss had instructed, having overridden Steven's view that, as it was on a stretch of high chalk, this house was clear of the risk zone.

'It's borderline. We'd be wise to monitor moisture on the higher chalk as well – precautionary approach, Steven.'

The property looked uninhabited: uncut grass, the porch blocked up with driftwood. No one from this address had called the office to raise objections to land access. He approached the porch. The bell didn't work.

Walking round to the cliff side he began to feel like a trespasser as he recalled the pilot's antics. It was as he'd remembered: a garden between the house and the red beach chalet, the two buildings connected by a pebble-lined path. His boots crunched towards the hut.

'Hello?' He called out, but the hut was locked.

He walked back to the house and knocked on the red door. All he had to do was explain CoDMaS and its procedures. The others would be here soon.

Steven knocked harder. The hollow echo of an empty house came back at him. A cold wind off the sea cuffed his hair.

He approached the end of the garden that was cultivated to within a few feet of the cliff edge and stepped over the flowerbed, careful not to crush the last of the snowdrops. At least he could work out where the monitoring poles might best be positioned: best for CoDMas, least troublesome to the occupier.

The uncultivated ground was thick with rough grass and tufts of wild sea thrift beginning to send up buds. As far as he could see, there was no exposed loam, which was a good sign. Here, the poles wouldn't interfere with her plants, though they might impede her view. He tested the earth, pressing hard with the heel of his boot.

'All right?' His boss called as the others appeared down the side of the house.

'There's no one in,' said Steven

'Are you sure?'

'Yes.'

'Have you thought about a position?'

'Here?' Steven pointed to the ground at his feet. 'But wouldn't it be better to wait for the owner?'

His boss eyed up the land, calculated the distance from the house to the cliff edge. He checked, as Steven had done, for exposed areas vulnerable to rain.

'It's always better to see who we're dealing with, but we'd never get anything done if we had to make appointments all the time for this kind of work.'

The boss walked back to the house, knocked on the door and peered though the kitchen window. Steven joined him. On the table lay the remains of breakfast – half a round of toast, a cafetiere, a white mug – and draped over the arm of a chair, a purple sweater.

The boss stood back, eyeing up the façade.

'See that,' he pointed to a crack in the wall above the kitchen window.

'Movement?' Steven was annoyed with himself for not noticing.

'We'll need access to the inside. Make a note.'

Under the heading, "Structural Survey," Steven wrote: Marine House.

'Is this where you want them?' shouted one of the gang, metal pole in one hand mallet in the other. The boss walked over to him, checked on the OS map as he went.

'There,' he pointed to the rough grass beyond the flowerbed. 'That's a public right of way – see,' he showed them the map, the route of the footpath along the cliff edge. 'Never mind this fence around the place. Sod it,' he said, zipping up his anorak. 'We're not hanging around with this weather brewing. We've had no objections to the land access letter have we?'

'No,' said Steven.

'Here?' The man with the mallet was ready.

'A bit further over, towards the hut,' said the boss. 'Steven, leave a card will you?'

*

'Hey! You!' Lydia shouted after the young man, but the wind was against her. He was the last of them hurrying towards the van, its engine running. She cupped her hands around her mouth,
'Hello, Hello – Wait!'

He turned and walked towards her.

'Are you the owner?' He seemed relieved.

'I am.' Lydia stood by the gate, out of breath. The first specks of rain fell on the backs of hands that were shaking.

'Following our recent letter – ' he said, sounding like a letter himself. 'We're from Northern Geophysics working for CoDMaS. Our letter, regarding the survey which includes your property – '

'Letter? What letter?'

'We wrote concerning land access – '

'Letter? I've had no letter.' Through gritted teeth she gave each word equal emphasis.

'It was sent first class, end of last week. We needed to set up poles to monitor moisture – I've left a card, explaining – they'll be there for a couple of months.'

'Monitor moisture – where? Look, what's this about?'

He led the way to the end of her garden.

'What the –' Five metal posts hammered into the ground, snowdrops crushed beneath clumsy boots.

'See how the yellow bands line up?' the young man spoke quickly, eager to explain that if any of the yellow bands slipped out of alignment she was to phone the number on the card he'd pushed under her door. 'But we'll check them regularly, anyway.'

'You can't just put them there – trample on my garden. Why here?' She took a deep breath, tried to collect her thoughts.

An older man, who'd been sitting in the car, joined them.

'Perhaps my colleague hasn't made it clear. This land needs to be managed in line with the revised coastal defence strategy. As we explained in our letter.'

'What do you mean, "managed"?' Her fists clenched at her side as she tried to steady her breathing.

The older man turned towards the house.

'How long has the crack been in that wall?'

'What? You can just inspect my house without me here?' Her voice a high-pitched shriek. 'You'll have to remove them and if you don't do it, I'll do it myself.'

The older man stood there, letting her rant. She clasped the first pole, cold metal on hot, damp palms; her heart thudded in her neck.

'Those monitoring poles are the property of CoDMaS. I must advise you not to tamper with them or you could be liable to – ' his voice a monotone, like a policeman reading her rights. 'And, what's more, we have located them on a public right of way. Have you had planning permission for this fence? And, in the house – any more cracks? Doors out of alignment?

'This is my home,' she yelled, hijacked by a full force-ten rage, her face on fire. He hadn't said it – *nutter* – but she could tell that was what he was thinking. Then, to highlight her agitation, came his flat-calm of a reply:

'We aim to work in collaboration with the public. It's for your safety,' his look said: *a danger to herself and to others.* 'We need to do a structural survey of this property, which means we need to get inside. Shall we say Monday at ten?'

'No way.'

'Like I said, we prefer to collaborate. We prefer voluntary agreements but even if we don't get them we have to carry on. If you have any complaints there are channels.' He gave her a card. 'Call head office. Someone will answer your queries. Then perhaps you could telephone my office to confirm that appointment.'

19

Fizzing, helpless, she watched them drive off. But for the geology lesson on the beach she'd have been back sooner, could have stopped them. She ran inside and grabbed the phone in the kitchen.

About to punch in the Regional Director's number, she noticed the pile of unopened post on top of the fridge. It was a polite, reasonable letter - *access to your property ... initial ground survey*.

She slumped into the comfort of her father's chair, angled it so she didn't have to look at the wretched metal poles. Storm clouds towered; the downpour wasn't far off. It would have made a good picture if the view from the studio hadn't been spiked.

Manage a coast? Being this close to the sea wasn't like living in some cosy tree-lined suburb. Who better than she knew that? That's why she didn't live at sea level like her grandmother had, or on the mud cliffs at Slayton. That's why she chose to live here on the high chalk. When she bought it she'd had the house checked over and it was sound.

Martin Dawson was due anytime. She moved the hyacinths from the table so he could set up his machine. She was pleased with the studies she'd made earlier, close-ups of the blooms with the digital camera, already thinking how, on the computer, she might merge them with images of the teapot. The hyacinths mattered – their scent – but she couldn't scan a fragrance.

She put the bowl of flowers on top of the fridge, next to the pile of post.

The wind was strong now. Raindrops pattered the window. It could still catch her out, the shock of it. She was in the world; they were not. Except, perhaps, as particles long since dissolved. Rain, river, sea, rain. Round it went, the same water.

She saw Martin coming and ran to open the door. After that gang of hard-hats, he seemed a friendly face.

'It's getting wild out there,' he said, hunched inside his coat, collar upturned. A sudden gust propelled him into the passage before she'd time to say, 'Come in.'

'Thanks for being accommodating about the time change.'

'Nothing serious, I hope? Your mother – I mean.' She closed the door.

'I don't think so, though she needs some tests – the posts in your garden, they weren't there before?'

'Don't ask.' She raised her hands, accidentally brushing his arm. 'Sorry.'

He smiled as he unbuttoned his coat, taking his time. He was looking along the wall, studying the line of her *Horizon* photographs.

'You can put it there.' She pointed to the coat stand in the corner, 'then we'll sit in the kitchen, like last time.'

He followed her through and put the recorder on the table. 'Those photographs – I hope you don't mind me asking – I mean, you're a photographer?'

'It's part of what I do.'

'Oh?'

'What matters to me is – looking from the same place over time – ' *I hope you don't mind.* She sort of did, he wasn't supposed to ask questions, but it seemed churlish not to answer. 'For that series I always shoot from out there – so the poles are, well – would you like a drink?'

'Maybe later? I don't want to delay you any more – '

They sat either side of her kitchen table.

'The transcript, it was all right?' asked Martin.

'I was surprised. As I read it, I kept remembering things.'

'Thanks for agreeing to another session.'

'I don't mind talking around images.' She'd like to talk to him about the hyacinths.

'Fine, let's see what happens. May I set this up?' He unwound the microphone lead.

'You want to hear about Luc today, right?'

He carried on fixing the microphone, thoughtful as if weighing up how to reply.

'It's up to you. Carry on from last time, it's your story.' Polite. He raised his eyebrows. He did this, she'd noticed, when emphasising a point. He offered her the microphone. 'Start from wherever feels right – an image? Ready?'

She nodded and looked up at the hyacinths sitting on the fridge. Their scent filled the kitchen.

He pressed record. Stated the date and time.

'Those hyacinths, they remind me of – ' She hesitated, not sure if she was ready to speak of her mother aloud to this stranger. Being with her mother in the morning-room, that's what hyacinths reminded her of. She closed her eyes, the scent took her there: her mother standing by the fire with a pile of fresh washing, she could touch her. *Say what you see.*

'Of what?' He prompted. She opened her eyes, surprised by his voice.

'Many things.' She stalled, too aware of him now to go back to the memory and half afraid if she spoke it, it would evaporate. There were so few memories of her mother.

'Luc,' she began again. 'The first time I saw him he was carrying a bunch of blue hyacinths.'

'Oh?'

'Yes, at one of Dora Manning's soirées.'

'Dora Manning, the poet?'

Was he going to interview her after all?

'I was staying with Bea – my mother's cousin – I think I mentioned her last time? In London. She lived in the house opposite to Dora. Everyone gathered at Dora's – poets, painters, writers. Georgia Keay, you know, who became such a prominent feminist? She was always there. That night the place was full, people sitting on the floor, drinking wine – I was perched on the arm of a sofa taking it all in and Luc arrived with a bunch of hyacinths. He picked his way across to Dora – he looked different, even among that Bohemian crowd – the old herringbone tweed coat, the white opera scarf wound around his neck, the mop of black hair spattered with blue paint. *Pour toi, jacinthes*, he said to Dora – he was half-French, you know, it wasn't a pose. As he reached across to give Dora the flowers I noticed he was wearing a bracelet made of thin strips of leather plaited to form a band. It was tied to his wrist in a loose knot, the ends trailing, each threaded with a tiny shell – '

No need to say aloud that, later that evening, Luc had given her the bracelet. She paused, remembering the moment for herself.

May I sit there?

I move along the sofa arm as far as I can but when Luc sits down I can feel his leg next to mine. He takes out a tin of tobacco, rolls up a cigarette.

Want one?

No thanks.

Bea tells me you're a painter?

I mumble about my interview for art college, can't look up at him so I focus on the wristband.

You like it. He holds out his arm. His hands are flecked with blue paint, he smells of linseed oil.

It's unusual. I've never met a man who wore a bracelet. *Where's it from?*

Tangier. A world away, though he tells me he bought it in the market at Aigues-Mortes, a place in France where the land is below sea level – the thought of it makes me shudder and I don't know what to say, don't want to show I'm bothered. I like talking to him. Like the smell of him.

Here, have it. He unties the bracelet and offers it to me as if to break my silence, but I still can't think what to say. He ties it round my wrist. It's warm. The heat from him spreads through my arm. My face colours up and I can tell by the look he gives me and the careful way he ties the bracelet that he knows my history.

It's good to meet you at last. Bea has told me all about you.
Dora's holding up the hyacinths she's arranged in a jug.
Lovely, Luc. Gorgeous.
As she wafts past, the scent hits me.

'The scent of them,' Lydia said, surprised at the sound of her voice, unsure how long she'd been lost in her thoughts. That night at Dora's she'd taken Luc's hyacinths as a sign that he'd been sent for her. Now, Luc was getting in the way of that memory of her mother. 'The scent – I think I'm prepared, but each year the first hit startles me.' Each year she planted bulbs to feel, again, the shock of those first hyacinths with their green tips pushing through black earth, telling her that her mother, who'd hidden the bulbs in October, wasn't coming back. 'My mother. You see, they remind me of my mother.'

She watched the rain on the window, waited. Would he ask another question, direct her back to Luc? He said nothing. She closed her eyes, took in the scent of the blooms.

'In the morning-room, by the fire – I remember so little – but things we did together come back – making toast on the embers, listening to the radio as she did her mending, darning my father's socks. She told me about a fishing boat – all the crew lost. A body, washed up weeks later, unidentifiable, except he still had his socks on – his wife recognised her stitching. I'd know my mother's stitching if – '

She glanced a moment at Martin, a pained looked on his face – sympathy for the lost fishermen, or anxious to get to Luc? Behind him rain streamed down the window in rivulets. Find a single drop to focus on, follow it down the glass. She'd have to keep her eyes wide open, not blink. No one could predict the path a single drop would take. The best mathematicians had tried; it couldn't be done.

Martin leaned forward as if to ask a question. She didn't want the sound of his voice breaking her thoughts so she closed her eyes.

'One day, I remember – I was thinking about it earlier. I can see us, both of us, in the morning-room, the fire is blocked by wet washing. Steam rises off small white towels on a clothes horse – you know, big wooden things, haven't seen one for years – which was odd because towels go in the laundry van. Mum's wearing her new dress, a maternity smock, dark blue peppered with tiny white dots; not dots, they were more like little asterisks. She runs her hands over the bump, reminds me that a new baby's on its way, as she lays out another of the white towels.

These are nappies, for the baby.

I want a sister.

You can't choose. Wait and see. Come on, we're going to do something special today, so you'll know when the baby is coming

She produces a brown paper bag, tips out the contents.

Look – bulbs. They look like onions to me.'

Lydia stopped. She couldn't say about the strangeness, that feeling as if something had edged into the room, like a nasty draught under the door, only it seemed to be coming from her.

The nappies meant there really was going to be another person, a baby who would sit on her mother's knee, want toast and stories.

'Inside each of these is a beautiful flower waiting to come out, my mother explains. We bury the bulbs in bowls of black earth. *In spring the flowers will burst through. They smell gorgeous. When the flowers come we'll have the baby.*

What colour will the flowers be?

They're a mixture, blue, pink, white. Blue is my favourite. You have to wait and see, like the baby.

We put the pots in the storeroom behind big catering cans of grapefruit segments.

They're asleep now but they'll wake up. You'll see.

She doesn't know she'll never see those hyacinths.

She produces another paper bag from behind the stone marmalade jars.

For you. She kisses me. It's a doll. A rubbery baby doll with chubby legs, dressed in a pink cotton nightie that she'd made.

Think of a name for her.

Is it a girl?

Yes.

Will the baby be a girl?

I've told you. We can't choose but you can choose a name for your doll.

Baby.

That's not a name.

Yes it is. I want to call her Baby.'

She paused, another glance at Martin. Dolls and flowers; he wanted her back in Dora Manning's flat with Luc. He sat perfectly still.

'The bulbs, did they grow?' he prompted.

'The following January, before – before we set off for Grandma Hutton's house, my mother suggested we take Baby down to the cellar to check on the bulbs, see if they're ready to come into the light. There are green tips poking through black earth, so we bring them up to the morning-room and put them on the windowsill. I sit Baby beside them and watch, to see if I can see them grow. Later, we set off for Norfolk. As we arrive at the station I realise I've left Baby on the windowsill. *We can't go back, Lydia. We'll miss the train.* We hurry across the bridge to our platform through a cloud of steam. I howl. And I can see my mother's tempted to give in, she's uncertain about going anyway. *It might be better after the baby is born, Ted.* But Grandma H hadn't come to us at Christmas because she'd had bronchitis so we carried on.'

Lydia closed her eyes, gripped the arms of the chair. The images in the film ran faster than she could put into words. The three of them arriving at Grandma H's. Already the wind is strong, wild rain, big waves breaking along the front, a high spume. *Come in. I'll put the kettle on.* Grandma H settles to her knitting by the fire, working on something that looks like a meringue. Booties for the baby. Now, the soundtrack: breaking wood, the rush of water.

'Afterwards,' she said, and waited. She couldn't go there, couldn't say it. Not yet. 'Afterwards, when Jennifer brought me back, I ran into the morning-room, thinking my mother must be there, that she'd gone ahead. The fire was out, the grate full of cold ash.'

She paused and shivered remembering how the morning-room had not simply been cold but that a terrible draught had sliced the air from every angle, a hundred times worse than the one she'd felt as they'd planted the bulbs. Had she done something wrong? What had she done?

'The doll was on the windowsill next to the hyacinths, green shoots had grown – '

There was no baby on her mother's lap. No mother, no lap.

Everything would be all right, they'd come back, that's what she'd told herself. If the hyacinths stopped growing, they wouldn't come back; as long the hyacinths grew, they were alive. If her mum had died, why had the flowers – made to grow by her – lived? She remembered that thought, clear as if it were yesterday.

' – so I watched. Out from the green tips came the fat spear of the flower. Green at first, it gave way to a dusty blue, getting bluer as each little floweret opened up into a bell, one after another, until there was a full bloom. Blue, her favourite – Of course the hyacinths died. One minute sweet, blue flowers, then a bad smell as they withered. One minute they were there, then they weren't. Not even a sock – ' She lowered her head, not sure anymore what she'd said out loud and what she'd only heard or seen in her head.

When she looked up she saw that Martin was checking his watch, a barely perceptible turn of his wrist.

'I've been rambling,' she apologised, but was relieved he'd let her capture a memory of her mother. She wasn't sure how, but it felt is if it might become part of the new work, a step towards what she needed to make.

'Not at all. What matters is what you remember.' His tone polite, considering they'd barely begun on Luc.

He looked again at his watch.

'You have to go?' The disappointment surprised her.

'No. I'm aware the disk has only ten minutes left – but I have another, if you want to carry on. It seemed like an important – '

' – why don't I go back to Luc?'

'That's up to you,' said Martin.

'Well, that's what you want, isn't it?'

A raised eyebrow, that was all. He said nothing.

'As I was telling you I met Luc through Bea. Bea had promised me that if things got bad with Jennifer I could always come to London, move in with her. I was sixteen, or maybe seventeen already. Anyway, the hotel was closed for winter and one evening I refused to get Bernard's newspaper. I ran upstairs through the empty hotel. If I still believed in the ghost guests I didn't care. I moved all my stuff into an attic room that was only used if the hotel was full. I felt safe, high up with a clear view of the sea. But Jennifer was already planning the next refurbishment.'

Martin signalled for her to stop.

'Just a second, while I put in a new disk.'

He took out the disk, replaced it with a blank one. The one full of her talking, he slipped into his bag. What had she said? It was all right. She hadn't admitted anything. If she had, he wouldn't be sitting there, calmly waiting for her to carry on.

20

'What time is it?' Her question surprised him.

'Just gone seven,' he said, 'but do go on, it's fine with me.' He was more than happy to continue.

'Well, you see, after jazz clubs and coffee bars in Soho I wasn't going back to serving tea on the lawn at The Marine.' Lydia paused, looked across at him. 'Mmm, actually, I think I'd like to stop.'

He was amazed that she'd agreed to go on after that powerful memory of her mother. Right up to the storm she'd gone, on their way to the grandmother's, the colour draining from her face. Eyes closed, she'd gripped the chair, sitting in silence for an uncomfortable few minutes. Should he interrupt, check she was okay? He'd decided it would be like waking a sleepwalker. *Afterwards,* she'd said, when she'd finally spoken, emphasising the word, *Afterwards.*

What had played in her head during the silence?

He'd offered to go on in case she needed to play the thing out, 'cool down' time, but when he put in a fresh disk, something in her voice switched. Talking about Bea and Luc her tone was conversational, yet when remembering her mother planting hyacinths it was as if she'd been talking to herself. He didn't exist.

He packed the disk away in its Perspex case and wrote the date and number on the label.

'Would you like a drink? Wine?' she offered.

'I was thinking more of tea – but, well, why not?' After such a long session, over difficult material, he ought to stay, see if there were any issues.

She opened a bottle of red wine and set out two large glasses, filling one almost to the brim.

'Really half a glass for me, less.' He still had the drive along the track and the weather sounded as if it was getting worse. How did she feel with a storm brewing, how could she bear it?

'Here, help yourself.' She put the empty glass and the bottle in front of him. 'Well, we've had our two sessions and we've hardly got anywhere,' she sipped her wine. 'I can see why you said it might take eight hours. How many have we done?'

'Around three.'

The quality of that memory of her mother would make her want to go on, he knew, but it had to come from her. If she could connect in that way to memories around Luc he'd be on to something.

'Could we do another?' she asked, looking away from him and out of the window.

'Would you like to?'

'We've hardly touched on Luc or *Taking in Water* – '

'I'd be happy to come back again,' he said rather too eagerly.

'Aren't you going back to London?'

'I'm likely to be here for another week.' He could be here a while, depending on what Eileen's tests revealed.

She said nothing and sipped her wine.

'I've been wondering – how did you get to be so interested in Luc's work?'

'That period has always been a key interest for me: the Sixties, cultural change – '

'You've told me all that. I mean, on a personal level?'

If this was a test, he couldn't afford to fail. He wasn't supposed to make personal connections, but the machine was off and she had asked.

'As a kid my favourite book showed pictures from all the

first space missions and the first moon landing.' Shame Luc missed seeing Apollo 8's "Earth Rise," he was about to say, and thought better of it. 'It was a gift from my father. Together we'd study the blue planet, the blue marble, the strangeness of the moon's surface, and I also loved those first images from Gagarin's trip, because they were the first – '

'Was your father an academic?'

'Oh no,' Martin smiled, 'he was a fisherman, worked out of Slayton Harbour. Though, in his own way, he was a bit of a philosopher.'

'Really? Go on – '

It didn't seem appropriate to repeat his father's words: *There's an order to things, and the sea is in charge.*

'The sea, the challenge of it, that was his life. I'd study those images and I'd think of my father out in his boat, a dot in all of that sea. I mean, what schoolboy wasn't fascinated by how much of the world is water and how gravity holds it there? So when, as a student – and it wasn't long after my father died – I first studied images from *Taking in Water*, well, I just got it – what Luc was trying to do – the connection between the minute and the massive, the sublime – '

'He died at sea, your father?'

'No, no. Lung cancer –'

'I'm sorry – '

'What you said, about the fishing boat going down, the one man being recognised by his darned sock,' he began, wondering why he was saying this, 'my mother told me that story, maybe it's apocryphal, anyway, she said that's why she was happy to darn my father's socks even though – sorry, I'm rambling,' he laughed.

'That's all right.'

They sipped their wine in embarrassed silence.

'Look, about this other session,' she began, 'I'd like to, but could I read the transcript of today first – would you mind?'

'I'll try to get it to you tomorrow.' He'd be going nowhere tonight in this weather and didn't want to spend the evening watching TV with Eileen. 'Do you want to fix a time?'

'Friday?' Lydia suggested.

'Friday might not work, my mother again – a clinic appointment. What about Saturday afternoon?'

'I *might* have a visitor this weekend,' she began, a puzzled look on her face. A visitor, a lover? 'Although it's looking less likely – so, yes, let's say Saturday afternoon, around three?'

'Good.'

'Why don't we pencil it in and I'll call you when I've read through what we've done today?'

'Sure. Thanks for the drink.' He stood up.

'I'll get your coat.'

He packed away his machine and followed her into the passageway.

'So, the poles out there, what are they for?' he asked taking his coat from her.

'Some coastal survey. They want to test the moisture levels in the ground but they also want to check my house. Why? I can't see why it's necessary for strangers to investigate my home.' She hugged her arms to her waist, looked at the floor.

Strangers. Did that mean he was no longer a stranger?

Then suddenly from nowhere: 'It's too much the way they barged in – no warning,' tears welling, she buried her face in her hands. He stopped buttoning his coat, the glow from the wine moving through him, he reached out – no curator's glove, no academic distance – this wasn't immortal Layla in the work of art but Lydia, here, and clearly distressed.

'Are you all right?' he said. A light touch on her forearm, he let it rest, but she eased herself away, slid her hands from her face, took a deep breath and repossessed herself.

'Thanks. I'll be fine. Sorry.'

'Are you sure you'll be all right?'

'I'm fine,' a touch snappy, then she added, softening. 'Thanks.'

'I'll be in touch.' He buttoned his coat. 'You take care.'

'Thanks,' she said and managed something approaching a smile. 'Oh, make sure you shut the gate, will you? Otherwise the wind'll have it off its hinges.'

21

Martin pulled the gate behind him and listened for the click.

Head bent against the squall, he ran to his car. Icy rainwater trickled down his neck, the shock of it clearing his wine-fugged head. The wind carried with it the roar of waves, relentless against the foot of the cliff. Would she really be all right?

He climbed into the car, slung his bag on the passenger seat, slammed the door and revved the engine, waiting for the heat to filter through.

Where Lydia had gone today was not quite what he'd expected; deep into memories before the storm, her mother; Luc in his herringbone coat and opera scarf; not only was he half-French, she'd been with him to France. She'd talked about Luc's obsession with The Camargue, and something Luc had said about how both their lives had been shaped by the sea. What had Luc known of her family history and had it influenced the making of *Taking In Water*?

He took out his phone to call Eileen. No battery. She'd be chewing over what the doctor had said, worrying herself into a cardiac arrest.

'Nothing sinister, Mrs Dawson,' the doctor had reassured. 'You've no other symptoms?' To be on the safe side, he'd given Eileen a letter to take to the drop-in cardiac clinic on Friday. Martin would drive her there. She'd snared him good and proper with her fluttering heart, though better it happened while he was here and able to get the information first-hand, not via her hypochondria down the phone to London.

Outside, rain cascaded down the windscreen; inside, the glass steamed up. He turned the fan to full blast, producing a rush of tepid air. Hardly able to see, he moved off, trusting he was on the right track. He was relieved, finally, to see the sodium glow of lights along the main road, to be moving away from such exposure to the elements. The sea had devoured Lydia's family and yet she lived on top of it. Why?

'Ectopic,' said Eileen. She was in the hall, on the phone to Monica. Eileen had gone one further than Monica's arthritic hip. 'That's what the doctor called it, he said my heart has an *ectopic* beat.' Eileen emphasised the word while signalling to Martin to leave his coat on; hurried hand movements that he ignored. 'Our Martin's back, just a minute,' she put her hand over the mouthpiece.

'I've nothing in for tea,' she said, though it was gone eight. Here, supper was a light snack before bed, dinner was what you had at midday. She was touchy if he called the evening meal supper or dinner. *Your London ways.* 'I was waiting for you.' Her voice full of accusation.

'You want me to go to the chippy?'

'Would you mind?'

'In a minute. Let me take this up first.' He held up his black bag of recording equipment.

'What do you keep in that bag?' Eileen called after him as he headed upstairs.

'Heroin.' The red wine talking. Well, to Eileen, his work was as disreputable as a Class A drug.

He ought to have said, think of the cholesterol. Setting off to the chippy he felt like a murderer and tried to imagine growing up without a mother. Lydia had talked of her pregnant mother as if she were there in the room. Her ghostly, twentysomething mother who was no longer alive but, he had the impression, she was not fully dead to Lydia, even after half a century.

Driving down to the harbour he could taste salt on his lips from the sea-laden wind that had pummelled him out at Lydia's place. Her house would take a battering tonight. How would she handle that after today's session? Perhaps he should have stayed a bit longer?

He parked and dashed across the road to the chippy, away from the waves pounding the harbour wall.

Eileen gathered up the chip papers.

'I'll put this lot straight in the dustbin, else it'll stink the place out.'

'Let me,' he offered.

'No, I should keep busy.'

'Mum, it will be nothing, I'm sure.'

'Easy to say.'

'Remember what the doctor said: "Nothing sinister."'

'It's easy for you to talk.'

'An irregular heartbeat doesn't automatically mean something sinister, that's what he said. And he was pleased that you've no other symptoms.'

'At my age, these things mean something.'

He thought of Lydia, a decade younger than his mother he'd admit, who swam in the sea, for goodness sake. Listening to Lydia today it was as if she was not subject to aging. She didn't look her age and, sometimes, her voice sounded young, vulnerable. Here was Eileen willingly queuing up in a line marked 'age and infirmity.'

'OK, let's consider the worst-case scenario: the heart is a pump. It's a pump, it can be fixed.'

'You make it sound like plumbing.'

'It is. You'll see when we go to the clinic on Friday.'

'Give me those as well,' she said, pointing to the congealed chips he'd left on his plate. 'Or else I'll never be rid of the smell.' She went out to the dustbin in the yard, rain lashing through the open door. 'It's a right gale out there,' she said coming back in.

According to the newspaper reports Lydia had been alone when rescued, trapped in the roof with the sea filling the house, aged seven. In the library he'd found out more about that night. The statistics were stark: along the east coast thirty-thousand homes devastated, hundreds of thousands of livestock dead, nearly five-hundred people dead, with over three times that number perished along the coast of Holland.

'Do you remember 1953, a big storm?' he said.

'I do. Such a wind that night. What's made you ask?'

'Something I came across – '

'No warning. That was the worst of it. People drowned in their beds. I remember seeing the pictures, on the news – '

'You had a television then?'

'No, I mean Pathé News. At the cinema. You've got me thinking.' And she was off remembering how it was around the time she'd first noticed his dad. Most likely a matinee at the Gaumont. She'd have been with her friend Janice. Bill and his mates in the next row, she'd watched him blow smoke rings, never did take much notice of the news, impatient for the main feature. 'But when that came on, well it was local, good as – couldn't believe what came up on the screen – bodies being carried off, whole families, villages under water, bungalows up-ended like toys, sheep and cattle lying dead in the fields. Worse down East Anglia though, worse there. We'd seen nothing like that on the news since the air raids.'

'The worst peacetime disaster,' said Martin quoting one report, 'but who remembers it now, who knows about it?' He'd only a dim recollection of his father once mentioning a storm so strong it smashed boats tied up in the harbour. 'I mean, people still talk about the Blitz but this – '

'Well, it was different then, not like nowadays, everything on the telly all the time. I mean, things happened, you didn't dwell on it; you got on with it. No warning. That was the worst of it. At least with the air raids you got some warning, at least some had a chance – if you don't mind, I want to call Monica back.'

'Sure,' he said resisting the temptation to say: don't dwell on your fluttering heart, don't make it into a disaster.

'You're not going to the pub then?'

'I've work to do.'

'You spend too long on that computer, it can't be good for your eyes.' She'd have him with a brain tumour before the night was out.

22

Midnight. Rain streamed down the window. Lydia watched the lighthouse beam strobe the blackness. On the table in front of her, where Martin's machine had been a few hours ago, sat her own small tape recorder. She'd give it one more try. She pulled down the blind and poured another glass of wine, finishing the bottle she'd opened for Martin.

She rewound the cassette.

What had she said out loud to Martin and what had been said only in her head? She'd talked about her mother and setting off for Norfolk. She'd seen teacups bobbing on the sea in Grandma H's sitting-room, but had she *said* that to him? No, she would have remembered.

If she could talk in front of Martin about her pregnant mother planting hyacinths surely she could go on now, for herself, speak the images of that night, admit it all to this machine. She pressed the record button: 'I want – what I want to – what I see – ' She couldn't, she simply couldn't do it. The sound of her voice talking alone to a machine – it was crazy. *Nutter.*

Rain lashed the window; the blind, lifted by a sudden gust, rapped at the frame. It reminded her about the crack in the wall, the wind and rain working its way in. It was a crack. A crack could be fixed.

Another gust and with it a bang, and again, a bang, bang. Martin must've left the gate open. She listened. No, the noise came from this side of the house. The studio – how could she have forgotten? Her work would be ruined.

She grabbed the torch from the cupboard beneath the stairs, pulled on wellies and searched the coatstand for her waterproof, the one that covered her head-to-toe and kept out the fiercest rain even though it was as light as a feather.

Outside, the lighthouse beam lit up the hut and she could see the door flung wide by the gale. Those damned surveyors distracting her, she'd forgotten to lock up. Rain stabbed her bare hands as she leaned into the wind to climb the verandah steps.

She stood in the doorway and shone the torch inside the hut – paper everywhere, sketches flying around. One flapped towards her. As she reached for it the door slammed, trapping her wrist, a sharp crack on the bone. The torch flew from her hand.

'Ouch.' A searing pain shot through her arm. The torch rolled to the other end of the verandah, still shining. She stumbled to pick it up.

Inside, she shone it round until she found the light switch.

Sitting at her worktable, whimpering, she inspected her wrist. A graze, broken skin on the bone, bleeding slightly. She sucked the wound as she looked around. The place was a tip. Rain had even wetted her "weather wall," her collection of cuttings that showed weather at work around the world: Florida, after a hurricane – a man clutching his small son's hand, running through waves, their wooden beach home upended behind them; Bangladesh – four women holding hands against the pull of water, wading waist-deep through a city street, soaked saris clinging to their bodies; Tristan da Cunha – the cliff over which the wind had blown a herd of cattle into the sea.

Too tired to deal with the mess, she switched off the light, locked the door and shone the torch along the row of marker posts. They hadn't budged, totally unmoved by the wind.

We try to collaborate. We prefer voluntary agreements.

If they could see her now out in this gale, crying.

A danger to herself.

She'd heard that before: Bea urging her to go to hospital, to be "voluntary" otherwise they'd take her anyway. Even twenty-five years ago medical records were confidential. Surveyors couldn't get their hands on them, surely.

She stepped beyond the posts towards the cliff edge and stared into the dark, the full force of rain lashing her face, the gale thumping her so she could hardly breathe. If the wind had been coming off the land she'd have been flung into the sea like the cows on Tristan da Cunha.

Even with a gale this strong, the sea couldn't reach her in bed. If water did scale the cliff, it would be foam, borne up on the wind, nothing that could knock a door down.

It was a Force 8 out there, at least, but nowhere near as strong as the hurricane that had pushed the sea and her life into a different shape. Living here, facing up to the wildest storms was preferable to living in London with the weather in her head building up. In London she'd needed medication to live, here she just needed this view, whatever the weather.

She turned to go back and as she passed them, reached out to kick one of the metal poles. 'Fuck you!' It stood firm against her flimsy Wellington boot. Her toe throbbed.

Back in the house she hung up her waterproof. Despite the rain on it, it still weighed nothing, not like Martin's leather coat. As she'd handed it to him the weight of it had surprised her, and the smell, that mix of animal hide, a spicy fragrance – deodorant or shower gel maybe – and male body. *I don't want strangers in my home,* she'd blurted out and from nowhere her eyes had filled up and he'd reached out, a genuine concern.

In the kitchen she washed her grazed wrist, put a plaster on it, then filled the kettle for a hot-water bottle. As she waited for it to boil she saw the light winking on her phone. Martin, her first thought, but he wouldn't call so late. She saw it was Howard's number, calling after his concert, no doubt. She didn't play the message, really didn't want to see him this weekend. She'd better make that clear, an e-mail? She turned the phone to silent and reached up for the brandy bottle that sat next to her blue cup on the shelf above the fridge. *Nutter.* No. She was not.

Up in bed she pulled the duvet around her, took a swig of brandy and turned the radio on for the comfort of a blameless voice. She listened to the newsreader giving an update on an Arctic explorer trapped on an ice floe. He had one last chance to clear a strip long enough for a rescue plane to land. Think of it: floating on a sheet of ice, alone. Without his satellite phone he'd be done for. If she knew his number she'd call him, urge him to *hold on*. She'd care about him for as long as the news let her, just as strangers had cared for her when they saw her seven-year-old face on the breakfast table. Mothers, serving their children's porridge, had maybe paused a moment to thank their lucky stars it wasn't their daughter being collected from hospital by an aunt, unaware she was now an orphan. *Clinging to the roof timbers – calling for her baby doll.* Back at The Marine, as she'd pulled the *Evening Post* from the letterbox for uncle Bernard, she'd seen how quickly the stories changed. The storm hadn't stayed news for long. The front page filled up with cheerful pictures: the bearded man who'd climbed the tallest mountain in the world, streets all over the country decked with Union Jacks for parties, and the Princess Elizabeth in her gold coach on her way to become the Queen.

Caught between sleeping and waking, it was as if she were underwater, yet her throat was parched. In front of her, a shimmering shoal of fish, formation dancers in the dark. The shoal parted revealing a baby, sitting on a wreck, alive, plump and naked. She reached to pick it up, but thousands of fish swirled into a huge ball, surrounding it. The baby was gone, leaving a rope dangling. She must catch the rope, tug, tug. She hauled, tried to pull the loaded wreck to the surface. She could do it, pull harder. Almost there but suddenly the water was beneath her, sea lapping in the room below. *Hold on to the roof beam, Lydia.* How, when she was tugging on the rope for all she was worth? Astride the joist, the rope in one hand, the other gripped the rough wooden beam. Splinters spiked her palm, waves licked her dangling ankles. If she hid in the roof, the water wouldn't get her. She needed both hands to hold on to the joist but the effort was too much.

Fifty-seven – but in her dreams, always seven again.

Fully awake now, she could see it was two-thirty. Hardly any sleep at all. Unreliable, unfathomable sleep. One minute a calm lapping into oblivion, next pitched up in a squall.

Parched, she felt along the shelf in the dark for the tumbler of water. She drank it all and still she was thirsty – too much red wine – as thirsty as she had been, twenty-odd years ago, in hospital when she'd woken up from days of sedation. The dry mouth then, they'd told her, was a side effect of the drug. No amount of water had quenched that thirst. Back then she'd reached for the jug on the bedside locker. Her drugged adult limbs heavy, yet, in her mind, she'd thought she was seven and back in that other hospital where Jennifer had stood at her bedside and Lydia had cried out:

'Mum, Mum. I want Mum. Where's Mum?'

'They're still looking,' Jennifer had said, as if they were all playing hide-and-seek. Then it had slowly dawned on her that this was a different hospital, a different time. Not seven, she was thirty-one and had given birth eight weeks before to a baby girl, stillborn. And with the baby gone, she hadn't slept. Days without sleep, images flashing, a crazy story. Her mind overheated, wires crossed, "hallucinations," they'd assured her.

Some of them were; some of them weren't.

That's when she'd glimpsed again what had been hidden for so many years, when the film in her head had started to flicker.

Now, the wind rattled at the skylight. This was the worst place for her, the inter-tidal zone between unfathomable sleep and the dry land of a waking day. She would get up and heat some milk.

Drink this, Lydia. Her father is offering her a mug of Horlicks. *Here, Mum,* and he has a cup of tea for Grandma H. *I've put a drop of whisky in.* Grandma H has a nasty cough. *Ted, that sea is getting higher, I'd swear it could knock the door down.*

The floating cups, the empty drawer, she'd seen them as Martin had sat there, and she'd almost told him. Whether he'd believed her or not, it would have been out there, on record.

After her breakdown she'd tried to tell them – nurses, doctors – only too willing to confess, but there was never time. The shifts changed. She'd managed once to get the attention of a young psychiatrist, a student. He seemed to be listening but, in the end, he said what they all said. *Feelings of guilt... surfacing now... unbearable at the time...you were only seven.* Focus on the present, they said, and sent her to Occupational Therapy where she'd made the tight-lipped blue cup sitting above her fridge.

Sleep. Let it come. Enough to protect herself from herself.

23

Martin pulled on another sweater. The heating had been off for a while and the room was cold. The rattling window was beginning to unsettle him. It was nearly two-thirty and still no sign of the storm abating.

He hadn't finished but he'd transcribed enough to e-mail something to Lydia for the morning, keep her keen to meet again on Saturday.

He had to let her follow a memory, talk to herself. His job now was to listen carefully, discover where he might prompt her to open up more. The key was in her shifts in tone. Listening back, he'd noticed, after the long silence following her account of her mother, there'd been a significant change.

Afterwards. That's how she'd broken the silence. The word had hung there. He'd replayed it several times trying to read the emphasis she'd placed on it. *Afterwards* – heard one way it seemed as if she thought that whatever private scenes had played in her head, she'd actually spoken. *Afterwards* – heard another, it sounded as if she'd been pushing thoughts away, making an effort to stay composed. Whatever had happened between planting bulbs with her mother and Lydia, newly orphaned, watching the flowers grow, remained hidden behind that word. It was beginning to interest him as much as his interest in Luc.

After that she'd talked, almost too consciously, of Luc, saying what she thought he or the Archive might want to hear. There were some great leads for him to follow up. One more read through that section to make notes, then he'd call it a night.

The crunch came because Jennifer wanted to turf me out of my attic room. She'd declared war on the new package holidays – "the garlic and olive oil brigade" – she called them. To her a foreign holiday meant a dirty room, undrinkable water and spaghetti for dinner. How could this compare with a decent British seaside hotel? Anyway, she wanted to make all the rooms *en suite*. I was ready to try for art college but artists were as alien as foreign holidays to Jennifer. It was Bea who encouraged me. You see, Bea was the link ... I've mentioned her before – my mother's cousin?

I knew about Bea and her family, but we'd never met. Her father was in the wine trade, her mother a painter – not a great artist but her work sold, she had followers. *Not like us*, was how Jennifer referred to Bea's family. They had a summer place in The Camargue which is how Bea's mother became a friend of Luc's mother, that's how come Bea and Luc were such close friends – known each other as children. As I said, he was half-French – I know people thought he'd created a persona – his mother's family were quite wealthy, they owned acres of saltpans around Aigues-Mortes, made their money harvesting salt from the sea. Have you ever been there? Such a weird landscape – fields filled with trapped seawater waiting to evaporate. "Both our lives shaped by the sea," Luc used to say. It connected us, early on. The mound of salt that I lay on in *Taking In Water* – that was a reference to Luc's past. He needed that, even though he'd given up painting because he thought his large abstracts were too introspective, because he wanted to look out at the world more. For Luc some personal connection mattered. There had to be a private layer beneath the elemental and the political stuff.

Luc created the mystery around his Frenchness because he wanted people to think his French side was Bohemian rather than bourgeois. Well, yes, his mother was an amateur watercolourist, but other than that they were business people, salt merchants. He was hooked on the south, the light, the blueness. The Camargue, where he'd spent part of his childhood, it obsessed him – "not quite land, not quite sea." Fresh mountain water, massing down the River Rhone, fanning into the delta as it met the sea. "You can be two different things at the same time," he'd say. He loved the place. No, that's not quite right. He loved the *idea* of the place, its uncertainty, its ambiguity. I went once with him to Aigues-Mortes. That's where *Taking In Water* started. It was the only time I had a row with Bea. But I'm getting ahead. I was talking about Bea, I'd like to carry on with that – Do you mind? Without Bea I would never have met Luc.

Next time he'd look for an opportunity to ask about that trip to Aigues-Mortes. Unless she had her own agenda on Saturday, that's where he'd ask her to start.

It was a pain having to go down to the kitchen to use the phone socket to get online but he'd promised to e-mail something by first thing in the morning. He felt his way downstairs in the dark so as not to wake Eileen.

Back upstairs Martin tore a page from his notebook, folded it and eased the wedge of paper between window and frame to stop the rattling. Would Lydia sleep through the storm? It would be ten times worse where she was.

He stacked up the *Taking In Water* reproductions and tidied the rest of his papers away. There had to be a private layer in the work for Luc, she'd said. What about for her? He picked out a close-up of her scooping the salt. Something in her face, eyes closed, a puckering of the brow, reminded him of how she'd looked when she'd gone silent today.

No warning. Eileen had said about the 1953 storm. Wasn't that what Lydia had said about the surveyors? Then the tears.

Were the surveyors really the cause of her distress?

24

Gulls squabbling on the roof woke Lydia. She turned over, tried to ignore them but they weren't going away. She checked the clock, nearly eight, and counted the hours. Five. It was enough. When she'd become ill, it'd taken days without sleep to overheat her brain enough to make her crazy. Sluggish, fuzzy, was how her head felt this morning, dampened down by just enough sleep.

No chance of any more with that racket. She sat up, inspected her wounds. The bruise was flowering nicely around the plaster that she'd stuck over the cut. Gently, she circled her wrist. It was sore but it moved. She pulled back the duvet to find her big toe reddened but not purple like her wrist. Had she really kicked at those metal poles out in the gale last night? Well, what did it matter, there'd been no one to see her.

She climbed down from the bed and got dressed.

Out in the studio she left the door open to let the cool morning air clear her head. A few thin clouds, that was all that was left of the storm, the sky rinsed clean.

She gathered up sketches and sorted through them. None of her important pieces was lost. On studies of the teapot and on her weather wall cuttings there was some puckering where rain spatters had dried but, like her wrist, no real harm done. Yet, last night, she'd howled like a child when the door trapped her arm and she'd assumed all her work would be ruined.

She sat a while studying the Marine objects on the shelf. She needed more, something as potent as the teapot. Her toe hurt too much to walk over to Slayton. She'd drive there after she'd checked her e-mail.

Martin had sent the first transcript at three am. Up that late? The message with it simply said: *Should have the second disk finished around lunchtime. M.* There was a message from Patrick with more on *Every Last Drop*, giving her the names of two digital artists who'd made studies of the sea and who would be speaking about their work at the conference. She moved it to the folder she called, 'For Later,' and opened Martin's attachment. She scrolled down, reading on screen. She'd have to read it all, now. As she pressed *print* the phone rang.

'Howard, hi.' She'd forgotten about his call last night.

'I was getting ready to leave a message,' he said. Was she imagining something in his tone that suggested disappointment at actually reaching her? 'I thought you'd be out walking. You sound groggy.'

'Bad night, I'm only just awake – '

'Yeh, I called, after the gig, were you out?'

'In the studio.'

'You're into the work, then? So what about London this weekend?' It sounded like a command.

'But Howard – you know, I said, London would not be good for me right now, plus I've got these surveyors coming on Monday and – ' Her eyes prickled again, tears too ready to come.

'Surveyors?'

'Didn't I say?' Had they had that conversation or had it been in her head, rehearsing what she'd write in her e-mail? She filled him in on the marker posts and the crack in her wall.

'Well Max is not happy – He's called for an extra rehearsal of the new piece, Saturday morning – ' Howard ploughed on, talking over her.

'That's all right, if you can't make it,' she said, and hoped she hadn't sounded too eager.

'We need to talk before I go to Italy,' he said.

She didn't reply; let his demand sit in the silence. Hadn't the energy, the headspace to ask: *about what?*

'Oh?' she managed.

'Depending on what time we finish the rehearsal. I might get away. I'll call you later, let you know. I probably wouldn't get to you before four.'

'Okay, but – ' Why didn't she say it? *Please don't come.*

She took the transcript down to the kitchen, sat at the table, the pages still warm from the printer and read it right through. There was her pregnant mother, airing nappies that were never to be worn, planting hyacinths; dried up things that had come to life. She read it again, allowing herself to see the images: the vapour rising off the nappies before an open fire, the two of them burying bulbs into damp black compost.

Her throat clenched. If she started crying for them now she'd never stop.

With Martin and his machine she'd talked these moments back into life; memories of before the storm, precious moments. She had remembered and dared to speak of what she remembered. The sky hadn't fallen in. She was still sane. She'd gone as far as Grandma H knitting booties on the afternoon of the day before – there wasn't much further to go.

At Slayton, she headed for the pillboxes and searched carefully, scrambling over broken slabs of concrete, inspecting the mud at the foot of the cliff, looking for a handle, a lid, anything. After the storm last night there had to be more.

Nothing.

She crawled inside the broken fortification. Nothing from The Marine, but trapped in the corner was the driftwood she'd left behind on the morning when Martin had startled her. A hollowed-out log, the wood quite delicate, it was no good for firewood, too thinned out, fragile, but the shape of it interested her. It was wedged behind a boulder; she eased it out, careful not to break it. How on earth had it survived last night?

Back at the car, she stowed the driftwood in the boot and headed off to the supermarket. She was almost out of food and wanted paint supplies. A plan was forming, how to deal with those surveyors. It was time to stock up, hunker down for what lay ahead.

On the track to her house, the car wobbled through puddles left by the storm; bottles and tins rattled against each other in the boxes stacked behind her; ahead, a clear blue sky and a calm sea.

In her pocket, the phone rang.

If it was Howard she would be straight with him, tell him not to come on Saturday. Relieved to see it was Jean, she stopped the car and got out, damp grass brushing her jeans

'Oh, Jean. Hi. I thought you were Howard.' She leaned against the car door.

'Sorry to disappoint – you sound cheerful anyway. Where are you?'

'On the track back to my place, just done a big shop. How's your mum?'

'No worse, no better.'

'I'm so sorry, Jean. It must be hard for you. If there's anything – '

A silence down the phone and the sense that Jean was trying to stop the tears.

'Thanks. Look, I'll speak to you later, when you're back at home, just wanted to sound you out, see if you could help at the Centre on Saturday?'

'Is that your first day?'

'Yes, but the way things are, I need to get over to Mum for a visit in the afternoon, if only for an hour or so. It's often when she's at her most lucid. I was wondering if you'd do the last couple of hours, from three? I'll be back in time to cash up and close the place.'

Now Lydia fell silent, as she juggled times in her head.

'Sure, sure,' she said eventually.

'You don't sound so sure – '

'Well, things are bit up in the air. Howard might be here and – look, it'll be fine. I'll sort it out.' Anyway, Martin still hadn't sent all of the transcript, and the time they'd agreed on Saturday was provisional. He'd have to wait. 'Don't worry, I'll be there. Talk later. Bye.'

She reached under the seat for her camera and walked to the cliff edge. There were no metal poles here to spike the shot.

Had she really stood on the cliff last night leaning into the gale, staring at the seething of this same sea, almost believing those surveyors knew her medical history? Weeping like a child because she'd caught her hand? What a difference sleep makes. Now, shopping done, all she had to do was call the surveyors, confirm their damned appointment. With the cupboards stocked and enough paint to do the hut, she was ready for them.

She eyed the horizon through the viewfinder. Not a boat, a bird, not even a vapour trail, just the glassy mass meeting the vaulting canopy of light. She angled the camera up a fraction. More sky today. Click.

25

She chiselled the scraper up the back wall of her studio, removing the last scraps of flaked paint.

Occupational therapy.

The surveyors were coming on Monday but she wasn't going to sit around worrying until then. She'd have the outside of the studio freshly painted by the time they got here, and when they'd gone she'd repaint the kitchen, fill in the crack.

Now this wall was prepared she could allow herself to check her e-mail again. *Around lunchtime.* It was gone two-thirty and she needed something to eat.

With the transcript tucked under her arm, she carried a plate of cheese sandwiches and a cup of coffee back to the studio, to have the hut's reliable weathered wood around her as she read it again. Something in the section on Bea had disturbed her.

When I first met Bea she'd have been in her early twenties — a graphic designer, working on magazines. Her father had recently died and she was living with her mother in a rambling house in north London, Fortune Green – not quite Cricklewood, not quite Hampstead – the place opposite Dora Manning's. I mentioned that last time. I still own the house, you know. Anyway, when I was about eleven, Bea turned up at the hotel one Friday. It was August, high season and the place was full. Jennifer, as always on a Friday, was getting ready for the changeover – finalising seating plans and all that. Guests had been arriving all afternoon, taxis in the drive, some in their own cars – wing commanders with their blazers and moustaches, the regular spinsters, all cardigans and liver spots. The spinsters were a challenge for Jennifer. She respected loyalty in her guests but single tables weren't cost-effective in high season.

At six she'd stand by the dining-room entrance, greet each guest with a handshake, dressed up in her navy linen suit, her hair in a tight pleat.

I'd gone up to my room to get out of the way and found a fold-up bed installed and made up next to mine. Were they going to put one of the spinsters in with me? I waited on the window seat on the main stairs because I knew that once the guests were all in the dining-room, Jennifer would check up on the chambermaid. As she passed me she said: *I meant to tell you, my cousin Bea is coming. I've put her in with you. She's due any time, why not look out for her?* Bea was to stay for one night on her way to Edinburgh. *All that way when the rest of us are making an effort to save petrol.* I guess that dates it: '56. Suez.

I lived in a sort of bubble at the hotel, had to piece the world together from snatches on the radio, glimpses of headlines as guests read their morning papers. Certain topics were forbidden by Jennifer: politics, religion, sex and foreign holidays. I wasn't supposed to ask *awkward questions*. There was a lot of mumbling among guests, the grown ups were worried, I'd listen in. *We might be able to reach Cairo, but what do we do when we get there?* I'd heard one of them say, and couldn't quite understand why he'd want to go to Egypt – that was one thing that attracted me to Luc, he always knew what was happening in the world – anyway – It was a muggy, evening. As the guests ate dinner, I sat in the empty lounge, sea-gazing through the open French windows, watching the birds getting ready to leave. The puffins had already gone. I saw a woman on the lawn, admiring the view. She turned, saw me and smiled. She was a vision: white polka dots bouncing on a crimson cotton skirt that swirled just below her knees, a white gypsy blouse slid off her tanned shoulders. *Hello. Are you Lydia? I'm Bea.* I stood up. *You're tall,* she said. She wafted in on a cloud of perfume. *Je Reviens* – that's what she always wore.

Once the guests had finished dinner, we had ours. *Urgent, then, your trip? With petrol the way it is.* Bea ignored Jennifer. I was impressed. Even more impressed because she was a relation. Family. It turned out she was on a rescue mission to the Festival, helping out friends, taking materials for a set, all the way to Edinburgh. She'd saved all her petrol coupons. I wished I could go with her in her silver car – a Hillman Minx – it stood out among the black Ford Prefects. *Minx is the right word for that girl,* Jennifer said, when she'd gone. Whenever I hear the word Suez, I think of Bea. Funny to think it was because of that crisis in Egypt, and her having saved her petrol coupons, that I met her at all. I doubt we'd have met otherwise.

Bea chatted away through dinner, her silver hoop earrings jiggling as she talked. She kept smiling at me. As we finished dessert she leaned across to Jennifer. *If Nasser gets the Russians involved, things could hot up. What do you think, World War Three?* She sat back, pressed the white napkin to her mouth. *Do be careful, Beatrice. Lipstick's the devil to wash out.* Bea laughed, *Come on Jennifer, it's all up for us Brits. Things are changing.* I couldn't take my eyes off her.

Next morning before she left, she walked down to the beach with me and we watched families arriving, setting up windbreaks, creating little territories. *Lydia, I'm so sorry –* She hugged me. *You don't like it here, do you? Would you like to visit me in London? If I invite you will you come?*
    What if there's a war?
    There won't be a war here.
    What about World War Three?
    That was to annoy Jennifer. It won't happen. So will you come? I told her I'd love to, though going away seemed daunting. I'd never been anywhere, not since –

You're too young and anyway, London's a lonely place was all Jennifer said. But after that visit Bea sent postcards, sketchbooks and paints – I'd told her that art was all I enjoyed at school. My teacher had encouraged me. I'd shown Bea some of my paintings and sketches. *You're good.* She sent me copies of the magazines she worked on. One cover showed a jazz club, a man playing the saxophone. I'd imagine myself into the pictures, be there at the club, dancing. It must have been over five years before I finally got there. Bea's mother got cancer, kept having remissions, then getting ill again. It was after she died that I really took up with Bea.

The first time I went – it was on the second visit when I met Luc, when he brought the hyacinths – Bea drove me round the West

End at night. By then she had a red MG Midget – we had the roof rolled back. I felt as if I was in a film. We drank frothy coffee in glass cups at a coffee bar in Old Compton Street; we passed the jazz club I'd seen in the magazine. We went to galleries – my head was full of stuff... When it came to leave, I cried all the way to Kings Cross. *Don't be sad. You're turning into a beauty. When you smile you're beautiful. With your looks things will come to you.*

Not long after that Jennifer wanted my attic room. *It's got a sea view.* I was to sleep in the basement. I refused. So Jennifer eventually agreed to let me apply to art college if I lived with Bea, but she was torn. She expected me to work for her in the business – half of it was mine – yet, with me gone, she could get back to the life she would've led if I'd not been washed up.

When I moved in with Bea I begged her to let me have the attic, I wanted to be high up looking down on rooftops, away from everyone. It could be my place, I wanted to be independent, Bea had her own life to lead, anyway. It had been a junk room but I cleared it, painted over the flowery wallpaper with white paint. I had a great view – I loved that – on a clear day I could see the dome of St Paul's. The other reason I wanted to be high up was because of the reservoir. The house looked over a field, only it wasn't really a field, beneath the grass was a reservoir – a great underground tank of water. I didn't know then, they're everywhere in London. I didn't like the idea of unseen water. Sometimes I'd lie awake, convinced I could hear water lapping beneath the grass but my room was high up and I wasn't going back. I'd met Luc – though we weren't together yet – I'd been to jazz clubs and coffee bars in Soho, there was no going back to serving tea on the lawn at The Marine.

The images, vivid in her mind: Bea young, full of life in her polka dot skirt. Without Bea – who knows? If Jean's family had kept her afloat as a child, Bea had carried her to safety as sure as the man in the rubber dinghy who'd lifted her from Grandma H's roof. Had she ever shown Bea any real appreciation, told her she loved her? Back then she hadn't known how to, hadn't dared; had craved her independence, her attic away from everyone.

Bea had given her a chance to become something of the person she was meant to be. With Jennifer she'd have stayed packed away inside herself, like neatly stacked bed linen back from the laundry, starched and folded.

She brushed her hands across her face, dried her cheeks, and laid the transcript on the table. A breeze through the open door ruffled the sheets of paper; she held them down under her coffee cup.

Reading this she could see how she'd always trusted her gut feelings. Her gut had told her to follow Bea, told her when to go with Luc and when to leave him. She'd carried on running until her past had caught up with her after her baby died. But even then she'd recovered and bought this place on instinct so that she could learn to live with the past, so it couldn't catch her out again. Now, every bit of her was telling her to dare to talk more to Martin.

With your looks things will come to you. Had she really said that out loud? The way Martin looked at her sometimes, that was how people used to look at Layla, admiring from afar. But then he'd laid his hand on her arm, concerned. In that moment she'd wanted to say something – what? Acknowledge the way he'd listened? But she'd said nothing and he'd buttoned up his coat, looking embarrassed – because she'd cried? Because he'd reached out to her? For now it would be better if he stayed on his side of the machine, indifferent, like the sea.

26

Steven walked along the fence by the side of the hut. It wasn't an official visit so he'd make his observations from here.

'You're parked up that way, Steven, see if she's tampered with them,' his boss had said as they'd packed up for the day.

He leaned over the fence. They were coming on Monday, anyway. She'd left a message at the office.

'She's up to something, wants to make a point,' his boss reckoned. 'I bet she's got rid of them, wants us to look fools when we show up.'

All five, still there, untouched.

'Can I help?' A voice behind shouted. He spun round.

It was her, coming along the cliff path, a towel draped round her shoulders, her face pink with cold.

'Miss Hutton.' He felt his face colour.

'I've called the office about you lot coming on Monday. Didn't you get my message?'

'I was – we were – I mean, we've been working in the bays. Just wanted see if everything was okay.' He pointed to the poles.

'Thought I'd remove them?' She gestured for him to follow her. 'Come and take a closer look.'

'It's all right. Thanks. I'm just going.'

She turned back.

'You did get my message?'

Scary lady, she is. Not nasty, but scary. Reminded him of

someone, that singer his mum liked, used to watch the video on MTV – the woman singing on a cliff with a shawl round her head. Annie something.

'Yes, yes. Like I said, not official, this, I was passing, on the way to my car. I'll be off.' He said taking out his car keys.

'What were you doing in the bays?' She stood in his way, wasn't going to let him go.

'S'cuse me asking, but have you been swimming in the sea?' He looked at her huddled into the towel, couldn't believe anyone could go in the water but she was definitely wet.

'Please, I'd like to know – what you were doing today?'

'Collecting data to estimate the slump rate.'

'Slump rate?'

'So we can work out the retreat line – '

' – sounds like a war,' she flashed back at him and moved closer. He could feel the chill of the sea on her. *Here Comes The Rain Again*, the tune was going in his head, he could see his mum dancing round the living-room, singing along.

'The retreat line is only one option and I ought not to be talking about it. Don't let me keep you, you must be cold.'

She was starting to shiver.

'I'm used to it. I have sea in my veins.'

'Must get bleak in winter, living here – '

'Bleak suits me.'

'I'd be scared living out here, alone.'

'What of?'

'Being on my own.'

'Being on my own is what I prefer.' There was something determined about her, the way she looked at him; it felt as if she was sizing him up, wondering where all this testing and measuring would lead. She knew, he could tell, that they'd not been entirely open with her. It would have been better to explain things. *Say nothing they can quote back at you*, was the boss's line. *On budget and on time.*

'I'll grant you it's interesting here, geologically,' he said. He found these cliffs fascinating but was always glad to get home in the evening.

'And this *retreat line*, means letting nature take its course?'

'It's one option. We're still doing the calculations. I doubt the chalk slump would affect you.'

'Too right. I'm on the high chalk. I had a survey done before I bought this place. It's further along, towards the lighthouse, that's where the chalk is vulnerable.'

She stepped even closer, looking hard at his face. As she rubbed her wet hair and pushed the towel from her head, he felt drops of water on his hand. He could smell the sea on her.

Eurythmics, Annie Lennox, that's who she reminds him of.

'We're still acquiring data, making assessments.' They won't easily slide anything past her.

'Assessing what?'

Flustered, he talked quickly about stress analysis, the balance of forces, the need to calculate the rate of change.

'You think the chalk along here might be unstable?'

'Nothing major, and a controlled explosion could...'

'Explosion! Blow up the cliff?'

'I'm talking hypothetically.' Why had he opened his big mouth? It was hard to keep someone informed without talking specifics.

'And,' she said, her voice all suspicion now, '*hypothetically*, what circumstances would suggest a controlled explosion?'

'You must understand, I've no authority to say anything – hypothetically, you might use a controlled explosion as a preventative measure – safely explode a potentially weak point and then the cliff can resettle. It's better than a cliff-fall no one is prepared for.' Steven looked down at the salt stains on his boots.

'Tell that to the birds as you demolish thousands of nests.'

'They'll come back.'

'And you think the chalk is weakening in my direction?'

'When the data is in, it could turn out you're not affected.'

'Perhaps your boss can tell me more on Monday?'

'I'd appreciate it if you wouldn't mention this conversation when he comes on Monday.'

'But I will be told officially, eventually?'

She sounded upset. He'd been trying to reassure her but seemed to have made things worse.

'Of course. Look, Miss Hutton, I appreciate this is your home but don't go worrying unnecessarily will you?'

'My name's Lydia, by the way – '

'Bye then.' Steven could feel her watching him walking away. He turned round a moment just to stop the feeling of her eyes on his back.

'I think you're brave,' he said, 'living here.'

27

'The puffin tea towels sold well, there's only one left,' said Lydia. If Martin thought he'd been talking to a Sixties icon he should have seen her today. She'd done a brisk trade in puffin keyrings too, all black and white nylon fur with orange felt beaks.

'I've plenty more,' said Jean. 'Thanks so much for coming. You go, if you want to. What time's Howard arriving?'

'He's not. Well, not today – ' said Lydia. 'Are you all right Jean – your mum, I mean, don't you want to get back? I can lock up, you could have stayed with her.'

'She needed to sleep. I'd rather have something to do. I don't want to dwell on it.' Jean disappeared into the storeroom.

'Well, I don't mind staying. Is there anything I can do?' Lydia called after her.

'You could bag up the cash.'

Jean emerged with her arms full of fresh stock. They worked in silence for a while, Jean filling shelves, Lydia counting coppers into £1 piles. She was in no hurry; going home meant having to phone Howard. Why couldn't she, this once, go down to London, his text this morning had demanded? She could catch a train back early on Monday. If she couldn't manage that he wasn't sure if he'd see her before he left for Italy. A reasonable request, she'd have to admit, but she didn't want to think about why she wouldn't do as he asked. Something's up, she could tell; this was not about the house. Not now, Howard.

'Well, now that's done,' said Jean. 'I've got a few beers in the fridge, want one?'

Outside, sitting at one of the picnic tables they drank straight from the bottles and watched the last cars leave the car park. Jean's eyes were weary.

'Are you sure you're all right?'

'I'm okay. Tell me about you – what's happening with the virtual Howard?'

'Extra rehearsals before the Italy tour. He wanted me to go down to London – as if. But there's this survey thing – '

'They're coming, then – you've agreed?' asked Jean.

'Yes, but I'd rather not dwell on *them* if you don't mind.' She'd thought the structural survey would be the worst of it, but then Steven turned up with his talk of explosions. She was tempted to tell Jean. *Nothing I've said is official.* 'They've not pestered you about The Centre, then?'

'We're too far back from the cliff edge. Okay, tell me about the stalker. Are you still talking to him?'

'We were going to meet today but I put him off – '

'Really?' Jean turned to face Lydia across the table. She laughed. 'You gave me such a hard time about the binoculars. And now he's at your house every day.'

'Hardly. I've done a couple of sessions.'

'Why? You were adamant - *I want nothing to do with him.*'

'Because – ' how to explain what she was only just beginning to understand herself. Since the memory of her mother with the hyacinths, talking to Martin seemed connected to the work.

'It's not –' Jean hesitated. 'Upsetting, I mean going back – '

'Of course it's difficult but –' She could do it now, tell Jean what really happened that night her father poked a hole through the ceiling. How hard could it be? Jean would understand, would agree with her own sane reasoning: How could she be held responsible for something that happened almost fifty years ago?

But she couldn't because Jean had enough to worry about with her mother. Jean wouldn't record it or write it out; that's what she needed, the evidence out there on record. Lydia needed to bear witness to that night, and Martin's machine was beginning to seem her best chance. She could approach it gradually, in between the bits of her life that Martin was after. Reading about Bea had affected her more than she'd expected. So determined to make a life away from Jennifer, had she really appreciated Bea taking her on? If only she could pick up the phone, call her and say: *Thank you, I love you.* Bea had been dead for over twenty years. Jean was here, alive and her own mother about to die within days. 'Talking has made me think about lots of things. Your mother – sorry.'

'Mother?'

'She was very kind to me.'

Silence for a while.

'It was a shock to find her drugged like that today, her face sunken,' Jean began. 'The antibiotics have done nothing to shift the chest infection. She hardly knew I'd been.'

'But she recognised you yesterday, you said, didn't she?'

'Sort of, there was a bit of sparkle – she took my hand and said, *you are thoughtful, dear.* But as I was leaving she said: *who are you?*'

'Don't you think she knows you at some level? Things can go on in the mind, even though not communicated –'

'Perhaps – but to have been so capable and lively and to come to this.'

'She was so kind. Always welcoming, no matter how busy. I can see her now, surrounded by bolts of gorgeous cloth – satin, crepe, velvet – a tape measure around her neck, cutting out another bridesmaid's dress, always by eye, no pattern. Think of all the pleasure she gave.'

'She was still sewing, this time last year – now she doesn't even know what a needle is.'

'She made a difference for people. Hers has been a good life until now. I've been thinking about your family, I want to say – you did so much for me. Between you, you saved my life.'

'That's putting it a bit strong.' Jean sat up right. Lydia had her attention now.

'When we were kids, coming to your house – it was, well, normal. Really, Jean, I mean it.'

'Has talking to the stalker brought this on?'

'It's making me look at things – differently.' Thinking about Bea's kindness had got her thinking about Jean's family and their kindness. She didn't want anything to stand in the way of their friendship now. 'Do you remember when we met in London that time, sixty-eight wasn't it?' said Lydia, taking a swig of beer.

'Did we?' Jean looked away, her eyes directed out to sea and a fly-past of gannets. 'Lyons Corner House, on the Strand. Why did we meet there?'

'Because I was catching a train from Charing Cross.' Jean's eyes were still on the birds.

'You *do* remember!'

'I was going to Mike's parents'.'

'You'd just got engaged.'

'Bastard,' said Jean. The force of it surprised Lydia.

'You didn't think so then. If you could go back would you un-engage yourself?'

'No point in thinking about it. I have the children and my adorable grandchild, how could I regret them?' There was an edge creeping into Jean's tone as she looked up.

'Late arrivals, young kittiwakes, probably first-timers.'

She didn't want to upset Jean, far from it, but neither did she want these unsaid things sitting awkwardly between them.

'When I went to live with Bea, I tried to stay in touch with you. I wrote to you, don't you remember?' Rambling, confessional letters and all she ever got back from Jean were neat notelets, pictures of birds or wild flowers.

'Oh yes.' The tone was odd, as near to sarcasm as Jean gets.

'What do you mean?'

'Nothing. We were teenagers.' Jean put the bottle to her lips and drained the last of her beer. 'Want another?' she stood up.

'Okay.'

Jean took the empties inside and returned with two more beers and two packets of crisps.

'Thanks,' said Lydia.

'Yes, you wrote to me from London.' Jean pulled open a packet of crisps. 'Long letters, on and on: coffee bars, art galleries, the clothes, as if you were – well, if I'm honest – showing off, rubbing my nose in it.'

'Oh Jean – '

'It felt as if you wanted me to feel small.'

'No! I was seventeen, excited and wanted to share it. Anyway, you hardly wrote a thing back. Polite notes, as if your mother had made you.'

'She had – ' said Jean, and stuffed a handful of crisps into her mouth. 'And when I complained about you showing off she said it didn't matter, I had to write back because we ought to keep a lookout for you. She said that you couldn't help it, because – oh, this was decades ago, forget it.'

'Go on.'

Jean went quiet.

'She used to say, "that girl is fixed on surviving".'

'She said that?' Lydia shifted in her seat, overcome by the odd sensation of stepping outside of herself, seeing how her one-track, teenaged self must have looked.

'Well you wanted to know. It sounds harsh now I say it, she meant it kindly,'

'I see – I can see that. I didn't intend to make you feel small.

You meant a lot to me, that's what I'm trying to tell you now, Jean. And that time when we met in London, I felt as if you'd dumped me – '

'I thought you were glad to be rid of us.'

'Jennifer and her awful business plans, that's what I wanted to be rid of. That day in London, in '68, we hated each other, and we've never talked about it and I'm beginning to see why.' Now they'd opened up the cellar, why not a full clear out?

'Hated is a bit strong,' said Jean taking a swig from the bottle. There was an explosion of birdcalls above the cliff. 'Fighting talk. Those young kittiwakes need to establish themselves.'

'It feels odd that we've avoided the topic all these years, an awkwardness, that's all I'm saying.'

'Look, ten years ago I came back here to start afresh, leave the past behind,' said Jean. 'Are you not going to eat those crisps?'

'No. You have them.'

Jean opened the second packet.

'I'm in your past,' said Lydia.

'Oh Lydia, now I hate the stalker. What's he stirred up? I'm not bothered about some awful meeting we had years ago when we were still kids.' Jean kept her eyes skyward, on the birds. 'Thinking about it, I remember the smell of fried bacon and worrying I'd be late for the train. And you, you being, well, odd, distant – '

'Me, distant? *You* were the distant one. It was as if you were behind glass. No, no, as if you'd put *me* behind glass. Like everyone else, looking at me as if I really *was* the person in those gossip columns. You didn't believe I was the same person who'd slept head-to-toe with you.'

'A lot had happened since our last sleep-over. You'd been seen by millions of people on television, with the Beatles, for

God's sake – '

'For a few minutes – '

' – while I was in the middle of finals. It was such a big deal, first television global satellite link. And who do I see? *You*.'

'I was still *me*.'

'You were different.'

'How?'

'You were sitting behind John Lennon, for a start.'

'All right, yes it was quite a big deal, but I was a tiny part of it. What do you think goes through your head when you know the whole world is watching you?'

'I can't imagine.'

'All those people who don't know you and probably every person you've ever met, all looking at you at the same time – I was thinking: I hope Jean's watching. Not to show off, I mean, the thought of you watching made me feel safe.'

'Well, I felt as if life was happening to everyone else – dropping out, loving-in – I was trying for a First and getting engaged.'

'I can see, now you say, how it must have looked but – it wasn't all glamour that summer.' 1967: a long hot summer of love that had ended with Luc's death.

'I'd no idea what to say to someone on first-name terms with Andy Warhol.'

'Everyone was on first name terms with him – '

'You had the whole world open to you.'

'No, no. That fame shit closed things down, cut me off. I might have been on first name terms with *Andy*, but he was no friend.'

'We were worlds apart – me with my "bourgeois" good degree and fiancé.'

'I *envied* you.' Lydia thumped the beer bottle on the table. It made more noise than she'd intended.

'Envied me?' Jean frowned.

'You'd been to university, you had a man who wanted to marry you, you came from a whole, loving, family. Nobody had died – why wouldn't I envy you?'

'Really?'

'The gossip you believed – parties, love-ins – no one checked facts. One story bred another. Chinese whispers. You know what I wanted more than anything?'

'Go on.'

'To be *unfamous*.'

'Really?'

'I longed for a Saturday evening at your house, eating fish and chips out of newspaper.'

'Rosy specs, Lydia.'

'Maybe. I will have some of those crisps.' She reached across and took a few. 'Of course I enjoyed getting away, getting involved in art, all that I loved. But then the fame thing, it was too much. Suddenly, Luc and I weren't people, we were, well – things. I felt battered by fame, I was looking for shelter.'

'With me?'

'I wanted to re-connect with you, your family. What hurt me was that you never asked what really happened.'

'So, are you saying that none of it happened?'

'I'm saying there were stories going round with me in them, but they were not my story. We didn't ask for what happened after *Taking In Water*. It happened *to* us.' It suddenly came to her: the only reason she'd survived the storm around her and Luc was because she'd known something worse.

'Oh Lydia – '

'That day – I was hoping we could have a Saturday night in front of the telly with fish and chips. Sad, eh?'

They both laughed.

'This is silly,' said Jean. 'Do you feel better?'

'I do. It mattered to say it, not avoid it, leave it unsaid.'

'You've never talked much about Luc. Did you love him? Did you want to marry him?'

Now it was Lydia's turn to go silent and sip beer.

'I adored him at first, but then fame changed him. I was out of my depth – I was so young. You've never talked about Mike.'

'And I'm not going to. Enough of men.'

They sat in companiable silence, gazing out to sea.

'Thanks, Jean, for – letting me get that off my chest.'

'You be careful with this talking to your stalker,' Jean said. 'I'm still surprised you let him in.'

'His name's Martin. He's not the press, that made a difference. Anyway, it was you who convinced me this Archive was highly respectable.'

'Hey, don't blame me.'

'Time to go.' Lydia picked up the empties. 'Are you sure you don't want a bite to eat at my place?'

'I'll be fine,' said Jean. 'Do you want a lift?'

'It's okay, I'll walk.' Lydia stood up.

'I'll come with you as far as the gannets.'

They walked across the field to the viewing post on the cliff path. Over the sea there was a soft, grey light. They stood in an easy silence for a moment watching the gannet colony on the chalk stack below.

'It's funny to think that's really affection,' said Lydia. Pairs of birds clattered their long beaks in a fencing movement.

'Amazing how they come back and find the same mate each year,' said Jean. 'In the next life I'll find myself a gannet!'

They laughed. She turned to Jean, touched her arm. 'I meant it, about your family saving my life.'

'Thanks. It was good to hear you talk about Mum. Oh, look,' Jean pointed as dozens of smaller birds fluttered to land on the cliff's ledges. 'More guillemots.'

See those guillemots, Lydia, Dad's voice fills my head. *Their chicks squeak and chirp inside the egg. By the time the chick is hatched Mum and Dad guillemot know their own, they know their call among all the thousands of other fledglings. Isn't that clever?*

'You've gone quiet, Lydia,' said Jean. 'Are you all right.'
    Lydia shuddered, staring ahead at the whirl of birds.
    'Cold?'
    'No, no. I'm okay. I have to go.'

28

Lying face down Martin's hard cock pressed against his stomach. More awake than asleep now but wanting only to be back in the dream with the woman, lying on some indefinable rippling surface – cloth, earth, water? In the dream he'd been watching her from a place far away, couldn't take his eyes off her. When he moved closer, reached out to touch her, she'd disappeared, sunk into a deep fold.

He slid further under the duvet. Had Lydia thought he was coming on to her last time? She'd e-mailed back to thank him for the transcript and to say that she couldn't make Saturday after all. *Needed elsewhere.* She'd mentioned a visitor the other day – a lover? *I'll phone you,* he'd interpreted as: don't call me. That was on Thursday. Sunday, now, and still nothing.

He rolled onto his back, lazily stroked himself. Eyes closed, he tried to summon up the dream's atmosphere but it had evaporated.

'Martin, I've a cup of tea for you.' Eileen tapped on his door.

'Thanks.' If he pretended to be asleep, she'd come in anyway. 'What time is it?'

'Gone eleven,' said Eileen, opening the door. He turned towards the wall. 'You've not been up all night working again, have you?' He didn't need to look to know she was eyeing the images of *Taking In Water* laid out on the floor. He refused, any more, to play the game of hiding his work under the bed.

He didn't answer.

'I'll leave it here, shall I?' She formed a solid presence at his bedside.

'Thanks,' he mumbled as he heard the mug chink on the glass top of the nightstand. She hovered and he realised, a beat too late, what she was waiting for.

'How's the fluttering?' He kept his voice cheerful, wouldn't say, *your heart*.

'Had me up at two.'

So, she knew he hadn't been working late. He turned onto his stomach and lifted his head to look at her.

'All right now?'

'Seems to be.'

'Try not to think about it. Can't be much longer.'

At the clinic on Friday they'd done their best to reassure her but they planned, anyway, to monitor her heart for twenty-four hours. That had worried her all over again. She was on the waiting list. 'All our monitors are out at the moment, Mrs Dawson – it might be a few days. Nothing to worry about,' said a cheerful nurse. The machine, when it came, would record the thud, thud, thud of her heart for one whole day. Sound waves to translate into marks on paper, reveal the pattern of her pulse, an image in black and white that she couldn't dispute.

'Easily said.'

'No more than a week, that's what the nurse said. They can't think you're in mortal danger.' He sat up. 'What about going out for an old-fashioned Sunday lunch?'

'Maybe. I've things to do,' she said in a tone that implied he was supposed to persuade her. 'I'll leave you to your tea.'

He lay with his face in the pillow, pressed his groin into the mattress but all he wanted now was to piss. As soon as she'd left the room he got out of bed, unplugged his mobile from the charger and took it with him to the bathroom.

Sitting on the toilet he checked for messages. Nothing from

Lydia, just the text from Nick that came yesterday. *How's it going with Layla? Call me at home over the weekend if you want to catch up.*

Layla. How to tell Nick, he was now engaged with Lydia, that the subject he thought he was after had shifted. If he called Nick he knew what his old friend would say, 'Have you asked the sex and death questions?' Nick was ambitious. He'd added collections of scientists, sex-workers, dancers, bankers and butchers; he'd gone digital, making it possible to create networks of attitudes across generations, walks of life, social groups. In particular, attitudes to sex and death.

Martin could hardly ask Lydia the standard question: what was your first experience of a death? There could be no going full-on into an exceptional event unless the subject led him there.

Afterwards. She'd shut the door on death.

Not that his experience came anywhere near what had happened to Lydia as a child, but if he found it difficult to talk about his close shave in New York how could he expect her to open up about her night alone in the roof, aged seven? He didn't talk about 9/11 either casually or sensationally because it sounded like boasting – look at me, I got away! It amounted to the opposite of reflected glory – reflected tragedy? He'd never told Eileen because she'd have devoured it: *Oh yes, our Martin was in the building only minutes before,* exaggerating for dramatic effect until she'd have him on the 107th floor air-lifted out. As it was she took every opportunity to ask: *You're not going on any more trips to New York?* She talked about the events as if she'd been there. *When that second building collapsed, Martin, my heart ...* The tumbling tower, the dust, these images were burned into the minds of millions. There had been no warning. When the storm hit Lydia there had been no warning but there were no cameras to film the sea crashing into her grandmother's home, no reporters giving live commentary as waves snatched whole families. It was only later that film crews recorded the aftermath: bungalows up-ended like toys; sheep and cattle lying dead in the fields was what Eileen remembered seeing at the cinema between the B film and the main feature and the smoke rings blown by his father sitting in the next row. There were no live images of the moment of impact playing in real time for the world to watch and to replay. At that moment Lydia, aged seven, had been utterly alone.

He washed his hands and splashed cold water on his face.

He couldn't ask what had been her first experience of death, but if she chose to go into the memory he'd be ready to listen.

Back in his room he smoothed out the duvet, then arranged the images of *Taking In Water* out on the bed to study again the close-up shots of Gagarin. Luc had taken a newspaper photograph and silk-screened it repeatedly but with each new image he'd cropped in closer until only Gagarin's eyes remained visible.

Luc had obsessed on what those eyes uniquely had witnessed: Earth at a glance, the tremendous blue of a globe against the black of infinite space. *I see Earth. It's so beautiful,* the first words spoken by Gagarin as he'd orbited had been Luc's mantra. Luc wanted us to keep seeing it, as if for the first time like Gagarin, not to lose sight of this marvellous watery world. And, to see it in perspective with a single human body, Layla on her mound of salt. The proportions were no co-incidence: the world and a human body, both two-thirds water.

As Pop Artists turned to look at mass culture, Luc had kept massive nature in view. It wasn't only the blue planet that evoked the sublime, but the technology that had taken Gagarin up there. Technology, culture and nature couldn't be separated, that's what Luc wanted to show in a single work. And yet, Lydia had been quite clear the other day about the personal connection, the salt that referred to Luc's background. He'd check whether the business in Aigues-Mortes still existed. There were several new leads on Luc from what Lydia had told him already. But now he was curious – had there been a personal connection for Lydia? It must have meant something to her, had to, given her history.

He reached for the close-up of Layla lying naked, her eyes closed, her arm cradling the dent that she'd scooped in the salt. Something of that quality he noticed the other day – with her eyes closed, so inside of herself she became compelling to watch. Yet, as in these pictures, she seemed unaware of anyone. Luc would not be drawn on the scooping gesture, it had been her improvisation repeated at each performance.

'Do you want this?' Eileen stood in the doorway holding up his ringing mobile as if it were a bomb. 'You left it in the bathroom.'

'Oh, Thanks.' He read Lydia's number on the screen.

'Hello. Sorry to call on a Sunday but – '

'That's all right.'

'I was wondering how soon could we arrange another meeting?'

'What about tomorrow morning?'

'Mmm, I can't do that, the survey people are coming round.' She sounded composed, matter-of-fact as if waiting in for a plumber. There was none of the distress of the other day. He calculated how long lunch with Eileen make take, aware of her straightening and re-straightening towels in the bathroom across the landing, listening in.

'Well, what about later today – any good?' he said.

29

'You've been busy.' Martin pointed through the open door to her newly painted studio. 'Your visitor helped?'

'Visitor? Oh, no, he didn't come,' she said, and noticed the way Martin's eyes opened wider on the word he. 'Howard – he's my, my – ' her what, what did she call him? 'My partner, he's gone on tour, he's a musician.' A rush of explanation that hadn't been asked for. 'Come in.'

'More decorating?' Martin stumbled against the paint cans stacked in the passage. He squeezed past her and she was too aware of his presence, that woody fragrance again, as if he'd come straight from the shower. No leather coat. It was warm. He looked relaxed in his blue linen shirt, loose over jeans.

'More like decontaminating,' she laughed. Clean white walls, that's what she wanted, to make the place hers again after the surveyors had been. As long as nothing new turned up at Slayton, her work in the studio was stalled. She needed to do something that felt like *making*. For the whole of Friday she'd happily painted the hut, a soothing task.

Martin headed for the kitchen to set up his machine. 'Oh, perhaps not.' The table was covered with pots and pans, cleared from the shelves.

'Sorry, I was about to shift that lot. I'm getting ready to paint in there.' She stacked bowls inside bowls and put them on the work counter. With her hands busy, not having to watch his reaction she dared to ask, 'I was wondering, could I have a copy of the disks, eventually?'

'Eventually you should be able to download – '

'This goes online?' She whipped round to face him.

'There's electronic access for most of the Archive. And all new material is recorded digitally so – '

'The whole world can listen? I thought you said – '

'Not open access, people have to apply. You needn't worry. All I was saying was that *you* could download it, for yourself. But it will take time. Meanwhile, if you want the disks, I'll get copies, when I go back to London.'

'Would you?' That's all she needed, to know that her words, those memories of before the storm could, potentially, become part of the work.

'Sure. Are you ready to start?'

'You know what, I'd rather we worked in my studio.'

'This is a great space,' he said, looking around. With shutters and door open it was flooded with a cool, north-easterly light. 'May I?' he walked over to her weather wall, scanning her cuttings. She watched as he ran his finger over the one of four women in Bangladesh, holding hands against the pull of water, wading waist-deep through the city, soaked saris clinging to their bodies. He lifted it up to see more clearly another cutting half covered by it: New York, four women again, in raincoats, knee-deep in water, holding hands, hair whipping their faces, shopping held high, the caption read: *Fish swim in Manhattan streets, scuba divers rescue trapped drivers.*

He turned to walk over to the Marine objects on the shelf.

'Work-in-progress,' she said.

He picked up the teapot.

'You've found all of this beachcombing?'

'All of that is from Slayton, near the pillboxes, where I saw you that day. It's all from the hotel, buried in the mud cliff when

Jennifer's extension collapsed – a whole dining-room sits inside that cliff.'

They sat at opposite ends of her work table.

'You mentioned signing papers after all this is finished,' she reminded him. 'I'd want a guarantee that this online access is secure. And, I want it written in that this is my last word on Luc. I don't mind telling you but, then – ' Eyewitness, he'd called her; she wanted witness protection, didn't want a stream of cultural historians beating a path to her door.

'The Archive would never give out your personal details.'

She wanted to say: *you found me.*

He fiddled with the controls, switched on the microphone.

'It's important because I've been thinking – I'd like to do more after this session. Maybe even the full eight hours – I want to talk about my own work if that's all right. Talking about my mother, the other day, that was important for me, and there's more I – ' she couldn't will the words into being either. If it were that easy she'd have admitted it all to Bea or Jean long ago. Talking to Martin's machine, working towards that night through the good memories, she'd get there. 'But first I think we ought to talk about Luc. I'm aware that you want me to tell you about *Taking In Water* – I'd feel more comfortable going on, doing more sessions, if we did that first – '

'If you want to.'

'I do,' she said firmly. It was asking a lot of him, to listen to what she had to say. She'd feel more comfortable, more prepared, once she'd given him what he came for. Besides, since yesterday she'd been thinking about Luc, since Jean had asked: *did you love him?* It seemed to matter now to look again at their time together, but where to start? 'Why don't you ask me questions today? What is it you need to know?'

'Luc's mother, the salt business, that's not in the literature,' Martin prompted.

'In the art world there was only Mantella, his dealer, and me that knew about the Aigues-Mortes connection.'

'But he was born in London, wasn't he?'

'Yes. His mother, Dominique, came to London to study art and English and fell in love with Luc's father who was Irish. Dominique got pregnant, and, being a good Catholic girl, she married him. They had Luc, who, at that time, was not known by that name.'

'Oh?'

'Kevin Devlin, was how he began life.' She paused to enjoy the surprise in Martin's eyes. 'It's true. Though he was half-Irish, that side never seemed to interest him. Dominique insisted he have one French name: Kevin Luc Devlin. He never knew his father; the marriage didn't last. Dominique stayed in London with Luc, but they spent summers in France. In his head he was French, definitely. He preferred to be in London because there he could feel exiled. That's what he used to say. He needed that sense of not belonging to feed his work.'

After all these years, what did it matter that she'd given the world Luc's real name? She waited for Martin's next question.

'You were telling me the other day about the first time you met Luc, at Dora Manning's. You painted a vivid picture of him – the coat, the opera scarf and something about a leather bracelet with shells. Do you want to pick up from there? How did you two get together? How did you become Layla?'

'Oh the wristband thing – it seemed so exotic, back then. I admired it and he gave it to me, but it was maybe a year later, when I started college, that we got together. But, from that moment with the bracelet I was very taken with him – '

Martin didn't need to know that she'd worn the thing constantly, that it had become a talisman that fuelled her fantasies – all night love-making with Luc, in her head, him kissing her body all over. By then she was no virgin, she'd let several boys go "all the way," down on the beach, longing for intimacy as much as for sex. Later, she'd been shocked to read in a magazine about promiscuity in orphans, how easily they mistook bodily contact for caring. Given the risks she'd taken, she'd been lucky. Once she got to London, Bea had been frank: *One at the same time every day. And you can still say no, the pill doesn't mean you have to leap into bed with everyone.*

'Luc invited Bea to a private view and asked if I wanted to come along, but then Bea had a problem at work so I went on my own. It was the show of an artist Luc'd once shared a studio with – large abstract canvases. After a couple of drinks, Luc started on about how painting was dead. I went over to listen in. He was passionate about the issues – he was in the process of giving up painting. It was so much more exciting than a college lecture. It was thrilling for me to hear real artists talking this way. He took me home, came in and rolled a joint – it was that joint that led to Layla. He started saying my name, over and over. *Lyd-i-a, Lyd-i-a.* Stretching it out so it didn't sound like me. *It's for an older person, this name.* Had I another name? My middle name is Alice – *Okay, Alice. Alice in Wonderland.* But that had been my mother's name – '

Through the open studio door she was aware of the screech of seabirds. Would the machine pick up their calls? She was aware of Martin watching her, waiting. That night with Luc, because of the dope, she'd suddenly had the urge to talk about her mother but, back then, there was so little that she remembered. Back then the storm was still buried. *You can tell me if you want to, if it helps*, Luc had said, but there was nothing to tell, it was mainly a blank.

' – anyway, Luc tore a sheet from my sketchbook and wrote LYDIA ALICE in large letters, then he cut out each letter and mixed them all up. *We'll make a name from your two names, from the soft sounds.* He threw away the D, shuffled the rest and came up with Layla. *Hi, Layla*, he said and kissed me. Lightly, on the forehead.'

He was nearly thirty, she was eighteen, and she'd understood that the kiss meant she must make the next move. *You should see the view from my attic, do you want to? Are you sure you want to show me?* She'd led the way, left him looking out at the city lights while, in the bathroom, she'd undressed. She'd walked back into the room, naked beneath her silk kimono except for the wristband he'd given her. *You like that?* She'd nodded. He barely touched the sash and the kimono fell open. He kissed her breasts. No fantasy. *Layla*. Naked, answering to her new name, for the first time she'd felt she might have a future.

'After that night,' she carried on, 'we were inseparable until I left in '67 – four years we were together.'

Until I left. After the controversy, the storm around Luc, she'd saved herself. *I left.* Climbed down from the seventh floor. What was it Jean's mother had said? *Fixed on surviving*.

'A few months after that we went to France and the idea for *Taking In Water* started to excite Luc. After that trip I dropped out of college. *Why learn to paint? Painting is a trap. There's too much happening in the world, it can't be contained in two dimensions.* I believed I'd learn more being around his studio.'

'The studio – that would be at the house in Primrose Hill?'

'Yes. One of those crumbling stuccoed houses – it was damp, never warmed up. Luc had the basement, where he lived, and one room on the floor above that was his studio. His basement had a room at the front, which was a kitchen: dark, old brown lino on the floor, one of those deep sinks in the corner, an enamel food chest. No fridge. The milk was always off. The room at the back was the bedroom and off that was a kind of storage area stacked with his paintings.'

'He still had paintings around – can you describe them?'

'He wouldn't let me see them. I knew from Bea that Luc's abstract work had always sold well but that had made him despise it even more. Those canvases, he believed, were too limited, too much his own inner world. He wanted to make art that looked out more. He was planning how to destroy them – to make that act a work of art. The bonfire was his first performance piece. You've seen photographs?'

'So what was in the studio?'

'The walls were plastered with newspaper cuttings – sputniks, space capsules, images of Yuri Gagarin. Luc re-photographed the Gagarin press images and enlarged them – Gagarin's face framed by the space helmet. This was before we'd even thought of *Taking in Water*, before we'd been to France. Luc longed to see Earth from space. When Kennedy announced there'd be a man on the moon by the end of the decade, he'd have signed up for the ride. *Imagine standing on the moon, looking back on Earth. It will change everything.* He'd be devastated to know there are only twelve men alive who've stood on the moon. Did you know that? Back then, it still hadn't happened. But Luc talked about it. He was a talker, ideas flying around about nature and technology. He could have recited nursery rhymes, I'd have listened. The not talking, mute Layla, it was how I was, a kid on the arm of a talkative, older man.'

'Did he talk about Yves Klein?'

'Klein was *God*. He had images of Klein's performances and blue pigment work around the studio. Klein had died the year before I met Luc. It was Klein's death that made Luc determined to break from painting.'

'So what was he working on?' asked Martin.

'Trial pieces towards some kind of *homage* to Klein's 'Blue Revolution,' a performance piece, a restaging of *Anthropométries*. You know, the living brush idea, painting bodies to roll on canvas. He was serious, committed. I admired his priest-like devotion. He asked me to do a trial piece in the studio, just the two of us. He'd paint me blue, and I'd roll against canvas hung from the walls or laid on the floor. Sometimes, we'd make love – '

'Those trial pieces, Mantella showed as *Traces* in his London gallery?'

'Yes. And then Luc developed the ideas in *Continuing Blue*, which Mantella showed in his new performance space in New York, the following summer.'

'You didn't perform in that?'

'No, I didn't go to New York until Mantella made the commitment to *Taking In Water*.'

'And all that remains of *Traces* and *Continuing Blue* is in the Sarton Collection, nowhere else?'

'You know your stuff.'

'There's plenty I don't know. What made Mantella commit to financing *Taking In Water*?'

'Luc had met Mantella in New York when Klein was still alive and a big show opened there, supposed to take America by storm. But Pop Art was happening – mass culture, advertising, all of that. Klein was seen as too European, too romantic. Mantella was a Klein fan, so he and Luc hit it off. At some point he took Luc on as one of his artists. When *Taking In Water* got started, he was so excited – this was the breakthrough, Luc finding his own language, going beyond Klein.'

'Mantella's backing was crucial?'

'The money, of course, and his belief in what Luc was trying to do: explore the sublime without nostalgia or looking back to the Romantics, and explore the man-made without being over-cynical. And to finally get beyond painting.'

'*Taking In Water*,' said Martin.

'Luc was in awe of the natural world, man in the universe, all that cosmic stuff, but he was equally fascinated by technology, mass media. He was as obsessed with Warhol as he was with

Klein. But whereas Andy declared himself a genuine fake, Luc, well, you could say Luc ached to be genuine. *Authentic*, he used to say. Luc didn't have Warhol's detachment. When we hung out at the Factory, his lyrical side dominated, he couldn't hide his passion. We should have left New York after *Taking In Water*.'

Martin signalled for her to stop.

'The disk's full. Want to go on?'

'Sure.'

'You mentioned going to France, to Aigues-Mortes – want to talk about that?'

'OK.'

'Give me a minute,' he said.

She watched him as he scribbled something on his notepad then put the new disk in the machine. He was getting what he came for.

Was she imagining that slight shake of his hand?

30

She was taking her time.

Perhaps he should have quit while he was ahead. He already had more than he could have hoped for: Luc's real name, glimpses inside the studio, the relationship with Mantella and the story of how she'd become Layla.

She hadn't *seemed* to mind him asking about Aigue-Mortes, but then suddenly wanted a break, *Give me a minute.* She'd been gone ten, at least.

He got up and looked at her weather wall, at the picture of the women wading through a flooded Manhattan street, their shopping held high. They were laughing, no harm done – seeing the funny side of having fish swimming down Second Avenue. A mild disaster compared to what happened last September.

Luc had tracked space travel and here was Lydia tracking the weather. Was she planning to make a work based on this material?

'Sorry I took so long,' Lydia appeared carrying tray with a jug of water and two glasses.

He joined her again at the table.

'Want one?' she asked holding up a glass.

'Yes, please.'

As she handed him the tumbler of water he noticed a bruise on her wrist.

'That looks painful,' he said, and couldn't help but have an image of someone grabbing her. Howard? Had he been after all, they'd had a row?

'Oh, it's nothing – not as bad as it looks,' she brushed off his implied question: *how did it happen?* 'Shall we carry on – you want to know about the trip to France, right?'

'That would be good.' He shook the silly fantasy of an angry lover from his head.

'The trip to France started as research for *Continuing Blue* – the *homage* to Klein, was to go ahead in New York that summer. Mantella was keen to stage the piece in his new gallery space – a loft off Canal Street. Mantella had a contact in Paris who'd been at Klein's original *Anthropométries* – a musician. Luc *had* to meet him. I was excited, I'd never been off this island, but then it rained the whole time we were in Paris – bounced off the pavement – I remember my feet got soaked, ruined a new pair of suede boots. *I might as well be barefoot,* I said. Luc laughed. *Why don't you take them off?* Creepy, when you think how I finally left him. Eventually we found the contact's place, up an alley. A concierge directed us to an apartment on the top floor. Me, barefoot, sodden boots in my hand. Luc and the other guy talked in French. Luc paced and chain-smoked, while I tried to dry myself in front of this tiny electric fire – stuffing my boots with *Le Monde*. The place smelled of cats and cigarettes. It didn't go well. Luc had expected more – he always expected more. Back at the hotel he became withdrawn. The room was cold and I was starving. I remember we went down to an Algerian café opposite and ordered couscous – I loved that, finally felt as if I was somewhere different. *Let's go south,* Luc said and his mood switched.

'It seemed like we were on the road for days. I didn't sleep much, which made me jittery. We were only a couple of hours from Aigues-Mortes but it was late and I was desperate to sleep. We stopped at a bar that had rooms. Outside old men drinking, inside the woman who ran it sat behind the bar, smoking. She had a glass eye. She stared at us – odd couple – with her good eye but she let us have a room. Luc thought it was a good place to stop because the next morning, he said, there was something he wanted to show me – '

She went quiet. Martin waited.

'Sorry, where was I?

'He was going to show you something?'

She paused again, seemed to go inside of herself. He waited.

'Well, er,' she took a sip of water. 'That was, personal, not relevant. So – Aigues Mortes. Luc and me were all right in our self-contained world, meeting his mother was different. When we arrived there, he left me sitting outside a café in the main square while he went to see her, sound her out. I sat under the shade of an almond tree wondering how I had got here, to this exotic, walled town. Around the square were bars and cafés with bright awnings. Above them the façades of buildings were painted soft colours – peach, apricot, olive green – there were wrought iron balconies at the windows, green shutters closed against the afternoon glare. I longed to know what was going on in those rooms –

'To be honest, Dominique and I didn't really connect. I was very young, and I think she may have been depressed. She had a migraine the whole time we were there, stayed indoors during the day but sat outside in her little courtyard in the evening. We had to tip-toe around her tiny house. It sat just inside the old town – painted pink, blue shutters, a red tiled roof, it was lovely. You could see the ancient stone walls from the room we slept in. Her courtyard was half-covered with a vine. She remained a shadowy figure for me; this was the only time I met her. Intense, dark eyes. Nervous hands, chain-smoking. Didn't say much to me and spoke French to Luc. I had enough French to know she didn't quite approve of me. She said things about me – '

She stopped, leaned back eyes closed. She looked strained.

'Do you want to stop?'

She didn't answer but shook her head to indicate no. She kept her eyes closed.

'We drove around through acres of salt-marshes full of pink flamingoes, it was hard to tell land from sea. Dangerous. There, the land is below sea level. No cliffs, no high ground. He took me to the saltpans owned by his family – fields with dykes around to trap the sea. The water evaporates, the salt remains.

'We climbed a heap of harvested salt – the only high ground around. Salt hung in the air, just breathing made you thirsty. At the top I relaxed, I could see the sea. *Soul mates*, Luc said. Our souls shaped by the sea. *Both of us trying to get away from it yet, drawn to it.* We lay on our backs staring at a big, blue sky. *See how impossible painting is? How can you represent this?* Salt clung to my hair, stuck to my clothes. I remember kissing Luc, his lips were salty –

'When we stood up I noticed the imprint of our bodies. *Can I?* I took his camera, and focused in on the shapes we'd left, took lots of pictures. *No illusion, only the trace of what has been.* I quoted his words back at him.

'Later, in town, avoiding Dominique, we sat for hours in the square, drinking red wine. As it got dark, shutters on the balconies above us were opened to let in the cooling air. You could hear music and chatter. I toyed with the salt on the table. This stuff had been part of the sea, dissolved in water, but now here it had come back as white crystals in a pot. *My family are like salt, part of the sea, only I can't recover them.* I was drunk, the heat, being in this place – I told him something – something I've never told anyone.'

She paused again, then looked directly at him.

'I told Luc about the wreck. Not a real wreck, it's something I dreamed up. It started when I was a child, at a friend's house; they had this toy wreck in a fish tank. No burial, you see, nowhere I could imagine them. I can think of them on the wreck, in the same place, all together. Luc started to scribble notes, said *We are going to make something, you and I*. The next day he had my photographs developed. Those images of the imprint our bodies had left in the salt excited him. That's how *Taking In Water* started. Though the title came later.'

Again, she paused. He held back his own thoughts; were others aware of how much she'd been author of the work? Now wasn't the time. She looked strained. This was costing her, dredging back, a direct reference to her lost family.

'Are you all right?'

'Yes, yes. Look, I'll tell you when I've had enough, Okay?' An edge to her voice, as if saying: let me speak, let me go on. 'Why don't you ask me something?'

He thought a moment.

'The scooping gesture you made in the performance, did that refer to those first photographs, the ones you took?'

She looked puzzled, shrugged as if to say: ask me another.

'Or, what about your time in New York? Wasn't that where *Taking In Water* finally took shape?'

She poured herself a glass of water. Again, he noticed the bruise on her wrist. It didn't look like nothing. And again, the wild thought as he pictured this lover, this Howard, gripping her.

31

'All done?' asked Steven.

'Yep.' The structural engineer had finished taking photographs inside the house and joined Steven who was in the garden eyeing up the crack in the wall.

'Won't take me a minute to fix these tell-tales,' said the engineer, unfolding his stepladder.

Steven walked over to his boss who was checking the marker posts.

'She's done that since we were here last,' he said, nodding towards the newly painted beach hut. 'So where is she – I thought she'd be all over us.'

'She said she had work to do,' said Steven.

'Work? What kind of work?'

'She's an artist, that's what she said.'

'That's not work. Wants to get away from it all – wouldn't we all? Anyway, I reckon she has a bob or two.'

His boss had a file on The Marine Hotel compensation – almighty fuss a few years back – reckons this woman had something to do with it. Seems far-fetched. *I'll have no big claims on my patch.*

'Tell-tales fixed on the outside. Touchy, you said, so I've not put them on the inside,' the structural engineer joined them.

'Better have a word with her before we go,' said the boss. 'She seems not to mind you. Training, Steven. Off you go.'

As he walked towards the hut Steven reviewed what the engineer had noted inside: minor cracks, a door that didn't quite fit, a few uneven tiles. His mum's house was on a hill and had worse signs of movement than that. The other day Miss Hutton had told him she liked being on her own, and here they were, all over her place. Of course she'd be touchy but she wasn't daft. *I'm on the high chalk. It's further along where the chalk has slumped.* If Steven were in charge he would talk to her, get her on their side. *Say nothing till we're certain,* that was the boss's line.

If he were in charge he too would have checked the stresses and strains on her house to rule her out of their zone of concern, not to alarm her. There was enough leeway in deciding where that zone began.

Steven stepped up onto the verandah and cleared his throat.

'Excuse me, Miss Hutton?' He called into the hut. 'We've finished, the boss would like a word.'

'Lydia,' she said, coming out. 'I told you, my name is Lydia.' She was dressed all in black, jeans and zip-up fleece. No smiles today, scary lady, but she did remind him of that singer. She followed Steven towards the house to join the others.

'So, what did you find?' she looked directly at the boss, her eyes suspicious.

'Thank you for your co-operation today. We'll send you our interim report just as soon as it's done,' he said. 'Now, my colleague has a few questions.'

The structural engineer stepped forward.

'How long have you had trouble with your door?' he asked, pointing to the red door at the back of the house.

'It's always tight after a wet winter,' Lydia shrugged.

'More than swollen wood is that, it's out of alignment, and the tiles under the kitchen table,' he carried on in the same toneless manner, ticking off items on a his checklist, 'is that lifting recent?'

'The house is eighty years old – all the floors are uneven.'

'And the crack above the window?'

'That's recent, but – '

'See,' the engineer said, turning to point to the crack, 'I've put studs either side of it – "tell tales" – that way we can take accurate measurements, see if it's getting any wider.'

'You're coming back?' Lydia eyeballed both men, each in turn, Steven edged round to stand at her side. Avoid eye contact.

'We need to monitor movement,' said the boss. 'Our interim report will be with you by the end of the week, though that's not our final decision, mind you.' And he went on to explain how, when all their investigations were completed, she'd be notified of their final recommendations.

'*Your* final decision? Don't I have any say in this?'

'We must balance personal and policy needs. There's preventative work we might need to do. Generally speaking, we take a precautionary approach.'

'And I'm in the way of your "retreat line"?' said Lydia.

Steven looked at his boots, wished they, along with him, would sink into the ground.

'Retreat line?' The boss laughed. 'Don't believe all you read in the papers. Speculation.'

Of course, the article in yesterday's *Evening News*, but it hadn't mentioned the idea of blowing up the cliff.

'So that's it today? You'll say nothing more?' Lydia persisted.

'Put it this way: I doubt you'd get planning permission to build here now.'

32

Lydia worked the knife blade around the rim, easing the lid off the can, *Absolute White,* chosen for its name and for the light it would create.

With the window wide open, a fresh breeze wafted around her bare legs as she climbed the stepladder. She pressed the brand new yellow roller into the paint tray and spread defiant bands of white across the kitchen ceiling. A week to wait before she had their "interim" report.

Don't go upsetting yourself, Miss Hutton.

He'd emphasised the *Miss*, as if she were some neurotic spinster like Miss Battersby who used to stay at the hotel. She edged the roller towards the junction with the wall. Above the window, a hairline crack mirrored the wider crack in the brick outside, now flanked with studs. *Tell Tales.* As if the bricks had secrets that could be tricked out of them.

She climbed down, shifted the ladder along and climbed back up. When she'd finished in here she'd make a start on her bedroom. She'd paint the whole house. That would see her through dealing with the surveyors, and with Martin. In the last session she'd talked about the wreck. *Tell Tale.* She glanced down at the table, imagined Martin sitting there with his machine waiting for her to speak.

'You remember I mentioned the wreck?' she said out loud to test the words she might use when the time came.

This morning she'd read the transcript and remembered more about that trip to Aigues-Mortes. She was beginning to see there'd been moments when her lost memory of the storm had tried to break through, especially on the journey when she'd had so little sleep.

After they'd left Paris, Luc had driven through the night. *Please, can't we stop?* She'd begged him. *You can sleep, while I drive.* She couldn't.

Eventually, he stopped near a church in a village, put his head on the steering wheel and slept straightaway. She paced around the churchyard reading memorials to the dead. After a couple of hours he woke and they carried on. She was jumpy, afraid, a feeling that something was about to creep up on her. She stared at the sky to blank off. The weather turned, heavy clouds hung above the road in front of them, felt as if they were coming for her. It went dark as night in the middle of the day, hailstones the size of mothballs clattered on the windscreen. *Stop them, stop them.* Luc pulled over. *Hey, relax.* He held her, kissed her neck. *Shsh, shsh.*

Had they sat out the storm? She couldn't remember. Being abroad for the first time, the sudden change of plan, leaving Paris, the journey – had it stirred something? And again, the following night, when they'd stayed in the bar with the one-eyed landlady, she'd slept badly. The next morning Luc had insisted on a detour.

Where are we going?
To the Source.

After a couple of miles driving alongside a wide river, he'd stopped the car. *From here, we must walk.* They set off, the cliffs of a gorge on either side of them. At the head of the gorge there was no more path, just a still pool. Deep, clear, turquoise. So calm, it looked like a swimming-pool. She wondered if it were real. Filled by a spring deep underground, the basin of perfect water seemed motionless but, imperceptibly, it spilled over the rim, into the stream, trickled onto the boulders, gathering momentum, churning white foam. Yet, the source of the water lay deep inside a dark cave.

No one has reached the bottom of the cave; divers have tried. Far below there's fossil water that's not seen daylight for forty-thousand thousand years. Luc telling her how he loved this place, had come here as a child. And he threw off his clothes, dived in, breaking the perfect surface. When his head appeared, he pushed his hair from his face and laughed. *Come on in.* She hesitated. *Come on.* Quickly, she undressed.

The cold of it was a shock. Freezing. Her lungs burned. She opened her eyes, saw her feet heading for the smooth rock below. As her toes touched down she pushed off, arms reaching up and soon her head broke the surface. She gulped a great mouthful of air. Luc was right by her, treading water. She tried to do the same but her legs were shaking. Luc held her. *You survived. Don't let it rule your life.* Remembering this, it was as if Luc had sensed what was still hidden to her. Not long after that she told him about the wreck and he began to talk about her energy, her 'aura'. Something else she remembered from that trip: overhearing Dominique say of her, *Elle a un regard hanté.* She'd looked it up: haunted.

She climbed down the ladder, scanned the freshly painted ceiling. It would do for the first coat. She shifted the ladder over to where she could reach the crack above the window. The man at the DIY store recommended she rake it out first. 'Make it bigger and it's easier to fill.'

She worked away with the scraper, opening it up. Then she spread the white paste and smoothed it into place. While it dried, she went to check her e-mails.

Dear Lydia

Attached is the final part of our last session – the New York section. I want to thank you for the time you've given to going back through a part of your past I know you were reluctant to visit. You have not only provided insight into the way Luc worked but also revealed your own contribution to *Talking in Water*. Your testimony makes a significant addition to the literature. Regarding your concerns about access/privacy – I will speak to the Director and should have more to say next time we meet. I'm pleased that you've agreed to talk further about your own work. I look forward to our next session tomorrow – let me know what time.

Warm regards, Martin

On the bench outside the studio, she settled down to read.

New York? At first, I loved it. We had the loft off West Broadway that Mantella had found for us – pretty basic as a place to live but a great studio, and we had access to the roof. I loved that. Luc was working on the Gagarin material and planning the layout for the final staging. We worked together on the canvases. He'd paint my body, then I'd sit or lie on it – whatever he wanted me to do. We had great rolls of the stuff. In between, well, I'd go out on the roof. I looked and looked – studied the rooftops, watched the pattern of the traffic down below. I liked that, reading the grid of the city. Gradually it became a life-size map in my head. I had my own camera by then and had picked up a telephoto lens from a pawnshop. I took pictures from the rooftop looking straight down. When Luc started work on the soundtrack he didn't like to be disturbed, so I'd head uptown. Walking. As the buildings got higher I'd take shots from the pavement, looking up. Or I'd visit Georgia Keay – by then she was beginning to make her mark. Her first book was out and she was teaching at Columbia. Her apartment was opposite the Natural History Museum on the corner of 77th and Columbus and beneath it was a 'Torn and Worn' that had the most amazing shoes – I was always buying second-hand shoes. Those few months, I was almost happy – working with Luc on *Taking In Water*, starting my own project, being high up. That's what I loved best about New York, being high up.

It all changed after *Taking in Water* attracted so much attention and Luc got sucked in by Warhol. When *Taking In Water* opened Mantella made sure that Kolker – the critic who'd been so keen on *Continuing Blue* – was there and he lined up Danny McCaig for photography. Well, you know what happened: major critical review, front covers on art magazines and Sunday supplements, big spreads inside. McCaig's pictures meant Mantella could commission the book – you've seen that, haven't you? Timing. All timing. What if Kolker or McCaig hadn't been there? Would Mantella have done the book? If Mantella hadn't produced the book the work might have been forgotten.

Luc was high on having made the piece, but the publicity knocked him out of orbit. I really believe it would have been enough for Luc to have pulled off the work. *Taking In Water* had it all: natural forces, the body, technology, mass media. It made the connections. *And it has us in it, our histories – the cosmic and the personal,* Luc used to say. He found that really satisfying. One good review would have been enough to spur him on to something even more powerful. He was already working on the 'Paradise' idea, you know, how to translate Gagarin's 'unprecedented encounter' into a philosophy, a way to live – if we could see the whole globe at a glance how could we possibly destroy it? *We are a part of nature, yet we live apart from it,* he'd say.

But, as you know, from then on it was less about art, more about, well, what was it about? The popular press attacked Luc for being anti-American. Why this obsession with a Russian, why not the American hero Shepard? Of course what mattered to Luc, to the work, was that Gagarin was the *first* human to see the Earth from space – not the space race. But America didn't want to be reminded that Russia had done anything first. Soon it wasn't about the work, it was about Luc. What toothpaste did he use? What cigarettes did he smoke? And the invitations – Luc didn't discriminate. He was riding high on the wave. It never occurred to him it could crash and take him with it. He believed the only way was up, he refused to see how random that kind of success is – like the sea, it can buoy you up, and it can dump you on the rocks. He couldn't see that mass attention is really a kind of indifference. What did he think – that everybody loved him? Fame, for him, was more toxic than weed, speed or acid. It was fame, not 'bad acid,' that killed him.

The controversy made Andy curious. We'd wander up to 47th, hang around The Factory. I was uneasy there – the tinfoil on the walls, the odd reflections. Andy had announced he wasn't doing any more paintings, only films. This drew Luc. The problem was, Luc wanted to talk; he was a philosopher. At the Factory people were too cool to talk. Well, not in the way Luc wanted to talk. People *watched* each other.

Georgia Keay warned Luc. She thought Andy was a creep, she had a thing about his hands: *unreal. Like a corpse. Who would want to be touched by those hands?* She didn't much care for the wig either: *you've got to think what's under there.* Andy's hands were white. But to me Andy seemed more nervous than creepy. He was hiding under the wig, the leather trousers, the pointy shoes. It felt like shyness to me, fear of people getting near him. He'd give the impression he was bored, but I'd say more scared.

After a few months of Luc hanging round, Andy was bored with him. Luc didn't get it because Andy always looked bored. Luc wasn't producing much in the studio. Like I said, he was obsessed with his Eden, 'Paradise' idea – how to live with nature but not some crude, back to nature thing – anyway, it was all in his head. He was doing uppers, downers, acid. He was thirty-four and he looked fifty. Andy liked to watch people self-destruct. The more Andy ignored him, the more Luc went back.

Andy knew Luc wanted to do a screen test and one day he called him over to the silver couch. Next thing, Andy comes over to me and takes me down to where he has this high stool in front of a camera. He didn't say anything, just pointed. I sat on the stool. Everyone knew what you had to do: look at the camera, just look. Andy set the film going and wandered off. Supreme indifference. Luc would have cracked, fifteen minutes staring down a camera lens. So Luc offered me. Everyone knew that sometimes Andy didn't put a film in. You know, it was about watching how people would react, wanting their fifteen minutes then telling them, after the ordeal, there'd been no film in, and you weren't supposed to mind. I hoped there wasn't any film in the camera. That's partly how I managed it. Luc wanted it, not me. I was standing in for him because he would have been compelled to speak, the one thing you mustn't do. Your face might start to reveal your inner life, but if you spoke – the end. Not cool. Some people found the stool awkward. You were high up, staring at a cold object. I kept my eyes steady, on the lens. That's what Andy wanted, that direct look – the only way he'd get eye contact – watching the films later, I mean. I don't know what Andy thought of me, I never heard, never saw the film – High up, staring, waiting – I knew how to do that. Fifteen minutes was easy.

Sometime in late '66 or maybe early '67 an English TV producer contacted Luc – did he have a new performance piece on the scale of *Taking in Water*? He needed some big idea for this global TV link-up, the first ever. *Our World*, I think it was called, contributions from around the globe, going out live for a whole day. But Luc was producing nothing. The new work was trapped in his head. He kept calling the producer. It was through that connection that we got on the guest list for the Beatles slot – *All You Need Is Love* – we still had status as a 'couple'. I was pleased because it meant we got to go back to London. I should have stayed, but I had my project to consider by then, my photographs of New York, looking down and looking up. I'd gathered quite a body of work. Mantella had put me in touch with a small gallery downtown that showed photographs, more commercial than cutting-edge, but I didn't mind. They were going to give me a show – people were already interested in buying my pictures.

That kind of success, or attention, whatever you call it, he'd had with *Taking In Water* meant Luc had a lot to lose. It paralysed him, but he started to believe *I* was the problem, said he was stuck because my energy was flowing away from him – that he could no longer feel my 'aura.' Looking back, it would have been easier if I'd stayed in London. Would it have stopped him killing himself? I – I've thought about that. Luc was on self-destruct. It was only a matter of time.

Back in New York Mantella started to put pressure on Luc – couldn't sponsor him forever – he wanted at least to see him working towards something. One morning Luc got up really early, went out and locked me in. I thought he'd just been careless. Anyway, I couldn't leave the apartment but I could get onto the roof, so I spent the day taking pictures of the rooftop water tanks –

those wooden barrels you see all over Manhattan – zooming in on any I had a direct sight-line to. All that contained water – it fascinated me. I followed what caught my eye. My work was always intuitive. I was never as conceptual as Luc. He worked 'head first.' Out on the roof that day I could see it – that's what Luc needed to do – get back into the world, look at what was under his nose – but how to tell him that? If you pay attention to water it always leads somewhere; that's what I wanted to tell him. He'd stopped paying attention. Luc's 'Paradise' would need water. Why not start in Manhattan, the most manmade place on Earth and yet the ocean is a bus ride away, there's the river and these reservoirs everywhere, in barrels on rooftops, high-rise water. Water rules the world. I mean, that's what *Taking In Water* was about, wasn't it? I decided that when he came back I'd remind him how, for a time, he'd got stuck in his head with *Taking in Water*. He always needed a title to clarify the concept. At first he'd wanted to call it 2/3. And, it had to be in figures, the proportions spelled out – body and Earth two-thirds water. It was too cerebral, so I reminded him why he wanted to make the piece – it was about *looking*, body connected to planet in *images*. Gagarin's brilliant eyes paying attention, taking in the vastness, the wonder of it. It was me who suggested *Taking In Water*.

As the day went on I forgot about being locked in, became absorbed in making my pictures, studying the great wooden barrels through my lens. They seemed so rudimentary, makeshift almost, from another time, yet they were vital. They became characters. I revisited each as the light changed, took shots of the shadows they cast. When Luc showed up I didn't hear him at first.

Layla, Layla, he sounded mad. *What are you doing?*
Taking pictures.
Pretty postcards of Manhattan to make money? What about our work? His voice was mean. I wasn't up to a heavy discussion about artistic integrity. I tried to talk about my water-barrel idea, about starting with water for his 'Paradise', but I'd lost confidence. I asked, casually, if he'd meant to lock me in. He said I was paranoid. Then he was all contrite, said he didn't know why he'd done it. The unpredictability was doing my head in. A couple of days later he did it again. The atmosphere was unbearable. I decided that, next day, I'd get up early and get out before he woke – I'd go to Georgia's. I was awake most of the night, planning what

I'd do. I had my passport ready. But I dozed off around dawn. Big mistake. He did it again. Went out, locked me in, only this time he took all my shoes. All of them. I searched the place, thinking there must be a pair somewhere. Nothing.

I went up on the roof, too upset to get lost in work. A voice inside me now was saying: *get out, now*. Between our building and the next, there was an alleyway that came out onto Thompson. I'd studied it often through my camera lens, taken shots through the fire escape that zig-zagged down the building. It was a hot day. I sat on the fire escape, which was still in the shade, a cool draft wafted up. I could do it. Seven storeys, I could do it.

I kept my eyes steady, didn't look up, didn't look down, held on tight, moved slowly, step by step. The fire escape finished half a storey short of the alley. The hardest part was the jump to the ground. All I could think was to keep my knees slack, not to resist. I was so relieved I hadn't broken any bones, I got up awkwardly, lost my balance, fell over and cut my arm. You've seen the blood in the pictures, no doubt.

I walked up Thompson keeping in the shade of the buildings, where the ground was cool enough to walk barefoot. I didn't even care about having no shoes, it felt so good to be out. My arm was stinging but I didn't pay it too much attention, I was focused on getting clear of the block, getting to where there were people. I was convinced Luc would turn up any minute and grab me – I hurried along Bleecker to West Broadway and up to Washington Square Park – no shade there and my feet burned on the hot ground. I stopped to cool off at the fountain, splashing each foot. That's when I noticed the blood on my arm and that's when he saw me, the man with the camera. I hadn't seen him, just heard him call out: *Hi Layla*. It wasn't Luc, I knew, it wasn't his voice but I was so scared. In the pictures I look deranged. And, of course, afterwards, after what happened to Luc, so much was read into the look in my eyes, the bloody arm, the bare feet. That photographer struck lucky, didn't he? He kept on clicking, all those pictures of my feet. Who would have wanted the pictures if Luc hadn't killed himself? I got as far as Fifth and took a cab uptown to Georgia's. I never saw Luc again. A week later he jumped from the roof – seven storeys. I was already in London.

Lydia walked the cliff path, a towel draped around her shoulders. Could she have saved Luc from himself? How could she? She was not responsible for *that* death. And, looking back now, how could he so depend on her 'aura,' feed off her pain? She'd been so young, so full of her own unresolved grief. At the time it had felt as if she'd been following Luc's lead with *Taking In Water*, yet reading back, she began to see how much had come from her. *Revealed your contribution* as Martin had pointed out.

She stood on the cliff edge overlooking the bay. It was later than she thought, not ideal to swim with the tide so far out but she needed the headspace only swimming could give.

She settled into the long slow strokes of a crawl, her hands scooping the water. Martin had asked her about the scooping in *Taking In Water* – Why had she scooped the salt in the same way each time? His question had surprised her. She really didn't have an answer. She needed to put herself back into the moment, remember what it had felt like as she lay on the salt. She would turn on her side, close her eyes – towards the end of a performance, wasn't it? She closed her eyes to shut out the audience, to concentrate on the soundtrack, yes, the soundtrack got louder towards the end – waves crashing – she'd call up the wreck, see it in her mind's eye. To stop the tears, stop her body shaking she'd scooped at the salt.

The sudden realisation broke her rhythm. She spluttered, her nose filled with salty water.

33

Eileen was cleaning the bathroom opposite his room. Martin lowered his voice.

'She had a *significant* involvement, Nick.' He enthused about the trip to France that had sparked the idea for *Taking In Water*, the way Lydia had worked on making the piece in New York. 'Even the title was hers.' He went on to explain about her water-barrel project in New York and her current work: photographs of clouds, the sea, objects and the recovered silverware from The Marine.

'Interesting,' said Nick, a noncommittal, detached tone. This was Nick, Director of the Archive responding, rather than Nick his old friend.

'There's more to come about her own work. I'd say it connects to *Taking In Water*. And, I have a feeling that embedded in *Taking in Water* is what happened to her as a child – but it's getting close to difficult stuff and she's wary.'

'Remember, Martin, you're not her therapist.'

'I know that, but there's more to *Taking In Water* and to her than anything recorded in previous accounts.'

'Is this getting personal for you?'

'I'm involved, of course, this is prime material –' and he deflected to his research: how he was thinking of persuading Sarton to show his collection of Luc's work; all right, so they couldn't restage *Taking In Water* but there were ways to present it, in the States at least – university galleries, East Coast, maybe.

And, they could get Mantella's movies digitised.

'Sarton might like the academic cred,' Nick said.

'Yes, and,' said Martin, the idea forming in his mind as he talked, 'what about an exhibition here – how contemporary artists respond to the sea. What do you think?'

'Is this all about the work, Martin, or her?'

'It's about *Taking in Water*, the ideas behind the work, the way it's been overlooked and – ' It was about writing a very different book, but his thoughts were not quite formed enough to speak of or to share with Nick. 'Anyway, can you do that, add something to the form?'

'What is it she wants?'

'Something that makes it clear this is her only and final word on Luc. She doesn't want to be pestered by follow-ups. Look, that last session was intense, she gave a lot and I wouldn't want her to pull back because of the privacy issue.' He and Nick agreed the wording of the new clause. 'You'll e-mail me the release papers, with that new clause inserted?'

He got out his laptop ready to go online downstairs.

'I'll need to unplug the phone for a minute, is that all right?' he called to Eileen.

'You'll not be long will you? Only Monica said she'd call,' she peered round the bathroom door, Mr Muscle in one hand, a J-cloth in the other and a look that said: *if you're not going to tell me who you keep e-mailing and rushing off to see, I'm not going to ask.* Then she surprised him.

'I'm wondering if it was the virus. The doctor reckoned it might be, and that chest of mine went on for weeks. Do you think I really need the test, Martin?'

'Yes, to know for certain, put your mind at rest.' Put his mind at rest. It was almost a week since they'd been to the drop-in clinic and yet she'd still not had the call.

'They must be very short of those machines, Martin. I don't

want to waste their time.'

'They said it could be a week and it's not wasting their time, even if it tells you there's nothing wrong.'

He glanced at the buff folder on the passenger seat. Was he wasting his time driving out to Lydia's, unannounced? He slowed down, kept to the speed limit.

Inside the folder was a copy of the release form she would eventually be asked to sign, including these new clause. He could just as easily have e-mailed it to her. He wanted to keep it separate from the transcripts, he reasoned, and to get it out of the way before the session tomorrow. She had real concerns and seeing the paperwork, with him there to address any outstanding fears, would clarify things. While there he could sound her out on the next session. *I'd like to talk about my own work. Talking about my mother was important for me, and there's more.* She'd said with a sense of urgency. An indication of a connection between her work and her past? Yet by the end of that long session she seemed ambivalent when he tried to fix a time.

'So what about Wednesday?' he'd offered, realising it would be Tuesday before he could transcribe everything.

'Wednesday, probably, yes. But why don't we talk on the phone when I've read everything?' She'd hardly been listening to him by then.

She'd looked genuinely puzzled when he'd asked about the scooping gesture. There were so many questions he'd like to ask: where had she gone after Luc died? Why had she come back to live in Flampton? If he was being honest, his interest wasn't entirely professional. Yes, it was getting personal for him.

Ahead, a sign that told him the turn-off to Slayton beach was imminent and that Flampton, and Lydia's place, was another three miles. What did he think he was doing: *just passing so I thought I'd drop in.* He took the turn to Slayton Bay carpark.

He'd turn round, go back and e-mail the papers to her.

Down on the beach he lingered around the pillboxes. How long was it since that day he'd walked Barley and seen Lydia through the mist? Not quite two weeks, yet it seemed far off. He'd become caught up in Lydia's time. Is that what he was doing here – hoping he'd bump into her again?

He examined the cliff. Mud, eroded by rivulets of water from above, lay slewed against the concrete ruins. As a child, he wasn't allowed near these things. One afternoon when Eileen had dozed off behind the windbreak, he'd run along the hard sand of the shoreline and climbed inside, peering out through the slit. It'd smelled of seaweed, damp and salty. 'Martin, Martin,' Eileen frantic. He'd waited, savouring the secret place, then tumbled out at the last moment and fallen, a sharp edge of concrete cutting him just above his mouth. 'I told you it was dangerous.' He still had the small scar.

Today, scrambling inside, the space seemed smaller. He crouched a moment while his eyes adjusted to the half-light: more broken concrete and, caught between the slabs, a tangle of seaweed. He went farther in and noticed washed-up objects: the husk of a mobile phone, a plastic bag, broken sunglasses, a watch. He picked up the watch. It was still working, the yellow second-hand ticked steadily round. He turned it over and read: *titanium, shockproof, waterproof to 300m.* Recently dropped. Could it be Lydia's? He put it in his coat pocket. As he turned to leave, his foot caught against something stuck in the sand by the entrance. He pulled, it out. A teaspoon, though it looked more like a soupspoon with its bowl flattened out. He ran his finger along the handle to remove the mud. The letters were worn but readable: *The Marine Hotel.* He looked around for more but found nothing.

He strolled back along the beach with the spoon in his hand

and the tide coming in. Offshore, a small boat hugged the coast, heading for the harbour. Twenty years ago that could have been his father, out there. His father, who saw the sea as a kind of god. *It's what I take to be eternity, Martin.*

But for his father's philosophising and the book he'd bought him as a child, would he have noticed *Taking In Water?* The book had fuelled his fascination with the watery globe seen from outer space. Images that made him think of his dad as a tiny speck out on the boat. But for the fact that his father had died just weeks before he'd first studied *Talking In Water*, would he be here now?

He crouched down, idly tracing in the sand with the flattened spoon. He'd spent hours on this beach as a child digging with his red metal spade, digging a great big hole to hide from Eileen. Since then, he'd made a career out of a different kind of digging. With Lydia he'd unearthed far more than he'd expected. *Lydia, Layla,* he wrote in the sand. It wouldn't work simply to splice new material into the chapters he'd planned for his book.

The book he'd planned suddenly seemed too narrow, too academic. He'd like to unravel and re-write the history of *Taking In Water*. No, its *histories*. The Sixties stuff, the break from painting, the space race, plus the personal histories of Luc and Lydia. *It had our histories in it,* Luc had said. And Lydia's history reached back to a shocking event – nature's terrorism – largely forgotten. *At least with the air raids we had some warning*, Eileen had said. Of course, thousands had died, but the warnings meant some were saved. Six years keeping Hitler out and yet, overnight, the sea invaded taking hundreds of lives. Added together the figures for Holland and Britain amounted to the same as for 9/11, and, like that day, there'd been no warning. No one would forget 9/11, an event burned into history. But the storm that had caused the worst peacetime disaster – who remembered it now?

There was no collective memory, it wasn't taught in schools. Maybe it was too much to bear, to think about how powerless we are against the sea, and yet that was becoming a pressing issue.

That's what he'd like to write: to take a piece of art as a way back into a piece of forgotten history and forward into climate issues. There was so much to consider from this one work of art, and though he would be rigorous and true to the material, did he really want to write a narrow academic tome, full of theory and footnotes? No. He'd like to write something readable, maybe something his father would have read. Something Eileen might want to read.

At the shore, he rinsed the sand from the spoon in the hiss of foam, wiped it on his jeans and put it in his pocket.

He knocked on the door a third time, but still no answer, so he peered in through the kitchen window: a stepladder, a paint tray and roller and the ceiling freshly painted; clothes strewn over the back of the chair. Her car was here.

He walked over to her studio, past the marker posts. She'd been exhausted by the session on Sunday, hardly time for her to recover before the surveyors came yesterday.

'Lydia?' he called out.

He listened at the door. No answer. It wasn't locked, which struck him as odd. Perhaps she was around, just hadn't heard him. He went inside. No sign of her having done any new work. It looked exactly as it had done when he'd left on Sunday.

He put the folder, and the watch he'd found at Slayton, on her worktable and took the spoon over to her collection of objects arranged. Looking now, he could see there was an order to how she'd arranged things. The teapot, at the centre, was the most intact, around it other fragments fanned out, getting increasingly unrecognisable. He couldn't simply add the spoon. He slipped it back into his pocket and went over to look at her collection of news cuttings. *Fish swim in Manhattan streets, scuba divers rescue trapped drivers.* He studied again the picture of women wading through a flooded street, skyscrapers rising behind them, and it came to him: the image of dust billowing along the narrow street, like a sea surge. He shook away the memory of it.

It really wasn't like Lydia to have left the studio unlocked. Luc's suicide was in that last transcript. He imagined her reading it back this morning – *jumped from the roof?* What effect might such a disturbing memory have had on her? Had she gone for a walk or a swim?

'Lydia, Lydia?' He called out, louder this time.

There was an uneasy silence about the place; the sense that she'd left in a hurry.

34

'You?' she exclaimed. It was with relief rather than accusation, pleased to find it was only Martin in her studio. He was studying that picture, again, the one of the women in Manhattan.

'Oh!' He spun round, obviously hadn't heard her come in.

'It's all right. When I saw the door open I thought it was those bloody surveyors. Didn't we agree tomorrow for the next session?' Her pulse quickened as the thought formed – why not now? Tell him what she'd realised out in the bay? 'I'm fine with doing it now if you want.'

'But you've been in the sea, don't you need a shower or something? Aren't you cold?'

'Won't take me a minute.'

'Well, really, I came to show you this – ' He picked up a folder from the table, 'I've spoken to the Director about your concerns – ' held out papers, talked in a rush pointing to the new paragraph on the form when all she wanted to know was: *where's your machine?* 'Thought it would reassure you, before the session tomorrow.'

'Thanks – but do you have your machine?' She was ready to tell him why, all those years ago, she'd scooped out a hollow in a heap of salt.

'Oh, no, I just wanted to clear all of that –'

'I see,' she said holding off disappointment. Trying not to sound over-eager, 'Could you come back later?'

'Well, yes – if you'd like.'

'I would, I really would.' She'd go back to his question, tell him it was her body trying to show her what her mind had locked up.

'– in a couple of hours maybe?'

'Okay.'

That long, she wanted to say.

'By the way, the photographs you took in New York – the water-barrel studies – do you still have them?'

'Somewhere – they're in London. Why?'

'Because of the connections to *Taking In Water*, certain preoccupations – and to your current work.'

'There's forty years between *Taking In Water* and the work I do now – '

'Well, we can talk about it when I come back.'

Yes, she wanted to say, *so go and get your machine* but he lingered, as if he wasn't quite done.

He held out a watch, offered it to her.

'I found it down on Slayton beach, wondered if it was yours?'

'No,' she took the watch from him. 'Probably some surfer's – looks like the sort of thing they'd wear.'

'Perhaps you'd like it – your photographs?'

'It's not a failed object. See, it's still working.' She held the watch face towards him. 'Where at Slayton did you find it?'

'Near the pill boxes – so I thought, maybe –'

'Walking the dog, were you?'

'Anyway, keep it. I don't know what to do with it.' Why had he avoided her question? If he wasn't walking the dog, why had he been down at the pillboxes? She needed to trust him.

'It might have interested me down on the beach. But I would need to have found it myself, shot it where it lay. So it's yours. What's washed up on the beach belongs to those who find it, there's some law – Flotsam and Jetsam Act.'

'Do you always photograph objects where you find them?'

He brushed his hand through his hair, the same nervous gesture she'd seen before, that first time he'd arrived unannounced and couldn't quite bring himself to say what he wanted. What was it he couldn't say now?

'It depends, things like that, yes. If they interest me.'

Martin left the watch on the table, put his hand in his pocket as if he was holding on to something.

'Those things from The Marine, your new project?' he nodded towards her collection.

'I like to get a shot of where I find stuff. Place matters to me, my work, keeping intimate with the place – there's been no more Marine stuff, not for days.' She wanted to add: that's why I need your machine, talking is becoming part of making the work.

'I think you might want this,' he said and handed her what she could see at once was a spoon from The Marine. A whole teaspoon, flattened but whole.

'You found this today?' She took it and went over to the sink to rinse off sand and salt stains. So, there *is* more. She wiped it dry then, at the shelf, tried different positions for the spoon among the collection.

'Sorry you weren't able to photograph it,' she heard him say.

It would be churlish to complain, be suspicious. After all, he had brought it to her, realised it was important.

He was back at her weather wall, his finger on the Manhattan picture.

'Why that one?' She left the spoon, went over to join him.

'Sorry?'

'You always look at that picture.'

He shrugged and then that nervous gesture, again; his hand raking through his hair as if he was holding something in.

'What's the matter?' She had the distinct impression he wanted to say something.

'Sorry, about the spoon, I mean. Picking it up and – and I

hope you feel reassured about the privacy, thing – you know, that you can speak frankly, don't be afraid –'

'Afraid?' she said. Right now it was he who looked unsettled.

'I'll leave you to get changed, you must be cold,' he said and turned to leave.

'What is it, what were you going to say?' She wasn't letting him go that easily. When he started on again about the privacy forms she cut him short, 'What's bothering you?'

'Bothering me?'

'You look, well, almost – ' Afraid, she wanted to say. She'd like to ask him if he knew what fear was. An awkward silence grew between them. What the hell, she would ask. 'Have you ever lost it, I mean really lost it?' She had to know, to see if he was up to hearing what she was about to tell. 'I mean, totally freaked out?' So out of your mind you forget it ever happened and do crazy things like sending yourself a message in a heap of salt.

'Not exactly, but – ' He took a deep breath, pushed his hand through his hair.

He pointed to the picture.

She moved towards him, close enough to catch the scent of his leather coat.

'Well, since you ask – ' He stared at the floor as he spoke. 'I was there, last September, in Manhattan –' he said, keeping his voice low and steady, as if measuring out what he wanted to say. 'I was in the South Tower just before – '

'Oh! You survived – ' She hadn't expected that. Questions formed in her head, all tactless, pointless to ask.

'No, it wasn't like that. I left before it happened, because – '

He was silent a while as if collecting his thoughts.

'I don't want this to sound, well, crass but the truth of it is this: I was in the South Tower about an hour before the attacks. I was in New York researching Luc and – ' He spoke fast, as if he wanted to get it over with: how he'd walked through the Village, then downtown to the Towers so he could see Luc's territory from on high; the phone call, a change of plan, the split-second timing of it all. 'So you see, it was *Taking In Water* that saved me.' He smiled, seemed relieved to have got it over with.

She looked at him, taking in the new information, this new side to him. He lifted his head, a half-smile.

'Yes, but it was *Taking In Water* that also nearly got you killed,' she said and reached out with both hands, touched his arms, as near as she could manage to holding him. He moved closer. She could feel his body slacken. He leaned forward, kissed her forehead.

35

The nurse guided Eileen into the cubicle. Martin settled down in the waiting area and considered Francine's e-mail: *If we can agree figures it should be straightforward, a matter of signing papers, but you'll need to be here – this weekend?* Yes, he could agree to her final figure for the house but couldn't commit to going back to London until he'd spoken to Lydia. And his thoughts were off again, back to her studio yesterday. He savoured the memory: the salty smell of her wet hair as he'd kissed her forehead. She would have been naked beneath the tracksuit. Where might that have gone but for Eileen's call?

'The machine – they've got one,' his mother, high-pitched, hysterical. He'd hoped Lydia wasn't able to hear. 'I've to go in the morning – I feel queasy. When will you be back?'

He'd sketched the situation for Lydia; they'd need to postpone the session. '*Go* – you must go.' There'd been clear disappointment on her face. 'I'll call you,' he'd promised.

Now, here was Eileen, accompanied by a smiling nurse.

'That took no time.' He stood up. Fixing the heart monitor turned out to be a simple procedure: four suction pads placed around her heart to hold in place the wires that fed into a recorder the size of his mini-disk machine.

'Remember,' the nurse said, 'no soaking in the bath, don't get the connections wet. And you must return it tomorrow. There's others waiting for it.'

Taking In Water

'Martin, will you fetch me tomorrow?' Eileen anxious already.

'You don't need to come yourself, Mrs Dawson. After 24 hours, you can remove the pads, just like taking off sticking plaster. Your son could bring it back.' Eileen's data would then be examined, and by the time she arrived for her appointment next Monday the doctor would have the full picture.

'Yes, I'll do that, don't worry.' He'd agree to anything that got him out of the house without interrogation. 'Now, let's get you home.' But Eileen was having none of it. She needed his help with errands, the library, Oh yes, and, while they were in the car, could he take her to the craft shop on the other side of town?

Martin parked as close as he could to the front gate.

'I feel like I've got one of those gadgets on,' said Eileen, 'you know, that lets you listen to music.'

'A Walkman?' said Martin.

'It makes an odd shape of me.' She lifted her jumper and adjusted the strap around her waist that held in place the black box: a stiff leather pouch with a tape recorder inside.

'It's worth being an odd shape for a few hours to put your mind at rest,' he said. His voice sounded distant, not his own. Inside, he was an odd shape.

'A few hours? It's a whole day.'

'You've done three, only twenty-one to go.' Would she make him suffer each heartbeat? 'Why don't you put the kettle on? I'll bring this lot.' The back seat was stacked with bulging supermarket carriers. 'Here, you take these.' He handed Eileen her library books, three detective novels: *The White Cottage Mystery, The Beckoning Lady, Sweet Danger*.

'Tea or coffee?' said Eileen, getting out of the car with exaggerated care.

'Whatever you're having,' he said, distracted, remembering

Lydia's cool brow against his lips.

He dumped what must be the tenth carrier bag on the kitchen floor.

'You've stocked up for weeks.'

'It soon goes when there's two. I'm going to lie down.'

'No. You must do what you'd normally do. Would you normally lie down at this time?'

'These damn wires. I'm not comfortable.'

'Try to forget it's there. Why don't you do some sewing?' He dug out the bag from the craft shop, the kit she'd bought to sew as a present for Monica's birthday. 'Here, why not start this?' Surely the movement of her sewing arm would register activity.

'Later, maybe.'

'Well, one thing's certain, when the doctor analyses your data, he's not expecting a straight line. You've got to move. They're looking to see how your heart behaves on a normal day. So, do what you normally do. I thought you were making tea?'

Eileen filled the kettle. Martin started to unpack the shopping.

'Leave it. I know where things go. I like things in the proper order,' she fussed.

'I can make a start,' he said, thinking of the uncanny order Lydia had created for her salvaged silverware. He must put her out of his mind. He concentrated on sorting the dog food out from the rest, cans of chicken chunks in jelly and pouches of rabbit in gravy, "special formula for older dogs."

Barley nudged and sniffed around the shopping bags.

'Don't come to me old girl, I'm just the errand boy.'

'She needs a walk,' said Eileen.

'You take her. Why not? Perfect, a gentle stroll with Barley, what could be a more normal activity?'

'Tea first.' Eileen put two mugs on the kitchen table. He sat down and watched the creases in her forehead over the rim of the mug as she sipped, and in between each sip came a world-weary sigh. He leaned over and offered her an encouraging squeeze of the arm.

'Go on, take Barley for a walk. It's what you'd do, normally.'

'In a minute.' She rested her hand on his arm, returned the gesture. It came to him, this is what Lydia had offered: a touch of reassurance, comfort. How had he configured it otherwise?

Why had he done it? As if his experience could be equated with hers. He hadn't meant to, but when she'd said, *Have you ever lost it? I mean, totally freaked out?* Not saying anything would have been like playing games, like the kind he played all the time with Eileen. After all, he knew so much about her it would have been odd not to speak. He'd answered her question, given an honest answer. She'd softened, come towards him with her touch. It surprised him. And he'd kissed her.

He thought about the women he would kiss politely on the cheek without a second thought: Maggie, the department secretary, Francine's mother, let's face it Francine herself, these days. The way he'd kissed Lydia had been more than politeness. Last night he'd replayed the disk, found the moment where Lydia had spoken of how Luc had kissed her the first time, *Lightly, on the forehead.* The older man testing the younger woman? Now here he was, the younger man – by how many years? It didn't matter. There'd been no test, he'd simply responded to the circumstance, to her gesture. What would have happened if Eileen hadn't phoned? *Go – you must go,* Lydia had said after Eileen's call had broken the moment. Meaning, go because your mother needs you or, because you've kissed me and I want you out of here?

'Penny for 'em,' said Eileen. 'You're miles away.'

'Sorry.' He drank the rest of his tea.

'Too much time on that computer, Martin, you look peaky,'

said Eileen getting up. 'Right. I'll walk Barley to the roundabout and back.'

Martin carried on unpacking the shopping until his phone rang again.

'Francine?'

'You got my e-mail?'

'Yes, yes – I was about to reply.'

'You sound stressed out.'

'I'm just back from the hospital with Eileen.'

'Hospital?'

'She's having her heart checked out, some tests.'

'Really? Oh, dear – sorry to push you then, but –' Not a beat more on his mother, no, no. As always, businesslike and cool. Maybe the warmth was there somewhere inside Francine, but he couldn't feel it. Certainly he didn't bring it out in her any more.

'Assuming all's well with Eileen's tests – she sees the doctor on Monday – I could drive back on Tuesday,' he said with certainty, though he wasn't at all certain he'd be ready to come back by then.

36

Lydia had tried to sketch the spoon. Nothing satisfied. She was trying too hard.

She went over to the shelf and laid the spoon next to the teapot. Then she moved the teapot to the back of the shelf and assembled the broken cutlery in a line, with the spoon at the end. No good. She tried arranging the objects inside the hollowed-out driftwood she'd found the other day. As if moving things around would make it all come right. How could she concentrate when she was listening for the phone.

Would talking to Martin be different now he'd stepped out from behind his machine? The sensation of his lips on her forehead – it was just a kiss. An affectionate, farewell kiss. That's what people did out there. It happened every day, a kiss on the cheek, said: I've been pleased to share your company; I'm marking my leaving with this slight touch of skin on skin. Had it had been more than that? Living alone for so long, she wasn't fluent in the language of touch, which was open to misinterpretation. Talking, listening, was intimate. Most likely it happened to Martin all the time, like patients and doctors, the intensity of all that talking.

He said he would call. He had a sick mother to think about.

If he did come back, where would she go after she'd explained the scooping? Back to the moment when her dad punched a hole in Grandma H's ceiling? No, she'd start at the hospital, at the point where the images in her head had begun to flicker, like a film. Frame by frame she'd show him the film. He would write out what she said, the whole film would be out of her head, the images laid down in words.

Back in the house she busied herself rearranging pots and pans in her newly painted kitchen. She couldn't phone him, his mother was ill.

Carefully she returned the blue cup to the top shelf. This misshapen thing had been enough to discharge herself from hospital. Its handle was out of proportion, its body bulged, bigger than a cup ought to be, and the rim turned in on itself, but it was recognisably a cup, well, more of a mug. On second thoughts, she lifted it back down and put it on the table, where she could see it.

Out in the garden, she cut a few sprigs of rosemary. The delicate purple flowers were just starting to bloom.

She wasn't imagining the sound of a car on the track.

*

'Morning.' Steven was relieved to find her outside. It really was beautiful here. She was reaching down to pick up the secateurs she'd dropped; cuttings lay scattered by the door.

'Oh – I thought –' she gathered the cuttings into a bunch.

'You're expecting someone?'

'No. You want to check those things?' She jabbed with the secateurs towards the marker posts, 'or these,' pointing up towards the tell-tales.

'Just the posts today, if I you don't mind?' Steven took out his notebook.

He could feel her eyes on him as he pretended to study each one in turn, his pen poised to make meaningless notes while he steeled himself to admit the real reason for his visit.

He wouldn't go as far as to tell her that the marker posts were there mainly for the effect they would have on her, even though that was becoming clearer to him with every discussion at the office. *Having them there keeps our work in view,* he'd overheard his boss saying to a colleague on the team who, like Steven, had wondered if the boss was being provocative. *Puts us on her property.*

Steven checked the alignment of the yellow bands, aware of Lydia going back into the house. He waited a couple of minutes then followed her. As he approached, he could see her through the kitchen window, arranging the cuttings in a pot. It looked handmade. Is that what she did in her hut? She went over to the sink and splashed water on her face, then stood a moment, her face buried in a towel.

'Finished, thanks. I'm off,' he called. Perhaps this wasn't a good time.

'Is that it?' She appeared at the door.

'All done,' he said.

'So when am I getting this report?'

'Actually, if you've a minute, I'd like a word. Only I thought you were expecting someone, and this is *strictly* confidential,' he said, chopping the air with one hand to underline the point.

'What is it?' she stepped into the garden.

'You haven't heard this from me. Okay?'

'Are you sure you want to tell me?'

'There are things you should be told. If you're not careful things could get nasty. By the way, thanks for not dropping me in it the other day, about the explosions.'

'Nasty – what do you mean?'

'The explosions option – it's where and how much of it that's up for discussion.'

'I get the impression your boss doesn't do discussion. He

didn't like me pushing him the other day, did he?'

Steven wanted to say: *the boss doesn't like you, full stop.*

'He's under pressure to deliver.' He couldn't go as far as to tell her that the boss would stop at nothing to cover his own back, including making something of her connection to The Marine Hotel. He reckoned she'd profited from a hefty lump of compensation. Avoiding financial settlements in the future was partly what CoDMas was about. 'The report should be with you on Friday. If it were up to me, I'd discuss it with you. The boss – he'll just send a letter and wait to see what you do.'

'You'd better come inside,' said Lydia.

'I'm late. I've got to meet the others.' He gestured towards the lighthouse. 'Look, this is already more than my job's worth but I think you ought to know, it doesn't have to be a foregone conclusion. Where they finally draw the line is open to discussion and you might not get that impression the way the report is worded.'

'Go on.'

'I can't,' he looked at his watch. 'You've a right to talk it through with someone on the team – '

'And I won't be given the opportunity?'

'Facts can be put in different ways.' She was the only private house involved so his boss was prepared to ride roughshod. And if she made a fuss, well, he'd already put it about that she was eccentric, and he'd say she was known for making a profit from public funds.

'Think before you reply, is all I'm saying.'

'Why?'

'He'll make it as difficult as he can, reckons he knows stuff.'

'What stuff?'

'Can't say anymore. Request a meeting. You need to get others involved – '

'Why are you doing this?' she asked, her voice was calm.

He'd thought she'd be angry but she looked puzzled.

'Because, well, it's your home – I can see the place means a lot to you.' Anyone could see she loved these cliffs, as he did, though maybe for different reasons.

'Thank you.'

*

Back in the studio she fingered the shell, a common limpet. It was all she'd picked up at Slayton this morning – how had she missed the spoon? Larger than most, the limpet shell had stood out, this abandoned home, the occupant long gone. Sitting at her worktable she began to doodle, fine etching marks with a pencil on paper to mimic its pattern.

They always settle in the same resting place, her father had explained. *They move ever so slowly over the rocks, grazing on algae – you'd have to sit still for a very long time, Lyddie, to notice. They always return to their own private spot, a dent made where their rubbery body has fastened on, over and over again. It's only when the creature dies that the shell is free to fall.*

This was her private spot. Was she up for a battle to keep it? If she made a stand there'd be publicity. Eventually someone would rake through her past. *Reckons he knows stuff.* What did that mean? She could see the headline: PARANOID CLIFF SIEGE WOMAN'S SEX AND DRUGS PAST.

She balanced the limpet shell on her finger – a perfect design – but neither did she want to let go of her home. *Lydia Limpet, don't let go.* She'd hung on to this hut, rescued it from The Marine. However cold it was outside, inside the hut she'd always felt warm watching her father swim in all seasons, a good swimmer, but, in the end, not good enough. Setting it up here had marked the start of her working again.

Her drawing was going nowhere. The sound of her feet on

the hut's wooden floor echoed back as she walked over to the shelf to place the shell among the Marine objects.

Running up from the beach, my feet slap on the wooden steps. A sudden downpour. I've been collecting shells, while Dad has his swim. Mum rubs my wet arms with a soft white towel that smells of soap flakes. *Soon get you dry.* I can hear her voice, hear the rain on the roof, but I can't see her face.

I'm tipping shells from my bucket, they clatter as they spill onto the floor.

Imagine carrying your home with you wherever you go. She's laughing.

Do they never come back, the things that live in them?
They can't. They're dead.

Lydia had relocated the hut once; she could move it again. She could move the house, brick by brick, build it further back.

This new strategy has to deliver, Steven had told her. Well, she had her own coastal strategy: facing out the sea each day; tracking the clouds; recording what the sea chucked back; keeping an eye on water at work on the world with her weather wall – upturned houses, floating cars, the look in the eyes of survivors. That was her work, keeping an eye on water, but what good did that do? Okay, so Patrick's architect wanted her photographs to hang in this new library and that might cause someone to pause for a fleeting moment. Was that it? Yet living here was how she survived, with her past around her in the hut, the cliff, the sea, the weather. If the surveyors redrew the coastline, she'd need a map of the past, something portable to take away.

37

Before he drove to the clinic, Martin phoned Lydia.

'Oh, hello,' surprise in her voice, and a note of caution.

'I'm sorry I didn't get back to you after the other day,' he said, then added hastily, 'I mean, my mother, it's been difficult.'

Eileen hadn't let him out of the house, as if he too had been wired to the monitor. Now, wire-free, she was soaking in the bath and once he'd returned the machine to the clinic he would be free. 'I could be with you in an hour, or anytime today – whatever suits?'

An awkward silence.

'Yes. Okay. About ten-thirty?' Nothing in her tone told him how she felt about his crass outburst or the kiss.

At the clinic, he was greeted by the nurse who'd attended to Eileen yesterday.

'How's your mum – everything all right?'

'Fine, yes.' Distracted he delved in his bag for the monitor and handed it to the nurse.

'I don't think so,' she said, handing back his minidisk recorder.

He walked down the side of Lydia's house. Ought he to greet her with a kiss because if he didn't, what did that say? If he did, well, it wasn't exactly maintaining a professional distance. The door onto the garden was open.

'Hello?'

'Hi, come in,' she called. She was at the kitchen sink, hands busy in soapy water, the kiss avoided. 'You can set that up,' she nodded at his bag, 'I won't be a minute.'

The place looked different – bright white walls and a lingering smell of fresh paint. She seemed different too: new jeans, a plum-coloured sweater.

He lifted the recorder out of his bag, grateful it wasn't a day's worth of Eileen's heartbeats he was placing on Lydia's table.

'Do you mind if I move this?' he asked, lifting a pot filled with sprigs of rosemary. She took it from him, put it on the work counter and carried on at the sink.

'I didn't ask for this,' she began, her back to him. 'I mean, you turned up,' she shrugged, thoughtful, almost talking to herself, 'and I started talking to your machine and –'

He wanted to finish her sentence: *now you're hooked*. He'd seen before how reviewing one's own life became compelling, addictive.

'I *was* beginning to make new work,' she carried on. 'The stuff from the hotel – that day when we first – when we met on the beach, I'd found so much I really felt I could do something with it.' She pulled the plug from the sink.

He looked across at the empty high-backed chair, her father's chair. If she would sit down he could start recording. Wasn't that what she wanted? To talk about her work? The other day, before the kiss, she'd been disappointed that he hadn't brought his machine, had been eager for him to go and get it, her need to talk, palpable. Now she'd had time to sleep on it.

She rinsed suds from the cafetiere and held up the clean pot.

'Coffee?'

He was jittery enough.

'Why not? Thanks.' He didn't need to drink it, but she needed to make it.

'How's your mother – any better?' she asked, tipping beans into the electric grinder.

'She was having tests – her heart – we're waiting for the results. Yesterday was difficult.'

'How old is she?' Lydia asked, switching on the coffee grinder. It was a reasonable enough question to see if his mother might expect her heart to be worn out. His thoughts whirred along with the machine. Age. It was a state of mind. He was forty-three, Lydia was fifty-seven. He didn't feel a decade plus between them.

'Seventy-one,' he lied as the grinder stopped. Suddenly he wanted to even out the years, make Eileen the same number of years older than Lydia as he was younger. *My mother's always been old*, he wanted to say. A state of mind.

'Well, I hope she's all right,' Lydia poured boiling water into the pot. 'Waiting can be worse than knowing.' She laid cups and saucers on the table and glanced out of the window.

'Have you – ?' He gestured towards the marker posts.

'I'm expecting them to deliver their report today.' She pushed the plunger down the cafetiere and sat opposite him.

'Milk, sugar?' It was the first time she'd looked directly at him and he noticed the light dusting, powdery blue, on her eyelids. She'd not worn make-up before. Had she dressed up for the surveyors?

'Black is fine, thanks.'

'The other day when you were here – I – I, appreciated what you told me.' She added milk to her cup.

'Look, it was clumsy of me. I wasn't trying to suggest – '

'It's all right,' she said. 'It makes a difference. As does knowing you have a personal reason for connecting to *Taking In Water* – your father – what you said about the book he'd bought you. I'm pleased you told me these things. Really, it matters – Do you want to switch that on?' She leaned forward, the eagerness he'd seen the other day returning, something in her voice that said, *okay let's get on with this*. He handed her the microphone.

*

She didn't need his questions today.

'I've been thinking about what you asked the other day, about the scooping in *Taking in Water*, what it meant. I would have said it was intuitive, which, I suppose it was, though now I can see it does have a – a personal meaning. To explain it, I need to go over some very personal stuff – ' The baby, the hospital. All of it, only that way would the scooping make sense.

He nodded.

'I need to take my time – '

'Really, don't apologise, forget I'm here,' Martin said.

Easier said than done, the way he looked at her.

'After Luc, I went to ground. I spent time in India, up in Dharamsala. I was into Buddhism – even shaved my head at one point. I was covering Layla's tracks. Early Seventies, and I was back in London. Bea was living with Ray by then, they had their own business, a design studio. They'd divided the house into two flats. I lived in the upstairs and helped out at the studio. I tried various projects of my own, carried on with photography. There were brief relationships but, after Luc, I was wary of getting too involved – I'd go to parties and sometimes people would say, you remind me of someone. I'd say, you mean Layla, yeah, people often tell me that. I wonder what happened to her? It always worked. I'd had my hair cut short by then and, for a time, I dyed it blonde. 1976, that long, hot summer. Lots of parties that summer, lots of one-night stands. I got pregnant. I didn't know who the father was.' She was tempted to say: it's okay, I never mistook all that bodily contact for caring. She looked up at Martin. His face was unreadable. He sat perfectly still.

'I think I mentioned before about the underground reservoir at the back of the house and how it had a field on top of it? That hidden water had bothered me at one time – in '76 it dried up, evaporated, the grass above it scorched. I was thirty-one, drifting, beginning to feel as if I was evaporating. My first reaction was – have an abortion. I even made the appointment. The woman on the phone asked, "and who will come with you, is there someone in the family?" Family? The word echoed around my head. Me, a mother – was I capable? But I knew I wanted the baby. Would I see my mother or my father in this new face?

'Late September and everyone was longing for rain. When it came, I watched the grass over the reservoir turn green, felt the baby growing inside. Nothing, for a long time, had seemed so right. Bea and Ray were supportive. They hadn't wanted children but they were excited about having a child around.

'November. I woke up in the middle of the night. Pain. Shooting pain across my back. Then bleeding. At the hospital they tried to reassure me but I could read the look on the midwife's face. Almost six months pregnant so I had to give birth. Give birth to a dead baby. A girl. A beautiful – '

Give birth. She'd given her death. Five hours to give birth to a dead daughter, who was never alive to be mothered, could she even call her daughter? She would not cry, not yet.

'They told me not to look, but I wanted to – I insisted they unwrap the cloth they'd bundled her into. I touched her tiny balled up fist, wanted to uncurl those delicate fingers, so I could hold her hand – ' Words falling out of her now, she stopped to catch her breath, glanced at Martin.

'I'm so sorry,' he said.

She could see the pained look on his face. Could she put him through it? How could she forget he was there?

'The day I came home from hospital was dark. Cold. There'd been a light snow. I stayed in bed long after my body had recovered. Weeks went by, me falling asleep all day, staying up all night. It was coming up to Christmas and I was dreading it. I hadn't slept for several nights in a row. I daren't sleep anymore for fear of dreaming of it, the baby's hand. I couldn't get that hand out of my mind. No sleep and my head was all over the place. I started to believe that Ray, Bea's partner, was a visitor from Mars, a trickster, who'd impregnated me. He'd tricked me, killed my baby and now he was going to kill me. Of course it made no sense, but I'd not slept for days, kept myself awake playing "Bohemian Rhapsody" over and over. I knew why I'd lost my baby, and now, it seemed, others knew too … *wish I'd never been born at all*…Freddy Mercury's voice pierced my thoughts, drowning out the small, sane voice: *you're not well*. I ignored the sane corner of my mind. The crazy story I was spinning made more sense.

'One afternoon – hadn't slept for four, five nights – I was looking out over the field, and saw a bright light in the afternoon winter sky, a spaceship coming to land on the reservoir, coming to take me to Mars. So, they'd camouflaged it as a traffic helicopter! Well, that didn't fool me. I pulled on clothes and my big winter coat, stuffed my feet into boots. Wasn't sure about driving the car, the front tires looked soft. What if the car was a trap? I would walk to the phone box by the shops and get help. As I hurried along, I was acutely aware of the cold. My legs were freezing. I looked down, pale flesh stood out between the hem of my black coat and the top of my boots. Winter-white legs. No tights. The sane part knew I looked weird but I had to get away.

'At the shops, there's a pram outside the bakery. Old fashioned, high-wheeled with its hood up. A baby was crying, an urgent voice. *Help me, save me*. Its cries came as words to me, calling out to me. This time I would do it right, this time the baby would survive. I would not let this baby die. I leaned over the pram, peeped under the hood. Soft, warm bundle, its tiny face surrounded by a woolly bonnet. The baby was a test. Get it right this time. I reached in to calm it – *hush, hush* – gently rocked the pram. I was about to scoop the baby into my arms. I glanced up. Through the plate-glass window, beyond rows of mince pies and Christmas cakes, a woman was watching me. She rushed out. Then the shop assistant followed her with a gold box. *Your Sachertorte.* It sounded like a coded message. She's not the mother, too old. Was I supposed to save the baby from her? She's the grandmother, said the sane part of me. *It's her crying time,* said the grandmother, settling the gold cake box at the baby's feet, elbowing me out of the way, glaring at my bare legs.'

She stopped again.

'Do you want a rest?' Martin asked.

'It isn't going to get any easier, if I do.' She finished her coffee and continued. 'I was "voluntary," Bea made sure of that. I could have left the hospital any time but something kept me there. In amongst the chaos of those sleepless nights, there'd been an odd clarity. My head full of images – like watching a film. Some of them were part of the psychosis but then I began to see that others might not be. I tried to talk about them but whatever I said sounded like a delusion. Anyway, there wasn't much time for the "talking cure " – St Barnaby's was a big teaching hospital – I knew I'd have to do it, find a way to cope. I could have discharged myself but when I tried, got as far as the main gate, a band tightened around my head, so tight I'd retch. I knew I hadn't finished in there.

'At night I'd look out at the row of solid Edwardian houses. Their gardens backed on to the hospital; I could see right into one house. Lights left on, curtains not drawn. A woman cooking dinner. She'd set pans on the hob, open a bottle of wine. Stirring with one hand, wine glass in the other. Two children: a girl about eight with long wavy hair, her older brother, might have been a teenager – wire-rimmed glasses, looked serious. The girl pestering him as he tried to read. I'd watch them all eat their meal. The father always finished first. I'd seen him gardening at weekends. It was like watching repeats of the same episode of a TV soap.

'In the hospital grounds, off-duty doctors and nurses played tennis. How did they do that? It seemed inordinately complex: hold a racket, hit a ball, add up the score. I couldn't do these things: cook dinner, play tennis. They required levels of concentration I didn't possess. My mind so full – and I – well – I had to prove to myself that I could at least do a reasonable impersonation of a person, fully in the world, mind and body co-ordinated. Prove I could get though a day, otherwise I'd never get out – never let myself out. I joined in occupational therapy – cookery, exercise class, art – anything to get away from the ward.

'Roz, the art therapist, had a frizz of red hair that made her seem chaotic, but she was calm, her voice soft and encouraging. She made us work round a big table, to encourage "re-integration," putting the bits of us back together. The sane voice inside was getting stronger. *You can do this*. To me, everyone else seemed a lot sicker. At least I didn't shout out all the time. One man – looked like a schoolteacher – drew rows and rows of stick men and kept shouting: *I'm leaking. Is it all right to swallow?* He believed his body fluids were leaking through his teeth. And there was Sara who wanted to be friends and she cried a lot. In her forties, overweight, but beneath it a once-glamorous woman. Wife of a shadow-cabinet minister, a socialist, kids in comprehensives so no private treatment for her. She recognised who I was – had been. In that state, you can't make friends –

'Roz would play music. Classical, usually. *Paint what you hear, paint what you see inside.* I stopped trying to use words to get heard. I painted to cover the images that had tumbled out of the cracks. I painted a pale blue wash, overlaid it with billowing white blobs. I painted clouds. I would learn to live with the flickering images in my head. I would prove to myself that I could do that, then I would leave.

'I wanted to make something solid, a well-made thing to speak on my behalf, elegant as a game of tennis or a family dinner. I took a lump of clay, knocked out all the air so my pot wouldn't explode in the kiln. I'd make a simple coil pot, fire it, glaze it and leave. *I'm leaking. Is it all right to swallow?* He'd make gagging noises. It spurred me on. I concentrated on the clay, rolled it evenly, to and fro, an even pressure with the heel of my hand. *I went to China once. It was very cold. If I was in China I wouldn't leak.* Too much for Sara. She fumbled in her bag for her purse, *I forgot to buy bread.* She ran out and cried in the toilet until Roz fetched her. I carried on coiling clay, making a spiral to form the base, then working upwards, creating a cylinder. I made a few so I could choose the best.'

Lydia looked up at the blue pot on the counter, thought of getting up. She wanted to hold it but didn't want to break her train of thought.

'I took fewer pills, did more exercise, tried not to walk in that timid, drugged way. I practised walking towards the bus stop, to see how far I could go before the band tightened round my head. One day I passed a woman with her little girl, walking hand-in-hand, laughing. It was them, the ones I'd been watching through their window. The band gripped my skull. Did they know what I'd done with the baby? Did it show? The girl, hair up in a high ponytail, was a miniature version of her mother. I wanted to say: you should close your curtains. Someone sicker than me might be watching you. They ignored me, didn't even give me that look that says they know you're from the hospital.

'Then it was time to choose one of my pots. I lined them up, deciding which to glaze. I needed only one to come out of the kiln and I would leave. He started up again: *I'm leaking, leaking.* I wanted to say: there's no leak, shut up and look, there's nothing there. *Leaking, leaking.* He was hysterical, knocked over his jar of water, flooding his painting. *Why don't you start again?* said Roz, her hands gentle on his shoulders. He wailed: *I loved my mother. I adored her.*

'Sara's head went down to her chest. I broke two of my pots, clay crumbling everywhere. I wanted to say: *swallow, just swallow. Hold on. We're all holding on. I'm holding on to a whole fucking ocean, trying to keep a whole ocean in this small pot.*'

*

He had to tell her, otherwise she'd go on talking and not be recorded. There was less than five minutes of disk left. But she was in mid-flow, where was all of this leading? *Images of that night.* What images? He had plenty more disks. He was relieved when she chose to stop. She stood up and reached for the blue cup on the work counter. She took out the sprig of flowers, poured the water away.

'This is it,' she said, her hand was trembling as she sat down again. She cradled the pot.

'The disk is full,' he said, softly, 'but I have more if you want to carry on.'

He put a new disk into the recorder. It was up to her now. He sat back. She picked up the cup and turned it around in her hands. Narrow at the base, it widened in the middle then narrowed again, the rim turned in. There were cracks forming in the blue glaze.

'Give me a couple of minutes.' She put the cup down. 'I need to go to the bathroom.' Agitated, she got up suddenly and her chair caught the table toppling the cup towards the edge.

'Oh – ' she gasped.

His hand shot out, blocked its fall. He stood it carefully in the centre of the table, next to the machine.

'Thanks.' It was barely audible. She went upstairs.

Nick was right, he was not her therapist and he didn't think she was asking for interpretation but what was his role – to prompt, to reassure, to disappear? All he could do was record for as long as she wanted to talk.

'Lydia, Lydia?' A woman's voice out in the passage. He got up to see who it was.

'You?' said the woman. She seemed familiar. 'Is Lydia here?' The woman was clearly upset.

'Jean, what's the matter?' Lydia stood at the top of the stairs.

Of course – the woman from the Bird Centre.

Lydia hurried down, put her arm around Jean. Martin retreated back into the kitchen, left them to speak alone, but he could hear every word.

'Lydia, I'd no idea. I'm sorry to barge in. It's Mum.' Jean started to cry as she spoke.

'They've just told me – hours they said. Sally's out and her mobile's off. I had to tell someone.' A confusion of anguish and embarrassment in Jean's voice.

'It's all right. What can I do?' Lydia said, her own voice not much stronger than her friend's. 'Do you want a drink? Come and sit down.'

'No, really, you're busy. I just needed to tell someone. I don't know where Sally is. I'm on my way home to pack a few things and then I'll stay with Mum. Until –'

'Do you want me to come with you?'

'I wouldn't want you to see Mum. She's all skin and bones. You won't recognise her.'

'I wouldn't mind, honestly. I'd like to see her. I'd like to say goodbye –'

'No. Remember her how she was, the best of her.'

'Of course. If that's what you'd prefer.'

Martin heard something that sounded like disappointment in Lydia's tone. The two women fell silent. He wasn't trying to eavesdrop but he hadn't much choice.

'Is there anything I can do, I mean for you?' Lydia brightened a touch. It sounded as if she were making an effort.

'You could keep trying Sally for me. I'll have to turn my phone off once I'm with Mum.'

'I'll get a pen.'

When Lydia came back into the kitchen, Martin was already tearing a sheet from his notebook. He offered her a pen.

'Ask her to phone reception at the Home, they'll pass a message on. Thanks so much.' Jean wrote down Sally's mobile and landline.

'Are you sure that's all you want me to do?'

'I must go.'

Lydia walked Jean to the door.

'Actually, there is something,' he could hear Jean saying. 'The other day, what you said, about Mum, you drew such a vivid picture. Keep that picture of her in your mind – her sewing, the tape measure round her neck, the frocks waiting to be hemmed. Keep that for her, for me.' Jean sobbed through the words. 'I'm sorry to have interrupted you, really –'

'It's all right. It's all right.' Lydia trying to reassure her friend. 'It can wait.' But there was an edginess in her words that said it was far from all right.

38

Martin sat on the sofa next to Eileen – how much longer must he linger before he could go upstairs to work on this morning's session? His thoughts reeled with what she'd disclosed today. He tried to picture Lydia with a shaved head. Eileen got up to fetch her sewing. After the News he'd slip away.

'That's coming along well,' he said, as she resumed work on the needlepoint kit she'd bought for Monica's birthday. On the box the illustration showed a stylised landscape of rolling hills, a stone path led to a red-roofed cottage, birds flew across fluffy white clouds. An image Eileen was colouring in, row-on-row of slanted stitches held in a grid.

'I've got the measure of it now,' she said, isolating a patch of sky, clamping that area of the canvas inside a wooden hoop.

'Are all the stitches the same?' he asked, making an effort.

'Oh yes, but the colours change.'

'Don't you get bored doing the same stitch?'

Eileen threaded white wool though the eye of her needle.

'Bored? No. You get into a rhythm, it's relaxing, gives me time to think.'

He thought, unkindly, *about what*? She stabbed at the canvas, pulling the wool through.

'I often think of your father when I'm sewing.'

He shifted, dissipating his discomfort into the sofa's plump cushions.

'It's all right. I won't go on. I know you don't talk much about your dad,' she said, without looking up.

That's not true, he wanted to say, but stopped himself

because, in a way, it was. Though he thought of his father often, he rarely talked about him with Eileen. He rarely talked with Eileen about anything. *Don't tell yer mam*. His dad's mantra.

'He admired you, thought highly of you,' she said, completing another row of cloud – *pity you couldn't have reciprocated* – reverberated between them. Yes, Martin had been an arrogant twentysomething at the time his father had died. Angry because he'd thought his dad deserved more for the hours he spent on that boat, but if he insisted on putting up with low earnings, must he send his money up in smoke, did he have to kill himself?

'Do you think he would have adjusted like Jack – doing pleasure trips round the caves?' he said, not rising to the bait.

'Probably, it would have kept him on the sea. He loved the sea. Loving the sea killed him, if you ask me.'

'Mum, lung cancer killed him. Forty a day. And, he died in this house.'

'I didn't say the *sea* killed him, I said *loving* the sea killed him. He smoked out of worry, he knew he ought to sell the boat, but he couldn't be doing with an indoor job. Sea or fags, it comes to the same thing.' She tightened the tension on the hoop. 'Don't mind me, off you go if you want.'

'I'll watch the weather first.' It seemed indecent to leave.

On the screen, a young woman in a green suit waved manicured hands over electronic highs and lows. He tried to keep track of her predictions, but lost the thread and waited for her summary. *Changeable*.

In his bedroom Martin woke up his sleeping computer. Was it only when she sewed, one hand safe on the wooden hoop the other following the canvas grid, that she dared to think of him? Nearly twenty years and he'd never understood that. He'd never seen that loving the sea had killed his father. He'd been angry, let down when his father died of what seemed a self-inflicted wound, leaving him without a buffer between him and Eileen. Now, he'd say, angry *on behalf* of his father rather than angry *with* him. Loving the sea might have killed him, but not the sea itself. He'd watched his father die in the bedroom across the landing. It had been hard to take in, even though he'd touched his father's waxy forehead as he lay in the funeral parlour and had thrown the first shovel of earth over the brass-handled coffin. There'd been talk of burial at sea, but Eileen had wanted a grave to visit. How must it be for Lydia – no bodies, no goodbyes, no ceremony, and to be so young?

He began to transcribe the disk from this morning, alert to the pain in her voice, and the urgency.

'Martin?' Eileen called from the landing, then a tap on his door. 'I'm having an early night.'

Not wanting her in the room, he went to the door.

'If you need a drink the kettle's boiled,' she said, a cup of cocoa in one hand, library book in the other.

'Are you all right?' he asked.

'I fancy a bit of a read in bed.' She held up a Margery Allingham, better than a sleeping pill. 'Fluttering a bit, though it's been worse.'

'You'll soon know the cause,' he said. There was all of Saturday and Sunday to get through. 'I'll be going down later to the kitchen, to connect up, send e-mails.'

'Do you have to work so late? I've laid for breakfast.'

'You won't know I've been there. '

'It's a mystery to me, these e-mails.' She turned to go.

'I thought you liked mysteries.' He smiled and pointed to *The Beckoning Lady*.

'The mystery I want solving, is what's wrong with my heart.'

In the kitchen, Martin cleared a space for his laptop, removing one place setting from Eileen's carefully laid table: plate, cereal bowl, cup upside down in its saucer.

If, after his father's funeral, he'd not immediately returned to college would she have started this ritual? By the time he'd come home the following summer, the habit had been established. *I wake up, I forget.* She'd said that was worse than his actual death, the daily waking up, thinking for a moment he was still alive. *He was often out at dawn.* Remembering was like being told again for the first time. Setting a place for one the night before reminded her Bill's absence was permanent. An everyday ritual to manage her loss, a message in a cup and saucer, bowl and spoon. That was nineteen years ago.

He put the lead into the phone socket and went into his e-mail. About to attach the document to his message, it occurred to him: she hadn't asked for a transcript. This morning, once Jean had left, even though he knew she wasn't finished, he'd sensed she didn't want to resume.

'I'd better try getting hold of Jean's daughter.' She hadn't asked him to wait, hadn't protested as he'd packed his bag and hadn't asked for a transcript.

He unattached the document and just sent a message:

Hope things are as well as can be expected for your friend. I'll be returning to London early next week but I'm available Saturday and Sunday if you want to resume. M

He knew Lydia had wanted to explain why she'd scooped the salt. She'd seemed eager. But then she'd gone back through the dreadful stillbirth and the breakdown – events that came after *Taking In Water*. How do they connect? In her head they must be connected, it was as if she were filling up the space she'd scooped in the salt. In hospital she'd painted clouds to blank out what she'd seen inside. What had she seen? Now she photographed clouds – was it still to blank out these images?

And the pot she'd made to test herself and held on to for all these years. *I'm holding on to a whole fucking ocean, trying to keep a whole ocean in this small pot.*

If it all connected, he couldn't see how.

39

In the bedroom, Lydia stood on the top of the stepladder with her arm at full stretch but still she couldn't reach the highest part of the sloping ceiling above the Velux window. Perhaps she could improvise, find something to lash to the roller, 'Ah yes! One of those bloody poles.' The thought of it was satisfying, but she really didn't have the energy. It was too late to be painting, almost midnight. She was putting off having to sleep downstairs on the sofabed. Besides, she'd told Jean to call her if there was any news or if she needed anything. She'd been listening out for the phone all day. *Hours*, they'd said.

This morning in the bathroom, she'd retched over the sink, overcome with a relief and terror, weighing up the risk of it, the danger of speaking of things she'd never said out loud before. She was about to say these things to someone who would give her his undivided attention. He'd listened to her recount details of her breakdown and hadn't flinched. The effort of that had drained her and she'd needed a pause to steel herself to carry on. She'd splashed cold water on her face, knew she must keep her nerve. She felt like a diver preparing to jump from the highest board, a few more steps and she would leap, no going back. As she left the bathroom and stood on the landing at the top of the stairs, there was Jean in distress. The shock of it had shut down her need to talk.

Of course she'd willingly turned her attention to Jean. What could matter more than her friend in the present? Yet part of her, the seven-year-old in her, was stuck, as if still standing at the top of the stairs, ready for the dive. Longing for it, dreading it. Down to the wreck. Would she feel the bliss divers speak of, the serenity of deep sea? Or would the pressure be too much to bear? She didn't have the chance to find out. Now, it felt worse than if she'd said nothing at all, a physical ache. She needed to keep on the move so had cleared the bedroom, made a start on painting. If she could just reach the highest part of the ceiling she would, at least, have the satisfaction of finishing the first coat.

She put the paint tray on the floor, climbed back up the ladder and swivelled the roof window open as far as it would go. Standing on the top step she put her head and shoulders out and breathed the chilly night air. A clear sky but not for much longer, blizzards over the next few days, the forecast said. She could smell the change in the air. But for now the night sky was a depthless dome, sprinkled with asterisks of ancient light. She savoured it and was back in New York.

In Georgia Keay's apartment on the corner of Columbus and 77th, she'd slept on the sofabed beneath stars and baubles pinned to the blue ceiling. Christmas 1977. *Why don't you go? It would be good to get away,* Bea had urged. Out of hospital for six months. She'd made her pot, made it to the bus stop. She'd had setbacks, could still get the sensation in her head, the band tightening, the retching.

That night, in Georgia's apartment she felt stifled, the whole building heated from a boiler in the basement that couldn't be turned off. She opened the window to let in cold air, listened to the night sounds: the hum of traffic, police sirens, and above it, the cries of gulls, the horns of ships. Opposite, on the turret of the Natural History Museum, stone eagles on guard, perched ready to swoop, like a warning. Getting sick had surprised her; she didn't want to be surprised that way again.

Next morning, freezing wind slicing her face, she walked

down Columbus – so many new bars and shops. She huddled inside her big black coat chilled to the bone, kept looking down to check she had her tights on, not quite trusting herself.

After a couple of days, feeling stronger, she came out of the subway at Union Square and decided, spur of the moment, to head for Washington Square. Ten years since she'd left, barefoot. She'd go back with her boots on. She walked the last ten blocks, enjoyed walking and looking around, the river air cutting along the cross-town streets, bringing a whiff of the sea. But as she got nearer, the band around her head began to tighten: after Washington Square, what then? Would she carry on? She could see the map in her head: Sullivan, Bleecker, Thompson. Would she go that far, to the fire escape, to the spot where Luc had jumped?

She needed to get off the ground, somewhere high. Up she went in the elevator of the South Tower, the car swaying in the shaft, wind whistling, ears popping. At the top she was calm again, a quarter of a mile high with nothing between her and the ground but a sheet of plate glass. She felt alive, shooting roll after roll of this brand new view of the city, zooming in on the Arch at Washington Square, approaching it, safely, through her lens. Outside, on the promenade deck, she watched a storm rolling in, a blizzard heading her way. She carried on clicking, walked towards it as far as she could go. Then her eye had caught sight of the long icicles that hung from the railing. What would happen if an icicle fell from that height? So sharp, it could hurt someone. Would it melt before it hit the ground?

The Twin Towers hadn't been there when she left in a hurry in '67; they'd been a novelty when she visited in '77 and now, they were gone. *Luc's neighbourhood, to see it all laid out*, Martin had said. She thought of him last September, waiting to go the top of the building. Chasing after her and Luc might have killed him.

An hour later and Martin might have been one of the 'jumpers.' Was it instinct that had driven them to smash windows, stand on ledges, breathing easier at last? Or, had it been a conscious decision – who wouldn't instinctively head towards air? No time to think, to see that survival and destruction could amount to the same thing.

She'd seen footage – hands clutching, feet running on air, garments billowing. Unbearable. She'd looked away. Yet that grainy photograph, full-page in the broadsheet had been compelling, the movement frozen, one frame, caught and cropped to fit the oblong of the page, the geometry of the building's vertical steel ribs creating a balanced composition. Unsettling, yes. But she'd stared at the dark form that drew the eye in: a man, upside down, his body perfectly in line except for the slight irregularity of one crooked knee. At that moment he was alive, the rush of air roaring in his ears, seemed in control, as if he'd been executing a well-rehearsed acrobatic feat. The appalling moving image had somehow been transformed into an awful, stilled beauty.

No image could tell what he'd felt, what had been in his thoughts. She'd heard that some had held hands with others. What if you had changed your mind? Had Luc changed his mind halfway down? She'd always told herself he would have been high on dope. His fall would have been a blur, not a decision.

No image, object, photograph could represent what it was like to make the decision to let go. No one survived to tell it, not Luc, not the 9/11 jumpers.

Had the falling on the night of the storm been her decision? Had she *made* a decision? Had it been a deliberate, wilful act and if so, what did that make her?

Fixed on surviving, Edna Thornton had said.

She thought of Jean sitting up all night, holding her mother's hand. Edna, at least, was tucked up warm in bed. Let her end be peaceful.

Out in the garden there was enough moonlight for her to see the marker posts. The surveyors' report hadn't materialised. She'd phoned, left a voicemail, her message not returned. Each slender metal pole was of the right proportion. She only needed one. She gripped the one closest to her, pushed it, back and forth. They'd been firmly planted. It might take a while but she wasn't giving up. The cold metal warmed, taking heat from her determined grip. Rotating it, she discovered, loosened the earth. She worked faster, increased the pressure, round and round.

40

Steven parked on the track in front of her car.

'This time, Steven, make sure she gets the letter,' his boss had said yesterday. 'Tell the post-room it's Special Delivery. Make sure it's signed for.' Bringing it himself might be stretching the idea of Special Delivery, but no more than his boss was stretching things. The report was already a day later than they'd promised. He'd picked up her voicemail late yesterday and called her this morning, reassured her he was on his way. He'd called as early as he dared; people like a lie-in on a Saturday, himself included, but today he'd rather see the report in her hands.

The way his boss had written the covering letter made the interim assessment sound final, and it was full of work-speak, *implications for human habitation*. Why not say: *how it affects your home*?

'I'll be in my studio,' she'd said when he'd phoned, so he went straight to the beach hut, his boots crunching on the path.

'Hello?' He glanced at the poles as he passed them. Four. There ought to be five. He'd pretend he hadn't noticed.

'It was perfect for a job I had to finish,' said Lydia stepping down from the verandah.

It was that kind of action – *attitude*, his boss would say – that meant a case against her could be made.

'My boss won't be happy.'

'I'm not happy with your boss.'

Yes, he wanted to say, but the boss knew how to play the game. She'd do better asking the right questions, not pulling up marker posts.

'In the end it's your business but – you might want to be careful about how you come across. To my boss, I mean. Think before you answer this,' he handed her the envelope.

'I'll wait if you like. In case you have questions.'

'Would you?' she took the envelope.

Steven sat awkwardly at the far end of the bench, beside him a blue beach towel, folded. She must be going swimming again. She leaned over the verandah rail, her back to him, and read the letter. He watched her shoulders tense up and braced himself, waiting for her to flip as she read: … *pro-active defensive erosion management … reactive retreat … instability… Flampton to Dunwick Bay.* Flampton to Dunwick was a broad brushstroke. His boss should have been more precise.

She turned to face him, fixing him with angry eyes.

'I'm assuming that "defensive erosion management" translates into controlled explosion?'

'Yes,' said Steven, 'but don't quote me.'

'Where exactly is this instability?'

Steven explained about the inlet that lay between her house and the near end of Dunwick Bay.

'But that's near Aztec City, half a mile from here,' she said.

'Aztec City?'

'Oh just a name I have for it. I know that stretch well, gets exposed to storm tides, takes a battering each winter.'

'Yes, but the plan is to come further in your direction.' His boss was proposing a generous margin.

'The birdwatchers won't buy this,' said Lydia.

'Don't rely on the birdwatchers,' he said. The cliff face was always changing naturally; the birds knew how to adapt. The explosions would be scheduled outside of the breeding season. The cliff would soon resettle. The birds would come back.

'So he's put me on the wrong side of the retreat line?'

'Yes, but "retreat line" doesn't mean a line, exactly, it's a zone. Think of it like the tidal zone: mean low to mean high water. There's no such thing as a coast *line,* it's a zone between land and sea, always changing,' he carried on. One side of the retreat zone there was a high risk, on the other side the risk was minimal. In between there was a zone of precaution.

'He's taking his precaution too far?'

'Ask for a grid reference, get him to be more specific.'

'Why has he done this?'

'He thinks the way you've been, well,' he wanted to say, "difficult" but it seemed rude to say it to her face, 'you might be hoping you'll get compensation – '

'He thinks I want *money?*' She was laughing hysterically now and turning away from him looking out to sea, shaking her head. He didn't know what to say.

'But won't it cost him money to get rid of me?' she turned, flashed back.

'Not as much as the compensation you could claim if your property was damaged by an explosion. CP is cheaper. Sorry, Compulsory Purchase. He has a budget for that.'

'Why are you doing this? Is this to soften me up?'

He tried not to get angry, but damn it, he'd given up his Saturday for her. He could feel all the answers rising up in him.

'I'm doing it because I like my job and want to do it right, because – ' And he was off, thoughts jumbled up, tumbling out, 'the sea is being stirred up by six billion human beings not thinking about what water can do, not thinking ahead.' Like his tutor at Uni said, it wasn't wars or disease that would get us in the end, but water. In the end politics could come down to who controlled the water. *Never forget the politics of water.* There was either too much of it or not enough. In China, one of the great rivers had dried up, no longer reached the sea. 'But we're an island with sea levels rising, we need to have our eye on the bigger picture. It's all about timescales. I mean, the water in this sea was once ice, half a kilometer thick, covering the ground we're standing on. The continental plates shift each year, a fingernail growth that pushes Mount Everest a fraction higher. A hundred, two hundred years from now, this cliff might be a different shape, nothing stays the same.' He was losing his train of thought, gabbling on. What was it he wanted to say? 'In the meantime, in your lifetime, if you don't mind the inconvenience of doors not fitting, tiles pinging up – that should be your choice.' Making an issue out of her was a waste of all their time. 'It's petty politicking and the politics of water, climate changing, and all, is bigger than that.' There, he'd said it. Why should this woman lose her home so his boss secured promotion?

'Have you finished?' she said. She looked upset.

'Sorry. I shouldn't have gone on like that. And,' he certainly shouldn't be telling her this, 'those poles, they're not vital to us, never have been, they're part of his campaign to wear you down. He's relying on you getting emotional.'

'He's a bully then, your boss.'

'Ask the right questions. If you want to stay in your house you'll have a battle, but it could be done.' He fished in his pocket producing his card. You can ring my mobile, but not in office hours. I can advise on the right words to use.'

'Thank you, thank you for coming,'

'Will you be all right?'

'I need to think,' she picked up the towel and wrapped it round her shoulders.

'You're not going swimming now, are you?'

41

She scrambled down to the bay.

Not vital to us, never have been. The poles, like the letter, a game. Could she trust Steven's youthful outburst – a sense of fair play or was he simply playing good cop? *Brave,* he'd said, that other time he'd called on her, brave to live here.

It was still bright, the sun out, though the air was sharp. She hurried into the water. The icy shock of it propelled her to move.

Arms beating the water, legs kicking for all she was worth, faster and faster she swam until "erosion management" became meaningless.

Brave? How fast could she go, how far?

Head turning, coming up for air, she glimpsed open sea. She was already beyond the headland, already farther out than usual. Her arms powered her on, longer, stronger strokes. One after the other, farther and farther.

Eyes open, as she took a breath, she glimpsed Aztec City along the coast, soon to be shattered by dynamite. On she went, couldn't stop, could go forever, on and on to where the sea curved over the Earth; to where it no longer mattered whether she had made the decision or not all those years ago; to where no one would know that she had let go, had not done what her father had asked.

As the tug of the water started to get the better of her she came to her senses. Treading water, she looked back to the land. If she didn't turn now there'd be no going back. What was she doing? *Brave? Nutter?*

Powered by reserves she didn't know she had, she fought

back with strong strokes, her arms beating the water. Gradually, she fell in with the incoming tide.

Heart thumping, she stumbled out of the water, raw sea air whipping her wet skin. Breathless, she slumped down on the hard sand just clear of the tide rush, then staggered to the boulder where she'd left her things and sat down. Hunched inside her towel she stared back at the horizon, grey-green storm clouds coming in low over the sea. *Possibility of snow showers,* the forecast said, last gasp of winter fighting off spring.

Behind her, on the cliff, screeching birds in a frenzy, busy parents feeding, teaching, sensing the storm. How many surge tides would it take to demolish this cliff? Hundreds, thousands of years. They could reinforce a cliff with concrete – were such a thing possible – but it would only deflect the sea's energy elsewhere. The sea's energy had to be played out, somehow.

She sat until her breath came easier, rubbing life back into her arms and legs.

If she admitted to Martin everything about that night, she'd have to tell him in such a way that would make him understand, realise that she'd tried but couldn't do it, hadn't done what her father had asked. *Hang on, Lydia limpet.*

Would Martin urge her to go to the authorities? Would official documents be required? What the hell, she was sick of it. If she'd committed a crime, it was time to turn herself in.

42

After a hot shower she poured herself a shot of brandy and checked her phone. One missed call. Jean. No message but she'd called from her home, not her mobile.

'Jean, it's me. I was in the shower –'

'Mum died an hour ago, I've just got home.'

'Oh, Jean, I'm so sorry,' she said, and felt the tears welling. 'Are you all right?'

'Well, yes. Well, no. I don't know –' Jean talked, a mixture of relief and sadness in her voice. 'Last night, around midnight, she'd seemed to rally. She was chatty; you wouldn't believe she was ill. Of course, she'd wander into the past at times but it all made sense. I told her I'd seen you yesterday and that you sent your love, and she said, "Is Lydia stopping tonight? I've nothing for tea." She sat up, searching the locker drawer, trying to find money for fish and chips and –' Jean went quiet. 'She said – '

'Go on, what?' Lydia took a sip of brandy and thought of Edna Thornton in her last moments worrying about what to give them for tea.

'Oh, it doesn't matter,' Jean carried on, 'then this morning she was sleeping, never woke up, just drifted away. So peaceful.'

'Shall I come round?' said Lydia. As the warmth of brandy spread through her, never had she felt more glad to be alive. What had she been thinking of, swimming so far out? How stupid, selfish, to have laid that on Jean as well.

'I've so much to do, the undertaker, and Sally's on her way, but tomorrow, would you come tomorrow?'

'Of course.' What could be more important now? *Available all weekend*, Martin had said. There'd be time for everything she needed to do. 'Your mum, she had a good life apart from these last two years.' And now Jean would plan the funeral, celebrate her mother's life. She'd weep, full of sadness for a while, but she'd carry on; it was in the natural order of things. Edna Thornton had had a full life, a good span. Not a newsworthy life, but a remarkable ordinary life. 'Think of all those frocks and gowns she made. Your mum's life is stitched into hundreds of lives.' She was trying to keep alive the image of Edna Thornton, making things. 'Think how special she made people feel.' No one would throw out a creation of Edna's. Lydia thought of all those bridal gowns preserved in attics and albums.

'Thanks for that, and for what you said the other day about what Mum had meant to you.'

There was silence on the line as each of them reflected.

'What she said about you, Lydia, I hope you don't mind – '

'I won't mind, but only if you want to, Jean.'

'It was as she was trying to find money for fish and chips, she said, "That girl, she's had to be mother and father to herself, we must make her feel at home."'

Late, out in the studio, Lydia ran her hands over the beat-up surface of the teapot. A worthless thing. A precious thing. Compressed into the folds of metal, her early life, the life before. It had a kind of touchable eloquence. It spoke to her, that connection to her mother. Whatever she made of the Marine fragments – and she would make something – they couldn't *say* what needed to be witnessed, not in a form others could understand.

Inhabit your memories, Martin had said at their first session. They inhabit her. Half a century of bearing witness, sole eyewitness to a crime never reported. Was it a crime? How would she begin? Like a police interview: name, date, time, those present.

She locked the studio. Time to go back to the house, try to sleep on the sofabed. Her body ached from her reckless swim. She stood a few moments by the four remaining marker posts. It was cold, a flurry of snow.

The effort of it warmed her. She gripped the first one with both hands. Now she'd perfected the technique they could all go.

43

Martin walked down the side of the house. Something looked different.

It was dusk. A beam of artificial light shone out from the end of the verandah of the studio.

'Hello?' he called.

'In here,' she called back, but didn't come out.

Looking round he realised what had changed: the marker posts had gone.

He stood in the doorway.

'Thanks for coming so late,' she said into a tissue, and then blew her nose. A single white candle flickered on the table in front of her. She stared into the flame.

'Are you all right?'

'I think so – ' She hugged herself.

'I'm sorry about Jean's mother.'

'Yes, it's very sad, even though it was expected. She'd had a full life – she was very much loved, such a kind, wise woman. It's sad, so sad – '

She looked up towards the objects on the shelf and he could tell she was holding back tears.

'You don't have to stand there,' she said. 'Why don't you come in?'

He put his hand on her shoulder, relieved that she didn't shrug him off, but reciprocated, reached up and rested her hand on his.

'When are you going back to London?'

'Tuesday. I have papers to sign.' He squeezed her shoulder,

a gentle pressure. On the table sat a small cassette recorder. 'What's that?'

'Trying to carry on without you.'

He sat down opposite her.

'I've brought this,' he said and took from his bag the sheets of transcript. 'I didn't e-mail it because you hadn't asked me to.'

'I'm glad you didn't. I don't want to read it until I've finished,' she said, reaching for a tissue. 'Finished explaining about – about the scooping, why I did that.'

He thought about getting out his machine but he'd do only what she asked.

'Digging into the salt like that, I can see now, was a message to myself – memories buried – as if my body knew what my mind had shut out, was making space – somewhere to put down – images – in hospital so many vivid images in amongst the hallucinations – images that flicker in my head like a film. Jumbled up. I want them out of my head – want to splice the film, show it all – I need to tell you something, I've never managed to tell anyone.'

*

Say it now or be forever trapped inside the roof.

Now it came to it, she couldn't look at him, not directly. She got up, walked out to the dark end of the verandah, leaned over the rail, the night air chilly on her face.

He followed her, she could hear the creak of his leather coat, sensed him standing in the light behind her. She couldn't talk; she must talk. She made conditions: if he moved out of the light, if he said her name, if he touched her. She wanted to feel again his hand on her shoulder.

He didn't move.

In her head she called up the ghost wreck, one last time.

Were they watching her? Could they see the bulk of the ancient chalk cliff, the abrupt end of land, and this hut? They would see Martin, standing in the light, but would they see her in the shadow? Would her twenty-seven-year-old parents know who she was? A woman older than they'd ever been. Did they know that in her head she carried their last moments, the home movie no one had seen?

It was up to her, not him.

'Do you have your machine?' she said, her teeth chattering.

'Give me a minute.' He went inside, fumbled in his bag. She followed, couldn't wait a minute longer.

'Use this,' she offered her own tape recorder. 'This is fine, this is for me.' She switched it on.

The last thing she registered before she closed her eyes was the tiny scar above his lip.

Let's go to visit the old lady with the mynah bird, Dad says. She lives up the road from Grandma H. I can't wait to hear the bird talk. A walk along the beach, visit the old woman and be home in time for tea. But it's windy and wet. So Dad says we might not go out after all. Mum's tired from the journey yesterday. Grandma H says she wouldn't dream of going out in this weather with her bad chest. They're both by the fire. Grandma H is knitting, casting-off a white woolly bootee.

Mark my words, that's a girl. I was tempted to do pink.

Can't we go? Please, Dad?

It's bad out there. Let me see.

Dad puts on his coat and trilby.

I want to hear the bird talk.

When Dad comes back he says: *I could hardly stand up.*

No thanks. Mum doesn't want the toasted crumpets Grandma H is handing round, there's a plate of them set down in the hearth. I spread strawberry jam on mine. *Time for bed soon,* says Dad.

Mum's gone quiet. Even though she's in the room, it's as if she's somewhere else. She stands, leans forward, with her hand on the mantelpiece. The new bootees are perched there; they look like meringues. She's standing to one end of the rag rug, the one Grandma H made. It has a picture of a seagull – blue background, big fat bird with a white breast, grey wings, orange feet and a yellow bill. I helped Grandma sort the colours the last time we were here.

Mum's standing on the gull's head.

Is it starting? Grandma H, says quietly.

I don't think so, says Mum. Her breathing is deep, noisy.

Contractions?

No pain, there's no pain, just this odd sensation. Cramped from sitting on the train, I expect.

She presses her hand in the small of her back. Her other hand is rubbing the bump. I want to hug her. I tug on her skirt. *Not just now, Lyddie.* I wait, counting the tiny white stars on her blue smock. I count to fifty, but it's as if she can't see me. She's gone inside herself.

I watch the seagull on the rug beneath her feet. Mum lets out a gasp. The rug turns darker, bluer. It's wet. There's water running down mum's legs.

Ted.

They all disappear into the bedroom.

I'll go to the phone box, call the midwife.

No, Ted. Not in this weather. No one will come.

Your mum's right, Ted.

I've seen a few babies into the world, says Grandma H. *Off you go. Nature will take its course.*

Dad comes out. He's trying to be cheerful but his voice sounds different.

Come on Lyddie let's have a game of snap.

We sit by the fire playing cards. He isn't concentrating. He puts down one card after another, never notices when two are the same. *Snap,* I say, *snap, snap,* my hand banging down on the cards. I win every time. He shuffles the pack. There's a noise, a groaning. Is it Mum or the wind? I daren't ask.

The baby, it's pushing, it wants to come out, Dad says.

The fire is getting low. Dad pokes the embers, stirring a flame, and throws on more coal. The wind is in the chimney; smoke swirls into the room.

More groaning, then a shriek, a sound that I can't believe is Mum. Dad's on his feet, walking over to the window and back to the fire, to the window and back to the fire. Then, a cry.

Ted, Ted. It's a girl.

Dad's put too much coal on, the fire's black where it had been red. I pick up the poker – I'm not allowed – and prod the coals until a flame licks around the black and I feel heat on my hand.

Lydia come away from that fire. Grandma H. rushes in and pulls a drawer from the sideboard, tipping everything onto the floor: envelopes, pencils, string. With the clean towel that sits on her shoulder, she lines the empty drawer.

Wind roars down the chimney, bangs on the window. The sea sounds nearer. It's dark but I go to the front door, peep through the letterbox. Waves breaking on the road, coming towards me. I can see the sea through the garden gate, white foam hissing and spreading and I hear Dad say, *high tide is an hour away.* High tide never comes as far as the garden. I try to think how big an hour is and if it is big enough.

I'm peeping through the crack in the bedroom door. Mum is on the bed with a baby sucking her bare breast. Her blue smock lies crumpled over the chair back. I want the baby to go back inside the smock. I open the door wider. *Lydia your Mum's tired,* says Grandma H. *It's all right,* Mum's voice is a whisper now. *Look,*

Taking In Water

you have a sister, a lovely little sister. We shall have to think of a name for her.

The wind shakes the house. The sea sounds too near. Mum's eyes dart anxiously around. She looks at my Dad. I want to cry but I can't. I want to climb on the bed with Mum. I grab the smock, run back to the fireside and bury my face in the cloth. It smells of her, creamy and sweet. If I don't look, will it stop? With my face buried in the smock the wind sounds louder and I can hear the sea crashing in the garden. I put my fingers in my ears. I don't want to hear anymore. I don't want to hear Mum crying or what my Dad is saying.

Even with my fingers in my ears I hear the banging.

Banging inside the house, banging inside the living-room. I come out from under the smock. Dad is standing on a chair, the chair is on the table. He's ramming the poker through the ceiling. His hair is white with plaster dust. I hold the smock up in front of my face. This time I'll count all the white stars.

Here Lyddie, put your coat on. Dad hurries my arms into the sleeves. *And these.* He means my slippers. He's buttoning my coat, so fast he gets all the buttons in the wrong holes. *Never mind.* He's pushing me through the ceiling. *Like Hide and Seek, you and your new little sister.* I'm squeezing between the timbers, I wriggle until I can sit with my legs on either side of a beam, the wood is scratchy on my skin and it's cold, even with my coat on, and my coat is too tight with the buttons done wrong. My legs dangle down into the living-room. I can see things on the floor that Grandma H tipped out of the drawer – scissors, string – the seagull rug seems a long way down. Dad goes back, then appears again, shoving the drawer though the hole. He balances it across two beams in front of me. Then comes the squirming bundle. *Don't fret little one, don't fret.* He says to the baby. *Hang on Lydia Limpet, don't let go.* He tucks a torch inside the drawer at the baby's feet.

Voices moving below, Mum out of bed, they are all by the front door. *I must try ... don't Ted .... Don't...*

A rush of freezing air. A growling sound as if a wild animal had broken through the front door, smoke down the chimney. A bigger roar, like a steam train. A crash.

It's dark. Slap, slap, slap. Cold water slapping my legs and it swallows my slippers my feet are freezing. Another roar, another train, water stings my legs. Grandma's living-room is full of sea.

The baby is crying, crying, crying. At first I can't see, but I know where she is from the crying. Then my eyes get used to the dark. There's moonlight through a hole in the roof where a slate has gone, and I see the torch my father left me. I shine it on the baby. She's getting redder and redder, her tiny hand beating the air, a little fist, fighting its way out of the towel she's wrapped in.

Hide and seek, Dad said. Find us, please find us. Come back you can hear us, you know where we are, the baby has given us away. Find us, go on, find us. I count to ten. Please don't cry, baby. I will sing. I will sing all the hymns we sing at school.

I'm squeezing hard with my legs to hold firm on the scratchy wood. I keep both hands on the wood too. I sing loud, louder and louder above the growling wild animal, above the baby's crying. I wish I had my doll, wish I hadn't left her behind at the hotel.

If I pick the baby up will she stop?

She's not much bigger than my doll. I'll rock her to sleep. They can't find us because it's dark. I balance the torch on the roof-beam, but the baby cries even more. Anyway, I can see her red face in the silvery light through the hole in the roof. It's cold, freezing. I can hear the water crashing below. I pick her up. She's cold. No wonder, because when I look up through the hole in the roof, I see snow flurries swirling in the night sky. She's heavier than my doll and hard to hold in one hand, but I need to hold on with the other hand. I lose my balance, wobble. I grip tight with my legs but I need both hands to steady myself. *Hold on Lydia Limpet, don't let go.* I grab the roof-beam. Steady myself. Crying. A thud, splash. Then no crying.

No, No, No.

It was an accident, I didn't mean to let go, didn't do it on purpose, she was heavy, I lost my balance, I didn't mean to –

She didn't even have a name.'

44

'Come on,' Martin coaxed, 'I think you need to rest, to lie down, let's go back to the house. A brandy, maybe?'

'You do believe me?' she kept saying, though her voice was muffled, slumped as she was on the table, head resting in her folded arms. He stroked her back.

'You do believe me?' She looked up at him, tear-swollen.

'Of course, of course, no more talking, come on.' He eased her from the chair, his arm around her, and they stumbled from hut to house through a spring blizzard and flashes of light from the lighthouse.

In the sitting-room he laid her gently on the sofabed.

'You're leaving?'

'No, I think you need a drink.' He didn't wait for answer. In the kitchen he found what he needed.

'Here,' he offered her a tumbler of water. She sat up and sipped, quiet now. 'And this, I think you need it.' He poured her a shot of brandy, then one for himself and sat down beside her.

They sat in silence. What could he say?

'I'm sorry if – ' he began but how to say it – had his academic curiosity about that gesture in the salt brought her to this? Had he pushed too hard looking for a connection between *Taking In Water* and that childhood trauma? 'If my questions – ' He put his arm around her. Held her.

'No, no. It's a relief, really, such a relief. Just tell me you believe me. I didn't mean any harm, I – '

'You were seven, alone in the dark,' he whispered.

She leaned into him. The lighthouse beam filled the room. He stood up.

'Don't go.'

'It's all right. I'm not leaving.' He went to the window to close the blind.

Back beside her, he put an arm around her shoulder to reassure. They'd both finished their brandy. He topped up her glass then his.

'Thank you.' She kissed his neck.

He could only follow her lead, couldn't get this wrong, not now. He turned, kissed her forehead and waited.

She reached for his face, turned him towards her, her mouth searching.

'Are you sure?' he whispered.

45

Heavy with sleep, Lydia sank into the sofa-bed, a blissful drowsiness. She stretched her legs, felt the dried stickiness of Martin on her thighs and inside a body-memory of him. She breathed him, on her skin, in the sheets. When she reached across he wasn't there.

Awake now, she remembered the surge of words, falling and falling, until his hand, firm on her shoulder, had pulled her back. Slumped against the certainty of his body, his arm around her, he'd guided her.

Brandy, her kissing him.

Are you sure? he'd asked.

Enough talking, she'd replied.

Silent in the dark, lips, tongues, skin, all touch. He'd moved inside her slowly, deeply, followed her, taken his time. Afterwards, he hadn't rolled away but had hugged her, kissed her hair as she sank into the deepest sleep.

Now, in her mind she formed his name, but couldn't bring herself to call out, didn't want him not to answer. She guided her hearing around the house. Bathroom, kitchen. Nothing.

It was Monday. He'd told her he was going to London on Tuesday. She checked her watch. Ten it said, and also that the month had changed. Naked, she wandered into the kitchen. Out of the window a canopy of grey hung low, more snow showers. April showers. March had ended. She was still sane.

She climbed the stairs, willing him to be in the bathroom. Had her body lied? She checked each room. If he'd gone, he

Taking In Water

would have left a note? No trace of him having been here except inside her. Could her body lie so convincingly?

Back in the sitting-room she pulled on the jeans and sweater she'd abandoned last night, tucking in the scent of him.

The studio wasn't locked, but the door was shut. His coat hung on the back of the chair. On the table, written on the transcript, he'd brought last night – *Back as soon as I can. M x.*

She picked up the coat, wanting the smell of it but it was cold. She draped it around her shoulders to warm it, enjoy its reassuring weight.

Her tape recorder still had the cassette inside it.

Her voice sounded like that of a frightened child, naming each frame, image after image: *bootees like meringues ... toasted crumpets ... blue smock... seagull rug ... hole in the ceiling ... moon through the roof.*

Stop. No, she'd hear it out.

Shsh, shsh, don't cry baby. No name for her to call out. A fierce hungry cry, angry. It wanted its mother's voice to answer. The voice it had heard as it sucked, getting to know the outside of its mother's body. Angry because this was a strange voice. Her sister. She could say that now, *sister.*

All the years the film had been stuck in her head she'd sometimes seen the last frame as her reaching to comfort the baby, be a mother to her, patting and smoothing the towel in the drawer to make a safe space for her. Other times, it looked as if she was pushing the baby away to shut her up. Sometimes the frames flickered so fast it was both things at once and she couldn't tell the difference.

You were seven, alone in the dark. Martin had said. Now he knew she'd had a sister who'd lived long enough to know Lydia and to lose her mother, but not long enough to have a name.

She switched off the cassette and walked over to the shelf of Marine objects, things from her first life. Seven years of home and love. Watching her mother polish silver, hearing her father whistle as he fried eggs. *Mother and father to herself,* Edna Thornton had said as she lay dying. She thought of Edna's frocks preserved in attics. Is that what this work meant? Should she put these things away, keep them to remind her she'd once had an ordinary life, until the sea barged into Grandma's sitting-room and washed her up in a different life?

She looked with fresh eyes at her weather wall, her one-woman water surveillance. *Six billion human beings not thinking about what water can do, not thinking ahead,* Steven had said. He'd been curious about why she lived here, seemed to understand it was important. She should've told him: *I don't ever want to be surprised by water.* It would be like being surprised by death, as if you'd lived not knowing death was part of life.

She settled into Martin's coat, hugged it around her. The wind was getting up, more snowflakes. She walked out onto the verandah, to where she'd stood last night against the rail, and watched the blizzard coming towards her.

'A blizzard in April isn't personal,' she said out loud and turned back.

As she walked to the house, she paused to look around at her home, her garden, her studio, all tucked inside the white fence. The thought hit her like the thump of a wave she hadn't seen coming. She hadn't put up the fence to keep others out; she'd put it there to keep herself in.

At the door, she sat for a while on the step to watch the snowflakes fall and melt almost as soon as they touched the ground, Martin's coat keeping her warm.

No. A blizzard in April wasn't personal.

It was air and water, not prediction.

And it wasn't punishment.

September 2002

1

Martin had left behind a crisp September morning in London. Here, it was heating up. With reckless confidence the driver dodged through traffic, his yellow cab swaying across the five lanes of Rockaway Boulevard towards Manhattan.

'I'm legal,' he told Martin, as he took a swig of water from a litre bottle. 'Green card since '87. Half-year, New York – half-year back home. Lahore.'

Martin looked through the windscreen, beyond the driver's head, at a clear blue sky, summer stretching into autumn. It was a year since he'd made this same taxi ride. He was here to make the most of the last couple of weeks of his sabbatical. He was going ahead with the new version of his book; it might not get him the professorship but it was the only book he could write. And, it had Lydia's approval.

'It's history, not gossip,' she'd said when he'd finally dared to show her the outline. He'd hoped she'd collaborate with him, be its co-author.

'You have the recordings we made, that's my contribution. I trust you to shape the material. I have my own new project, and a lot to learn.' Of course he understood, was delighted that she was developing her digital piece, exploring a new medium.

Tomorrow he'd meet Alex Markovski to agree which items could be photographed for the book – trial pieces and the panels with the Gagarin images, for sure. And they'd arrange for copyright clearance on the images Lydia had helped him to select from *Taking In Water Documented*. Most importantly, he hoped Alex would have sounded out Sarton, see whether he might lend items for exhibition in the UK. There was still funding to figure out, but there was reason to hope that Sarton himself might want to pitch in.

'I can tell you now, though,' Alex'd said when they'd spoken last week. 'Mr Sarton has agreed to have Mantella's films transferred to DVD. I'll have a copy ready for you.' Taking stills from that would evoke the atmosphere of the performance. It seemed a lifetime since he'd viewed the images, alone in the guest suite, numbing himself from the shock with whisky.

A walk downtown? He wasn't going to make a big deal of it.

The driver took another swig from his bottle of water.

'This city, it dehydrates. Two litres a day, I drink. Never get colds. Human body mostly water.'

Two-thirds, Martin wanted to say, like the Earth. *No one should be surprised by water,* Lydia had said back in April.

The blizzard in April had surprised him; huge snowflakes dissolving as soon as they hit the ground. He'd driven as fast as he'd dared to get back before Lydia woke and found him gone. He could hardly see, but he knew the track to her house well enough; his car filled with the scent of the hyacinths.

Earlier, he'd tiptoed out into a bright spring day, silently shutting the door so as not to wake her. He'd gone to the studio to collect his coat and left a note saying he'd be back later. He'd left his coat so she'd be in no doubt.

He'd driven Eileen to the cardiac clinic.

'Are you warm enough in that sweater?' Eileen had asked as they said goodbye at the hospital entrance, her check-up complete, the sky darkening, the first flurry coming down on their heads.

'I'm fine,' he smiled.

The news was good: no damage, no disease, just a little disorganised. An irregularity in the rhythm of her heart that had, no doubt, been there all her life and the flu virus had amplified its presence. More irritating than harmful, it would most likely settle down. There was medication if it bothered her.

Eileen used his mobile, called Monica who was coming over to meet her. They'd go shopping and have a coffee at The Grand.

Outside the hospital he pulled up at the flower stall and bought all of the blue hyacinths in the bucket.

Back at Lydia's he stood for a moment at the gate, words crowding his head. Listening to her recount the horror of that night, her clinging on to the roof timbers, he'd seen how much she'd clung to a child's view of events. Her memories buried, the storm never spoken of – did she realise that she'd been caught up in the worst peacetime disaster in modern British history? Did she understand about the sea defences in disrepair after the war? Or that the Met office had known about the wind and the Navy had known about the waves, but they hadn't talked to each other? If they had, they could have worked out between them that a wall of water, surging down the North Sea, would make the next incoming tide three metres higher than the highest recorded high tide. Did she appreciate that, as she sang hymns alone in the roof, the storm inflicted devastation the like of which is only seen in war? And, a nation sick of war, didn't want the memory of it, so it had been left to those who'd been there to remember alone. A terrible burden. A burden she'd been trying to put down ever since, unconsciously scooping away at the mound of salt, searching for lost silverware on Slayton beach.

She was standing, in the garden, his coat around her shoulders.

'I brought you these,' he offered her the flowers then felt clumsy, crass. He'd intended them in remembrance of her mother – *I have so few memories of her* – but might she find them an intrusion? She said nothing, but had taken them, held the blooms to her face.

What could he say, what would be the right words?

'The tape,' he said, wondering how else to refer to what she'd told him yesterday. How to say it? You might not have saved her but you didn't murder your sister – unlikely a newborn baby would have survived the cold. Finally, all he said was:

'You did your best. You were seven. You sang and someone heard you and –'

'I know,' she said, speaking for the first time, and something he took to be relief passed across her face.

'How did you get that scar on your lip?' she asked, reaching out, touching it.

On his left a vast cemetery, its brown tombstones prefiguring the skyline that would soon come into view. He could make out the pinnacle of the Empire State but nothing else, because the road dipped. As the gradient increased – he'd noticed this on his last trip – the midtown skyline would suddenly appear. He was thankful it was only midtown that was visible. The Towers never did figure at this point so their absence would also be out of view.

It came leaping up in front of him like a giant pop-up book, a city that seemed to come from nowhere, as if the buildings had been extruded from the bedrock; then it was gone as the taxi nosed underground through the tunnel.

He'd call Eileen, as agreed, once he got to the apartment.

'I don't believe you – going to New York? Do you have to?' She'd made such a fuss before he left.

'Yes.'

'Please, Martin. I don't know that I could take it if anything happened. I mean, you've been lucky once.' The whining tone had set his teeth on edge.

'Yes. Very lucky.' It was then he'd decided to tell her. Withholding the truth of his life was corrosive. 'Last year I was about to go up the South Tower, just before the attack.'

'What? You never said – ' Her hand clutched to her chest.

'I said what you wanted to hear.' He paused to let it sink in. 'But for a phone call to do with my work I would have been in the building when the attack happened.' At least now she might be more sympathetic towards his book.

'Martin.' She slumped rather theatrically into her chair. 'I don't know what to say.'

'No need to say anything. Be glad of my good fortune.' He couldn't stop himself, pressing home the point: how people cope with shattered lives, deal with unimaginable horrors after such appalling events. 'So, please stop worrying in advance about things that may not happen and don't make a big deal now you know the truth.'

She went very quiet.

'You'll call me, tell me you've landed, won't you?'

He'd left Lydia all the information she would need. It was up to her now.

'In London getting a licence, it's hard work, too much study,' the driver announced. 'Here, test is easy. All grid, except downtown. Downtown is complicated.'

'Yes,' said Martin. 'It is.'

As they surfaced on Second Avenue, he looked ahead at the synchronised traffic lights punctuating the view as far as he could see. Red, green. Red, green shunting traffic along, one block at a time.

2

Lydia turned into the narrow street of tall Victorian houses. Up ahead, a milk float blocked her way. It wasn't yet seven. She'd left, like the puffins, during the night, made her way along the track with the lighthouse beam behind her and driven non-stop. The motorway still hummed in her head.

The milk float moved off and she found a parking space. There wasn't much to unload – a holdall, a small suitcase, some of her photographs. Most of her things were already here. She reached into the glove compartment for the keys.

She'd expected to see the hall lined with the boxes she'd sent ahead. It was empty. Martin must have carried everything to the upstairs flat before he left for New York.

There was one more delivery to come.

The door to the main room of the downstairs flat was ajar. She peered in. The floor was stacked with Martin's papers and piles of books. On the dining-table lay her copy of *Taking in Water Documented*; yellow tabs protruded from its pages, indicating the photographs they'd selected.

In the upstairs flat she found all of her boxes neatly stacked in the corridor. She carried on up the narrow staircase to the attic bedroom, her old room. Martin had unwrapped her father's chair and set it by the window. On the table next to it he'd left a note. *Welcome.* He'd typed out the phone number of the apartment where he was staying and another number for flight bookings: *in case you decide to take that walk downtown.*

The room was full of stale air. She pushed at the sash window. It was stuck, not quite square in its frame. She eased it to the point where the balance lay and the old weights glided into action. She leaned out on a clear September morning, fine after yesterday's rain – October tomorrow. In the distance, she made out the dome of St Pauls.

'A childhood fall,' Martin had said back in April, explaining the scar above his top lip, the scent of hyacinths filling her kitchen, 'on Slayton beach, near the pillboxes.' They'd talked all day, and the next, lazing in bed. Over dinner the night before he'd left, she'd talked about the work she'd been trying to make with the Marine objects.

'Maybe those things are for some other work,' he suggested. 'Wasn't *Taking In Water* about that night?' She felt goose pimples rise up along her arms and a shift as if her whole body, her whole being, was moving into a new space. For a moment, she seemed to be looking from outside, seeing herself quite differently.

While he went back to London to sign papers, sell his house, she slept for hours on end, as if catching up on a lifetime of broken nights. At Edna Thornton's funeral she cried. Cried for Edna, but also cried, at last, for everyone.

Martin had visited several times over the summer. She even persuaded him into the water one hot June afternoon. As they lay sunning on the beach afterwards he said:

'I know you have a lot to consider with this survey business, so stop me if this isn't the right time.' He explained his idea for the book, his voice alive with passion for the project. He'd take the gesture of her scooping, start with that single action in the work of art, and tease out its meanings, writing more than a history of that work. He'd excavate the histories clustered within it – personal and political. *Taking in Water* was about more than what Gagarin had seen, it was about what she'd seen and buried; about what history had buried – the worst peacetime disaster. *Taking In Water* meant looking forward too, asking questions about the future of water in the world, but only if she agreed.

She pulled the window down a little now the room was aired. Below, beyond the garden fence, water had pooled in the middle of the field above the reservoir. Was it rain on saturated ground or the reservoir beneath seeping through? She took her camera from her bag; that was an image she might want for her project. She was happy for Martin to write his book but, for herself, she needed to play, experiment with the computer, explore the potential for layering and animating image, text, sound. Keep paying attention to water, keep collecting material – a new work would emerge that would speak beyond herself. Steven's words had stayed with her: *Six billion human beings not thinking about what water can do, not thinking ahead.* For years she'd had her weather wall that hardly anyone had seen. With a digital piece her water-watching might come to have a purpose.

Maybe she'd have something ready for the *Every Last Drop* conference next March. Patrick kept reminding her of it, encouraging, and Martin had submitted a paper. She was looking forward to meeting others – artists, dancers, writers – seeing how they paid attention to water. All this talk of weapons of mass destruction in the news now, what if it turned out to be a mistake? *The threat is never where you think it is,* Luc used to say. One thing she couldn't quite go along with was the title Martin had suggested for his paper – *Taking Back Taking In Water* – reclaiming the work from Luc. She could see now how much of it had come from her, and yes, maybe alone she would have made some other work back then, but she made *that* work with Luc.

She sat at the small table, arranging the chair so she could look out at the skyline. No horizon here, but now she didn't need that daily fix on something that didn't really exist. She took out the postcard Jean had sent from the airport.

Dear Lydia

Flight delayed. Never mind, I have many people to catch up with so happily writing here in departure lounge. Have met all the others on the tour - a good group. Still can't quite believe I'm going to have a whole month in Oz. Feels indulgent but Sally was persuasive. Still having wobbly moments about Mum, but I'm grateful she was released from that dark world she'd disappeared into. Hearing your memories of her helped – it's good to know she lives on for others too. I want you to know I'm thinking of you as you decide what to do about the house. Sorry I'm not there to give support. Keep in touch. Love Jean x

Lydia had been waiting for the right moment to reply. She dug out a pen and some paper from her bag.

Dear Jean

Thanks for your card. I'm picturing you hot and dusty, attached to your binoculars. Well, I've done it – gone for compulsory purchase. By the time you get back the place will be boarded up, maybe even demolished – who knows.
I strung them out until the last moment, let them think I was going to fight it, didn't want to give that old bastard the satisfaction of seeing me leave. Steven – the young one I told you about – right up to last week was still saying I could make a case. Having him care made it easier to leave in the end. I didn't want to turn my life into a battleground, certainly didn't want the

Taking In Water

publicity. All that negative energy. No thanks.

For now, I've moved everything to Bea's house, sorry, my house. I've a few things to sort out here, then I might be off on a trip myself. I'll let you know.

Martin did me a favour moving into the downstairs flat over the summer after Howard walked out. Can you believe it? He wasn't in Italy all that time, he was in London with his young violinist. Barely out of music college, I gather. It seems she'd only let him move in with her if he promised never to see me again. Not difficult, since we hardly saw each other – anyway, you were right, he was more 'virtual' than lover.

I'm not sure where I'll end up, but I do know leaving Flampton was the right thing to do. Eventually, I think I'll want to be near the sea for some of the time. Whatever happens, we mustn't lose touch again. I'm so pleased we talked about your mother and that it helped. As I cleared the house, she was often in my thoughts. Do you remember the day we climbed on to the roof of your garage and I tore my dress? Your mum ...

The chime of the doorbell echoed through the house. She put down her pen and moved quickly down the stairs.

Through the stained glass panel of the front door she could see two men carrying what was clearly the verandah rail.

'You'll have to come through the house,' she said and led them through the downstairs flat and out down the narrow garden. She watched, carefully counting the pieces: four walls, door, roof, verandah. Now the studio had been safely delivered she could think about what to do next.

'I'd like to walk across Washington Square with my shoes on one day,' she'd said to Martin over dinner on his last visit to Flampton in August. He said there was a walk downtown he'd like to make, too. They'd left it open. She had to sort out the business with the surveyors before she'd commit. And now she was here, the studio stowed in the garden and there was Martin's note with all the information she needed.

He'd transcribed the last tape so she wouldn't have to listen again to her voice. He'd put the images into words. The film was no longer flickering. Instead, she saw stills, faded like old photographs. She could look at them now they were no longer animated by terror, trapped in her head.

She had yet to tell Jean about her sister. Jean had been too raw with her own grief and sorting out her mother's house for Lydia to lay that on her. Of course she would keep in touch and when the time was right she'd tell Jean – the sister she'd chosen – about the brief life and silent death of her baby sister and how wrong the newspapers had been – the baby had been in Lydia's care, not her mother's belly, when she'd died. There was more truth in the scooped out salt in *Taking In Water* than in a single column inch. Strange how the truth, though lost to memory, didn't go away but stored itself in the body. Holding on to a terrible secret had lodged a weight inside her, an awful compression. She was adjusting to the new, bearable weight of her loss.

Back upstairs in the attic she stood at the window and looked down on the stack of red-painted wood. She must find a tarpaulin; it might be a couple of weeks before she got round to having it rebuilt – she'd no doubt have to apply for planning permission. It had taken time to work out what to bring, what to leave behind; hardest was deciding what to do with the Marine things. She didn't want them in London but she couldn't simply bag them up with the rubbish. Then it had come to her – she'd create a performance, in which she'd be both artist and audience.

She'd found a white linen sheet that she'd had for years and had come from The Marine. She cut it up, wrapped each object in turn, strange shaped parcels tied up with white ribbon: the teapot, the toast rack, a serving spoon and the teaspoon that

Martin had found. The teaspoon, for her nameless baby sister.

She loaded the parcels in her canvas bag and took them, along with it the hollowed out driftwood she found trapped in the pillbox, down to Dunwick Bay. As the beach swarmed with school parties at the start of the new term, she made her way round the headland, to Aztec City. On the lowest ledge of the chalk, she laid the parcels into the driftwood boat. The next tide would take it. She touched each parcel in turn, called up a moment from each life, a living memory rather than the moment of each person's dying. A small celebration of each life: her mother polishing silver, her father with his mug of tea, her grandmother knitting by the fireside. Touching the spoon was the hardest. She saw the baby, briefly content, sucking. 'Perdita,' she said out loud.

If the parcels were washed up, she wouldn't be there combing the beaches to find them. It was for others to imagine why on earth anyone would wrap battered silverware in torn bedsheets.

Now, she looked up as a solitary seagull landed in the pool of water on the reservoir field, an odd sight against the city skyline. She smiled. It stood quite still, resting, a touchdown before it took off again.

Reviews of Pamela Johnson's previous novels

Under Construction:

Irresistibly readable. Pamela Johnson writes with great feeling and wit about Amy Beardsley's return to life after her husband's sudden, shocking death. The dilapidated house which Amy takes on is a character in its own right. The relationship between Amy and the infinitely desirable Irish carpenter is beautifully done.
Helen Dunmore

A touching story about the relationships we construct with people and buildings.
The Times

A well written, sensual first novel of more than usual promise.
The Good Book Guide

The slow, yet dizzying slide into love makes for a compelling read. Under Construction is a book that is true to the way lives can change so greatly almost without our knowing.
James Friel

Johnson portrays Amy's daydreams and Angst with imaginative sympathy, but is best when slyly mocking her right-on tastes.
Harper's & Queen, London

You get to know every corner of the house – the fireplaces, the ruby and emerald stained glass in the front door, the crazy half-levels – but as the work gets underway, it becomes not only the central character but a metaphor for a woman's life.
Hampstead & Highgate Express

I read this novel on a recent holiday and although it takes a while to get into it, once you do it's pretty compelling reading. It charts the progress of a 40 something widow and her two daughters who move into a large Edwardian house needing a large amount of renovation. The mother meets a carpenter and becomes obsessed with him, sparking a dalliance. I loved the imagery the author used and I was almost transported to the locations she mentions - Dungeness, North London etc. A good read by a promising author and I'm sure we'll hear more from Pamela Johnson in future.

Amazon reader

Deep Blue Silence:

Compelling reading. The novel looks at the complex sources of inspiration that inspire new work.

Liz Hoggard

An elegant novel.

Belfast Telegraph

The preoccupation with the work of art and confrontation with her mother's past makes for an enjoyable read.

The Oxford Times

Pamela Johnson's first novel Under Construction *showed her to be a writer to watch and this second confirms it. Maddie is an artist working with shards of broken glass - part of the intrigue of the novel is where that glass has come from. Finding herself pregnant, unexpectedly, she starts searching for the secrets of her own mother's life. It's beautifully-written.*

Amazon reader

Maddie is intelligent, sexy, risk taking. The description of her making a work of art and the interweaving of her unpicking her mother's history through glass is fascinating. Johnson opens to us a whole section of Northern history and keeps a rapid pace. This novel is a real page turner at the same time as being full of ideas. Highly recommended.

Amazon reader

Acknowledgements

Taking In Water was written with support from an Arts Council Writers Award for which I am extremely grateful.

I would like to thank my first readers – all the current members of ReWord and former members of The Clink Street Writers plus Mary Stacey, Philippa Pringle and Anatol Orient – their support, encouragement and incisive comments have been invaluable.

Thanks too to Jill Foulston for perceptive editing of the final manuscript and to Frankie Wynne for meticulous line-editing. Any remaining mistakes are all my own.

Cover design by Sam Sullivan

Blue Door Press

bluedoorpress.co.uk

About the Author

Pamela Johnson has published two previous novels, plus short stories, poems, non-fiction and journalism.

For over 15 years she has devised and run writing workshops in a range of contexts – schools, community groups, U3A, residential courses for The Arvon Foundation – and is currently Associate Tutor on the MA in Creative & Life Writing, Goldsmiths, University of London.

She previously worked as an independent critic, curator and lecturer on contemporary visual art. Her essays, articles and reviews on contemporary visual art and craft have appeared in journals, broadsheets and gallery publications. She has curated national touring exhibitions and reviewed for Radio 4's *Kaleidoscope* and *Front Row*.

She is working on her fourth novel and a collection of poems, and runs a literary website, which has an archive of her many interviews with authors:

Words Unlimited
http://www.wordsunlimited.typepad.com/

New editions of her previous novels, *Under Construction* and *Deep Blue Silence* are forthcoming from Blue Door Press in 2017

Pamela Johnson

Printed in Great Britain
by Amazon